A CONTEMPORARY ROMANCE

THE KISMET SERIES - BOOK TWO

K. ALEX WALKER

CONTENT NOTICE

Hello, my pretties
(and your little dogs, too),

The Woman He Wanted touches on subjects of childhood trauma, sexual abuse, alcoholism, and suicide. As always, I want to make sure you're informed; we all have our own crosses to bear. I did, however, do my very best to make it *beautiful*.

Be safe.

With love,
- K. Alex

PREFACE

The Woman He Wanted is a reworked, re-release for anyone who might think, "Hmm, I believe I know these characters."

Kellen Edwards also shows up in *Moonlight Retribution*, you can find Ethan Stewart in Book One of this series—*Fated*, and everyone knows where you can find Tayler Diaz—*Angels and Assassins: The Wolf*, complete with its new cover. Make sure to check out Gage's wolf tattoo.

That thing is *nice*.

Okay, I'm done.

Please enjoy!

<u>*One more thing:*</u>

The Woman He Wanted was initially released in 2016, and I started writing it even prior to then.

At the time, I wasn't aware of the history of Lake Lanier that's recently become more widespread.

*Therefore, I've updated
that information.*

However, please understand that sometimes, authors don't know. It's not that they don't care, especially when it's related to things that affect them on a personal level.

Healing often takes a lifetime.
It's not something we simply grow out of
like our shoes from elementary school.

Thank you for allowing me
to tell part of your story.

-K

PROLOGUE

Kellen Edwards pulled his car between the two white lines outside the Starbucks across from the hospital where he'd now be continuing his career. He had a new position, three new positions, actually, and a new life away from the stressors that had plagued him in Louisiana.

Technically, one stressor.

Trisha, his ex-girlfriend.

His last image of her was her naked, lithe body pinned between three men in the bed they'd once shared. One had been behind her with his hairy knuckles gripping her hips. The second had positioned himself alongside her olive skin with its hints of caramel and the rose tattoo beneath her ribcage. The last man, the most memorable of them all, had dangled his uncircumcised penis in front of her mouth like a twisted fisherman.

He had a soft spot for women the size of Texas, but that

would no longer be the case. Sex would just be sex, no strings. He'd go back to his college days of unscrupulous behavior, tearing at his sleeve until only the threads of his heart remained.

When that familiar loneliness interfered, washing over him when the temperature outside was perfect and the spot next to him empty and as cold as a winter morning, he'd ignore it. Maybe, if possible, he'd pick up more shifts at work, although his schedule was already so full, he had to schedule time to sleep and visit his family.

He stepped out of the car and made his way to the coffee shop's glass front doors. Although he wasn't much of a coffee drinker, with his new lease on life and his dreadful hours, it made sense to at least try to pick up the habit. It was also shameful to be both of Spanish and French ancestry and spurn the idea of coffee.

A woman headed his way, and he held the door open for her to walk through. Unnaturally long lashes partially obscured her dark blue eyes, and red lips set off evenly-tanned skin. She flicked a look his way, started to roll her eyes, but then their gazes held.

"Oh." She glanced downward, tucking a strand of brown hair behind her ear. "Thanks for holding the door."

"You're welcome," he said, flashing her a smile. "You know, I've been in Atlanta for several months now, and I just started a new position at the hospital nearby. Do you come here a lot?"

"All the time. You?"

"Nope. Today's my first time."

"That's probably why you've never seen me. You'd remember me."

He grinned wider.

"What are you waiting for?" she asked, cheeks flushed. "Ask me out. You know you want to."

"It's that obvious?"

"I mean," she motioned to herself, "I'm hot. You're hot."

"So then, have a drink with me to—"

Laughter carried across the café, stopping him in the middle of his sentence. His head turned, almost helplessly, toward the sound, and every single thing around him came to a screeching halt. The blushing woman in front of him blurred as the pair of dark eyes behind the counter met his.

Oh.

You. Are. Mine.

He mumbled a quick, "Excuse me" and brushed past the red-lipped woman without looking back. The woman behind the counter's dark eyes remained on his as he drew nearer. While he didn't have a clue what the inside of the coffee shop looked like, he knew those eyes swirled even darker the closer he came.

"And how may I help you," she squinted at his chest, "Dr. Edwards?"

He looked down and yanked off the name tag affixed to his blazer from a mixer at the hospital earlier. "Uh, I'd like a," he glanced up at the menu, "grande, medium roast. Nothing fancy. For Kellen."

Head bobbing, she placed his order.

When their eyes met again, he knew he wanted them to one day sparkle only for him. She smiled, and he wanted that smile to belong to no one else but him. He wanted her scent, her touch, and to be the one who made her laugh. The only one who made her laugh. His entire no-strings-attached personal declaration, along with his memories of Trisha, went flying out the window.

"A grande, medium roast," she repeated. "Is that it?"

A response started to form, but it rapidly disappeared. For the first time since...he actually couldn't remember the last time...his mind went blank. Not so much as an ounce of the charm and ease he'd possessed a few minutes ago tossed him a lifeline.

"Um," she squeezed her lips together, "anything else?"

This woman had beautiful lips.

"What about something from the bakery? Maybe a slice of cake?" She gestured to the glass case next to them. "If that's too sweet, we have croissants."

Hopefully, that wasn't a nervous smile faintly tugging at the right side of her mouth. She also kept shifting from foot to foot, which had better not have anything to do with her heart racing at the same speed his currently was.

She looked away, chewing on the inside of her bottom lip, before making eye contact again.

And those eyes of hers.

Those fucking eyes of hers.

"Kellen?"

"Uh," he squeezed his eyelids together, head shaking, "yeah. Yes, that's it."

For now.

CHAPTER ONE

There she was, standing in the middle of a heavy, late-night shower in the hospital's parking lot when he'd assumed he would forever be relegated, week after week, to seeing her at the Starbucks on the corner. When he walked in, she would smile, point to him, and rattle off his order as he neared the counter:

"A grande, medium roast.
Nothing fancy.
For the doc."

She'd then write his name on his cup, adding a small heart at the end. He'd been seconds away from asking for her number until he saw it—another man with his name on a cup, the same heart doodled at the end of the "Chris" scribbled in her handwriting.

He wasn't the man who stopped at coffee shops, stealing minutes here and there from long shifts, only to see a woman's face, no matter how drop-dead gorgeous he found her.

But she made him feel odd.

Weird.

Sixteen.

She made him *nervous*.

He never got nervous, at least not since his balls had dropped and the braces had come off, but he lapsed into a mangled mix of English, French, and Spanish whenever he tried to talk to her. Sometimes, even trying to say the words "good morning" came out as though the words had grown necks and were being choked to death.

Kellen slowly approached, footfalls heavy, making his presence known to avoid startling her. Beams of moonlight turned the droplets on her skin into diamonds. The rain had plastered her hair, which she'd flat-ironed, to her face, and a pair of red pumps hung from the tips of her fingers.

She stood as still as an oil painting, the matching red glare of her dress igniting the landscape like a wildfire blazing through a drought-ridden forest. The dress was tight, date-night tight, and he shoved away a surge of jealousy.

"Hey, you okay?" He extended his umbrella over her head. "Let me walk you inside."

Mascara lines streaked her face, nowhere near potent enough to mar what he personally considered an excellent combination of attractive features—silky brown skin, sultry almond-shaped eyes, coal black lashes, and lips he fully intended to kiss, bite, lick, and suck until they swelled.

Lightning flashed through the sky like electric spider webs. Seconds later, thunder roared. The lamps in the parking lot sparked and went out, blanketing them in darkness.

He dropped the umbrella, lifted her into his arms, and raced toward the hospital doors.

As he walked her through the lobby, he challenged every inquisitive stare that came their way. Then, once inside his office, he fished a spare work shirt from the closet.

She took the shirt from his hand, her movements mechanical, and reached for the zipper on her dress. By the time he turned around to give her some privacy, wet skin, soft breasts, and mahogany areolas had already been imprinted in his brain.

He waited a few moments before facing her again, only to find his shirt hanging from her shoulders in a way that couldn't have been more seductive in his dreams. She'd left it unbuttoned, giving him a glimpse of the swells of her breasts and a full view of the treasure between her thighs, sprinkled by a light dusting of curls.

She walked toward him, beautiful mascara-stained face and all, grabbed his wrist, and brought his hand between her legs.

Wetness bathed his finger.

Wetness that had nothing to do with rain.

"What do you want to do now that we're alone?" she asked, her voice husky in a way that, of course, he would find sexy on this woman.

There she was, *the woman he fucking wanted,* virtually naked in front of him, his finger inches away from sinking into her body.

"Do you need me to call you a car?" he found himself asking. "Maybe I can help you get an Uber? A Lyft?"

She went completely still. "Oh, God. *Oh, God.* I'm an idiot."

"Hey, wait." He reached out. "Don't say that."

She flitted about the room, scooping wet clothes into her arms. When everything had been accounted for, she looked directly into his eyes. At some point, tears had fallen onto her cheeks.

"I'm so, so sorry, Doc," she said.

Then she left, sprinting down the hall, barefoot and wearing only his work shirt. Unable to help himself, he followed.

She didn't look as odd as he would have expected, half-naked in the elevator, standing next to an elderly man gripping the handles of an elderly woman's wheelchair.

"Bailey."

At the sound of her name, her eyes flicked to his. It had taken him three visits to learn because he, regularly, got lost in her eyes the minute he walked into the coffee shop.

"Don't go," he said. "Please."

The doors closed, leaving him standing alone on the polished linoleum.

After weeks and weeks of pining for her, she'd given him the opening he'd been waiting for. He'd then taken that opening, doused it in gasoline, and tossed a match on top.

Still, she would be his, and he felt feral, *brutish* as he settled on the conclusion.

But fuck if he cared.

CHAPTER TWO

Bailey glanced back at the hospital, at the dozens of lighted windows, and wondered which one belonged to Dr. Kellen Edwards. The man was downright beautiful, his eyes a curious blend of cinnamon and green. He had a headful of dark, luscious hair and a low-cut beard that she'd imagined, on more than one occasion, scrubbing her fingers over.

The "doc" was tall and broad-shouldered, the thing of romance novels, and carried himself with an air of confidence. However, that air of confidence was completely upended by the almost-bashful smiles he sent her at the coffee shop.

She'd assumed he'd been flirting when sending her those almost-bashful smiles.

Evidently, she was way off the mark.

A black sedan came around the corner, and she prayed her Uber driver didn't ask why she was wearing a man's shirt that she had no plans to return. She'd watched Kellen grab it from his office closet, yet it smelled like his cologne. Whenever he left the coffee shop, the whole front area would smell like his cologne. She could only imagine how it felt to be held by him, nose near his collar, basking in it up close.

"Bailey Green?" A young man, head lowered, peered at her through the passenger window from the driver's side. "I'm Caleb, your Uber driver."

She slid onto the backseat, shut the door, and took one more glance at the hospital windows.

"Did you get caught in the rain?" the driver asked. "Man, I know how that is. It almost got me."

She faced forward. "That's Atlanta for you."

"Right, right."

He pulled away from the curb.

Eyes closed, she sank further into the seat. Hazel irises appeared behind her eyelids, and her heart thrashed in response.

CHAPTER THREE

He'd been trying to talk to Bailey, at least get one word in, for the past week, but the minute he became the second-to-last person in the heavy morning rush, she disappeared in the back. So, this time, he did something he never did.

He took the day off.

If she ran, he would wait, even if he had to wait until her shift was over.

The line slowly inched forward.

Bailey avoided looking at him, her eyes as black as raisins and her skin like it had been produced by amaretto and honeybees. Her mouth—Jesus, her mouth—curled into a smile that caused a physical sensation inside his body whenever she steered it toward him. A sensation he didn't dare refer to as *butterflies.*

She wasn't anything like the women he usually went after.

Bailey worked behind a sales counter with a face he was

sure was completely free of makeup. Her curly hair struggled to remain underneath a green Starbucks cap. Plain studs shined in her earlobes, and she wore black shirts, black pants, and black sneakers underneath her apron.

He was used to dating attorneys, corporate executives, and fellow MDs. Women with corner offices, makeup applied by professionals, and long, straight hair. Despite Trish making it her life mission to deplete his finances and send his heart through a paper shredder, she'd been a junior partner at a law firm.

However, none of them had ever filled his head with helium. He'd never gotten tongue-tied or felt awkward, even when first meeting them. Seeing Bailey was the first time he'd learned there were different types of beautiful.

Some types drew people in.

Others rendered them speechless.

She smiled at a frazzled, middle-aged woman standing on the other side of the counter. The woman shouted her order across the countertop, and Kellen felt his mouth go dry.

By now, Bailey would have left. That meant, once the woman was finished, her eyes would be on him. He'd be expected to look into them, be charming, and try to speak, all while trying not to think about how his finger had felt touching her where he wanted to taste her.

"What's up, Doc?"

That was her voice.

She was talking to him, looking at him.

"Is it the usual again today? Grande, medium roast? Nothing fancy?"

There were words, somewhere. Probably outside underneath his car's rear tire.

This was the problem.

How could she be his someday if he couldn't even get the words—

"Hi." The word stumbled forth as though shoved from behind. "Can we talk?"

She counted the people in line behind him. "Sure. My fifteen's coming up, and I'm skipping breakfast, so, yeah, we can chat for a few. We can meet there," she pointed to a group of tables just outside the entrance doors, "but, in the meantime, will it be a grande, medium roast? For Kellen?"

He would not say *um*.

"Uh, how is the oatmeal?"

"Pretty good for a coffee shop. I mean," she shrugged, "I like it. I eat it all the time."

"Then a bowl of oatmeal and two coffees."

"Both coffees the same?"

"The second one's for you."

She chewed away a smile.

A memory of a buck-toothed Bugs Bunny, red-faced and sporting a sheepish grin, crossed his mind, punctuated by the classic Goofy *hyuck*.

"Thank you," she said. "I'll be out in a minute."

After grabbing a handful of napkins and a spoon, he headed outside to take a seat.

Although he didn't have to wait long, his leg tapped so hard it threatened to rock his life away, as his mother would say.

Bailey appeared from behind his right shoulder, the

13

oatmeal and two coffees in hand, and took a seat on the other side of the tiny outdoor table. She pushed the bowl and his coffee toward him, and when he reached out, their hands brushed.

His chest, stomach, and groin constricted.

Aside from the night in his office, it was the closest she'd ever been to him. This close, he could smell her—fragrant rose with a hint of something citrus. He could have done better at pinpointing it, especially after spending high school summers helping his mother craft soaps from essential oils and silicone molds. But his brain was sitting on the passenger seat of his car, wondering why he'd left it behind.

"I don't make yours as hot." She pointed to his coffee cup. "Wouldn't want you to burn yourself right before you have to, I don't know, perform brain surgery or something."

"Actually, the oatmeal's for you." Was that his voice? He sounded five years old, handing a boxed Valentine's Day card to his kindergarten teacher crush. "You said you were skipping breakfast. You, ah, shouldn't do that."

She tried to chew away another smile, but he noticed everything about this woman.

"Ever the doctor." She submerged the spoon into the steaming, creamy cereal grains. "Thank you. For this and for...that night. I also want to apologize for that. I, um, don't know what came over me. Can't say I've ever been that," she let out a shaky laugh, "bold."

She nibbled on the inside flesh of her top lip. He wanted to do that for her, pull that tortured lip between his teeth, explore her mouth with his tongue, feel her warm breath against the skin on his face, and listen to her sighs of contentment as she turned to mush in his arms.

Mush.

Oatmeal.

Shit, he was still silent.

"So," he shifted in the chair, "exactly what happened that night?"

She stirred circles in the bowl. "I'm not sure how to answer that, to be honest. Faux assertiveness that turned into cold feet, maybe?"

Again, he would not say um.

"Would you like to, um," *shit*, "talk about it?"

She brought the spoon to her mouth, pulled it through those *beautiful fucking lips,* and licked them as she swallowed.

"Are you upset?" she asked. "Offended? I'm really sorry. I really am. That was...I'm an idiot."

"You're not."

"And it was pretty left field for me. Bold isn't my forte, which is probably painfully obvious. I guess you could say," she met his eyes, looked away, "I was otherwise distracted. I hope you're able to forgive me."

There was nothing this woman needed forgiveness for, as she certainly couldn't be asking him to be upset about developing acquaintances with her pussy. But he saw his opening and took it.

"Do you like basketball?" he asked. "Can I take you to a game?"

To a movie?

A play?

The beach?

That jewelry store across the street?

What size ring do you wear?

Marry me. You're perfect.

She smiled, and she would have to stop doing that if she wanted him to remain a whole human while sitting across from her.

Another spoonful went into her mouth, and again she licked her lips as she swallowed. "Do you mean the Hawks game this Sunday at seven?"

Good Lord, she even knew when tipoff was.

"I have an extra ticket," he said. "A few friends from work and I are going. If you come to the game, we'll be even."

Lies.

Like he would go out with her once and leave everything at that.

The plastic spoon scraped the bowl as she dug up the last few ounces of oatmeal. When she was done, she brought the coffee cup to her lips. Hours passed inside him, and he figured she was searching for a way to let him down easy. His intentions weren't as obvious as he wanted them to be. Still, many women could intuitively pick up on a man's desire. It also didn't help that he probably hadn't blinked once since she sat down.

"I'd like that, Dr. Edwards."

"Just Kellen."

She nodded. "Kellen, I'd love to go to the Hawks game with you."

He couldn't remember the last time his poor heart had worked this hard in such a short period of time.

"Perfect. I'll need your number so we can meet up." For this date and the ones he was already planning.

They exchanged information.

When her time was up, she reached across and wrapped her fingers around his knuckles. He caressed the base of her thumb with the side of his.

"Thanks again for breakfast. I'll see you on Sunday."

She stood, tossed her trash, and sent him a wave as she headed into the coffee shop. Then, slowly rising to his feet, he brought his cup to his lips and headed to his car with that sensation coursing through his body.

He'd be damned if he called those things poking him in his stomach *butterflies*. Stomach flutters were reserved for teenage crushes and college public speaking class presentations.

But when he slipped behind the steering wheel, he caught a glimpse of his face in the rearview mirror.

Hyuck.

CHAPTER FOUR

Bailey set aside the college brochure and flopped back on her bed, still wearing her work uniform, although she'd been home for over an hour. Was she really ready to go back to lectures, homework, midterms, and finals? It had been so long since she'd last sat in a classroom or even thought about raising her hand to answer a question.

Her last attempt at higher education had been nothing short of a disaster, but something had spurred inside her ever since the first time Dr. Hazel Eyes walked into the coffee shop. Something that made her dream, made her see possibilities where she'd before blinded herself to them.

"Bailey, are you still at it?" Her mother peered into the room, then stepped aside to let her father enter.

She discreetly dropped her pillow on top of the brochure. "Hey, Daddy. You look *dapper*. Where are you guys headed?"

Nigel wore a gray suit with a blue handkerchief in the

pocket, as fashionable at fifty-six as he was at twenty-six. Her mother had gone with an orange cardigan and a knee-length brown skirt, and Alice had roped her long, dark hair into a single, thick braid that hung to the center of her back. Her beautiful mocha face glittered, her complexion the same as Nigel's, and a cute stub of a nose and deep-set eyes rounded out the rest of her features.

"I'm taking this pretty young thing out for a drive and then dinner," Nigel proudly said, hooking elbows with his wife. "You in for the night?"

Bailey tipped her head to the side. "Just about."

"All right. Make sure to lock up. And listen out for Erwin, would you? I found his key in the kitchen."

Maybe she would.

Maybe she wouldn't.

She gave him the smile she'd practiced over the years. "I will, Daddy. Have a good time."

"You too, Sweet pea."

They left, and she retrieved the brochure, her beacon of happiness gone, stolen from her like so many other things.

So her cousin had forgotten his key. He was only a few years younger than her mother, which meant he could get a hotel if necessary. Alice and Nigel had let him stay at the house in Barbados, but a few years ago, he'd joined them and appeared to have zero plans to branch out on his own. Not that Alice made any effort to push him from the nest.

No longer feeling inspired, she put away the brochure and went to lock the front door. On her way back, she passed Erwin's key on the marble kitchen countertop.

Though they'd known lean times, her father had eventually done very well for himself. The beautiful white countertops with gray marbling, the massive kitchen with gorgeous wooden cabinets, and the pristine stainless steel appliances were evidence of that.

However, that type of success came with a lot of work, which had often taken him away from home for several weeks at a time. It was probably why he didn't know and never found out about what had lived in the house in Barbados.

Bailey made her way down the hallway to her bedroom. Just in case, she locked that door as well.

CHAPTER FIVE

The dying charcoal of barbecue smoke, and the perfume of oil and gasoline from the cars littering the Philips Arena parking lot, hung in the air.

Kellen scanned the crowd, sure he looked too eager, standing at the bottom of the steps leading up to the entrance while the rest of the group waited for him at the top.

"Isn't that her?" Sariyah Nelson asked, one arm wrapped around her husband, Marcus.

He'd shown them exactly one picture. One he'd found on the Starbucks Instagram page. Yet there was Bailey, walking toward them wearing a Hawks jersey, *fitted* jeans, and Converse sneakers. She'd pulled her hair into a low ponytail with a braid across the front, the curly strands tumbling in bundles.

He loved her hair and often felt sorry for it, trapped underneath that Starbucks cap when it obviously wanted to spring free. He'd also wondered, randomly in the middle of Atlanta traffic, if her scalp was an erogenous zone. A few times, he'd found himself reflecting on what sounds he believed she would make as he tugged her hair, while massaging her naked hips and back from behind.

All of a sudden, she was in front of him, smiling, and he wanted to pull her into him and bury his nose in her scent. That scent followed him home, tormenting him in his sleep and when he woke up the next morning.

"Hey." He reached for her hand. "I'm really glad you came."

"I'm really glad you invited me," she said.

They walked up the stairs, hands joined.

"Bailey, these are my friends, Catalina and Henry White and Marcus and Sariyah Nelson," he introduced. "Everybody, this is Bailey. We all co-own a family practice, but I also work as the Associate Director of Pediatrics at Piedmont Atlanta."

He needed a full work schedule. If he spent too much time focusing on his own issues, he would quickly drive himself mad.

Bailey squeezed his hand. "Hi, everyone. Nice to meet you."

"Let's get inside," Henry said. "We only have a few seconds before Cat and Sariyah start embarrassing our poor friend here."

Catalina sidled up next to Bailey. "So, you're the cute girl from Starbucks. Let me tell you how much this man talks about y—"

"Like Henry said," Kellen cut in, "let's go inside."

Bailey looked up at him, smiled wider, and she *really* would have to stop doing that.

They bought wings, sandwiches, water, and beer, then took their seats a few rows from the basketball court.

He and Bailey sat book ended by the two other couples, Sariyah and Cat trapping them in intentionally, so close their thighs touched. Hopefully, it wasn't too much for Bailey. The night in his office lingered in his mind.

The crowd roared at tipoff.

Not ten minutes later, Catalina started up, shouting and cursing in long links of Spanish, the brunt of her ire directed at the refs.

Bailey sat slightly pitched forward in her seat, zeroed in on the game, her fingers flexing with suppressed excitement he wanted her to release. He wanted her comfortable with him, even if it meant her standing next to Catalina, shouting plays and yelling for players to "watch for the screen!"

The noise died down for a timeout.

"Is this your first game at the arena?" he asked, leaning forward.

"It is." She looked around the packed stadium. "There's so much energy in here. It's amazing."

"Have you lived in Atlanta all your life?"

"No. I spent the first ten years of my life in Barbados."

"Ah. Makes sense. That's why you're so beautiful."

A flush of color burst onto her cheeks, which came together perfectly with the brown, red, and gold elements in her skin. "I pegged you for a charmer," she said. "Didn't peg myself as easily charmed, though."

"Doesn't mean I'm not being honest."

She bumped him in the side with her shoulder.

The players returned to the court, and he saw approximately twenty-five percent of the first half. There was no way she would agree to a second date. Not with the way he creepily stared at her every chance he got.

At halftime, the players retreated, and his friends strategically went for bathroom breaks and more food, giving them a moment alone.

"So, Kellen," she faced him, as best as she could, in the packed space, "did you ask me to the game because we needed to be even, or is it because, as you say, I'm beautiful?"

"You didn't do anything wrong that night, Bailey."

"I came on to you."

"Trust me, Bailey, there's nothing wrong with that."

If he didn't stop himself, he would stick her name in every sentence. It tasted amazing on his tongue.

Her forehead wrinkled. "You weren't offended?"

"The furthest thing from it. I'm just an old-fashioned kind of guy. Blame my mother."

Had he taken her up on her offer, without a doubt, she would have regretted it the following morning. He could even see it play out, him nudging her awake, hard as stone, waiting for her to open herself up to him again, only to realize he was alone in his office.

Giving up one night was easy when he wanted mornings, afternoons, *and* nights with her. So many mornings, afternoons, and nights.

"Bailey, if I can be honest with you, I haven't been able to stop thinking about you since the first time I saw you," he said. "I walked through the door, and you looked up and smiled. It wasn't even at me, just in my direction. Still, I just about died right there and then. So yeah, if I was a different man, maybe I would have taken you up on your offer that night, but I could tell something wasn't right. I didn't want to ruin my chances of doing what we're doing together now."

"And what are we doing together now?" she asked. "Is this a date?"

"It is. Our first one."

"First?" She laughed. "First assumes you want more."

"I do. Interested?"

She nibbled on her bottom lip, and he tried not to let his gaze linger too long on her mouth. Her lips looked soft and inviting, and he'd bet every penny of his annual salary they were.

"So you just want to get to know me? No sex?"

"Well, wait."

She broke out into a fit of laughter that made him grin.

"I'm not saying I want to be friends," he clarified. "I came here with friends. I'm saying that I want you."

"All or just the good parts?"

"Bailey," a wave of heat passed between them, "I'm sure every single part of you is good."

He noticed the group returning as well as Sariyah's eyes asking if it was okay for them to come back.

"I'm interested," Bailey said, nudging him.

He smiled, found Sariyah's gaze again, and nodded.

After the game, the six of them lingered outside for a few minutes talking about work, the game, and current events. Bailey tucked her hand in his, returning the gentle caresses he passed over her knuckles. Marcus caught their subtle playfulness and disbanded the group, leaving them alone for him to walk her to her car. They didn't say a word to each other, bumping gazes before turning away, smiling like they shared a secret.

When they arrived at her car, he grabbed her other hand and held both between them. She shivered, and he loved that he could see her physical response to him.

"Did you have fun?" he asked, making small talk to keep her with him a bit longer.

The air crackled between them.

His heart galloped in his chest.

"I had a great time," she said.

She stepped into him and wrapped her arms around his midsection, her chin pressed into his chest. He reciprocated, squeezing her tight, releasing a mist of that rosy, citrusy scent. They remained that way for a while, holding on and sharing small talk, until the parking lot had nearly cleared.

"You're too tall."

He smoothed her hair, trying to tame a bit of frizz that popped right back up the minute it left his touch. "Too tall for what?"

"To kiss."

"Let me make a slight modification."

He leaned down until her fingers slipped into the hair at his nape, her sweet breath grazing his cheek. Their lips came together, gliding over each other, his soft against her satin. She gripped his shirt, melting into him, giving him more than he expected, but everything he wanted.

She fell into his arms, restraining a hunger he could sense bits of. That, he wanted as well, but in time. With how he craved this woman, anything further right now would be more than she could handle.

They separated, and he traced her top lip with his thumb. Sighing, she closed her eyes and grabbed his wrist with both hands as though she would keel over without the support.

"I'll see you again," he said, pulling her in for a kiss on her forehead.

"So sure of yourself," she teased.

"Will I?"

"Yes. So much, yes."

He laughed. "Good."

She got into her car.

He stood watching until she was out of sight, then walked to his car on the other side of the parking lot with a noticeable lift in his steps.

CHAPTER SIX

She'd been kissed before.

Of course, she'd been kissed before.

She was thirty years old.

But she'd never been kissed like *that*.

Bailey touched her trembling lips with trembling hands. Her entire body rippled. Kellen was kind and sweet, yet sinful and masculine. His kiss, though chaste, had turned her into warm honey. They might have been on two opposing ends of the social hierarchy, but their chemistry had them meeting in the middle. When his lips touched hers, for once in her life, every single iota of darkness disappeared.

She sighed, rested her head against the car seat, and sat for a few minutes before stepping out. Her legs quivered on the walk up to the front door, even as she stuck the key into the lock and entered the foyer. Her heart ricocheted so wildly, it rocked her as she floated through the house, up the stairs, and down the hallway to the last door on the right.

"Bailey."

Alice stood in a prim, white nightgown, arms folded across her breasts, at the mouth of the hallway. A spot of light from the partially closed master bedroom door gave just enough illumination to make out the rage in her eyes.

Not tonight, Alice.

"Where were you?" Alice asked in a voice that could cut glass. "And didn't I tell you to rearrange the kitchen?"

Always telling, never asking.

"At a basketball game," Bailey said. "And I'm pretty sure I did."

Alice's neck drew back. "Excuse me?"

"I'm sorry, Alice, but I did rearrange the kitchen. Right before I left."

Alice took a few steps down the hallway toward her. Bailey braced herself, a reflex.

"Do it again," Alice ordered. "I don't like it the way it is now."

"Fine."

"Fine? Keep giving me a," she lowered her voice, "fucking attitude, and see if you have anywhere to rest your head in the state of Georgia. Maybe, had you applied yourself, you would be able to afford your own place."

She would have been able to apply herself had it not been for trauma so potent, it warped her brain, and now she had to spend years reshaping it. Some of that damage was permanent, but she prayed enough working parts were left for her to one day make something of herself. Good parts she could share with Kellen.

"Is that Bailey?" Nigel called from the bedroom. "How was the game, Sweet pea?"

"The Hawks won," she yelled back.

"Ah, good. Come on to bed, Alice. Let Bailey be."

Alice eyed her with that look—the one that told her she would never see what she longed to see. The look that told her that although she'd been raised by this woman, she'd never experienced what it felt like to be raised by a mother.

"Goodnight...*Mom*," she taunted.

Eyes wide and glistening, Alice spun around, the tail of her nightgown flailing behind her, and disappeared inside the master bedroom. Bailey stared at the empty space for a moment, a knot growing in her chest she'd been harboring for three decades.

Sighing, she placed her hand on the doorknob to her bedroom and turned.

CHAPTER SEVEN

Bridgetown, Barbados
June 1987

The sun threatened to leave blisters on Alice's back as she sat on the front porch of the first house she hoped she and Nigel would share—a wooden, chattel house.

She hated wooden houses.

She hated the wooden blocks the house sat upon even more, and the galvanized roof that leaked whenever Nigel went out of town. Two weeks ago, her living room, if one could call the litter box-sized space a living room, had been as full as a pool. Last night, with him cuddled in the bed next to her, the heavens had drenched the earth with their wrath. All that rain, lightning, and thunder, and not even a drop had seeped in.

The yard, she loved.

It was large and always green. The grass grew slowly,

which meant it wasn't often she had to pull out the mower, at least whenever Nigel was out of town. She was looking out onto it now, watching cars pass by and women in colorful skirts chatting and laughing loudly as they walked down the street. Bailey played at the end of the yard, rapidly moving between tugging on a daisy that had popped up from the ground and chasing butterflies. The girl had the attention span of a puppy.

Today, she had on a red jumper printed with flowers that Nigel had brought back from Aruba when he'd worked on a project there. Her chubby thighs barely made it through the foot holes, which had made Nigel giggle and kiss them. He only giggled when he played with Bailey, unmistakable love for the toddler in his eyes whenever he looked at her. He was a gift, Alice knew, but she wasn't as sure about the child now tumbling in the grass, flinging her legs into the air over and over again.

She didn't know how it happened, but in an instant, she was across the yard. All she'd heard was Bailey's shriek and had barely consciously registered it before being pulled toward the child.

Bailey rolled onto her stomach and wobbled to her legs. Then, crying and swatting at her hand, she came running.

Alice felt the tether linking her to the girl, a tug in her chest with almighty strength. But, as the girl drew nearer, she backed away.

And away.

And away.

The closer Bailey got, the farther she became until Bailey

finally stopped running and looked at her with her little head cocked to the side, her curls, in bows, bouncing in the wind.

Bailey took a tentative step forward—smart little girl—and Alice, on the same foot, moved back. Bailey tried again, meticulously lifting that tiny leg, but waited too long to find the ground. She lost her balance, falling onto her bottom.

Nigel appeared in the doorway, roused from his sleep. When he noticed Bailey's tear-soaked face, he rushed down the stairs, crossed the distance in two bounds, picked Bailey up, and held her close.

"What happened, sweetheart? Come, let Daddy look at it."

Alice stood watching them.

"It's a sting, Alice." He turned to her. "These damn honeybees, and of course, she would be allergic. Get her medicine."

She didn't move.

"Alice, go get the pen," Nigel repeated, his voice like sandpaper grit.

She rushed into the house, searched through a basket on the bedroom dresser, and ran back out with the pen.

Bailey's face had begun to swell, her skin as red as the blood that ran beneath it. Nigel exposed a thigh, and Alice stabbed the pen, as hard as she could, into the child's flesh. Bailey yelped, and Alice felt it again, that tether, telling her to take the child. To hold the child close to her breasts. There was almost an overwhelming need for her to give that comfort, to smooth the silky hairs on the child's head and kiss the tears from her cheeks.

Instead, she watched and waited until Bailey's color came back.

"I'm still taking her to see Dr. Tinsel," Nigel announced, walking into the house to grab his key and a hat. "Alice, you stay here. We'll be back soon."

Soon was seven hours later when the sun kissed the horizon, the darkness breached by lights pouring through windows. He walked in, Bailey in his arms, now dressed in a pair of pink cotton pajamas. She was fast asleep, the bows gone to reveal a soft mound of hoops and loops.

Nigel still didn't hand Bailey over as he walked past, without a word, into the bedroom. Alice followed a few minutes later to find him on the queen bed, Bailey tucked into his side, him twirling her hair around his forefinger.

He didn't look up at her in the doorway.

That night, she slept on the loveseat. In the middle of the night, a gush of water seeped through the ceiling, splashing onto her nightgown.

On a night when Nigel was home.

CHAPTER EIGHT

Kellen dreamed about Bailey often.

Tonight, brown skin poured into his palms as soft as he'd remembered it from the arena. She was on top of him, her hair free and shining, untamed, through the light behind them. She pinned those sultry eyes on him like nothing else in the room existed, and he held onto her waist, waiting in anticipation for what he would find underneath.

Round, full breasts with dark-tipped areolas emerged with each tug of her shirt over her head. Then there was nothing but the skin he traced with his fingers, shoulder to fingertip, collarbone to belly button. He hesitated to touch her breasts, knowing he was dreaming, wondering if everything would dissolve the moment he indulged.

Yet, Dream Bailey took his hand and pulled it to the mound, which was heavy on his palm. He made circles around her areolas, the brown tips perfect as they, of course, would be in a dream. His circles grew tighter until his finger was on her nipple, and her back arched the minute he flattened his thumb along its peaked edge.

He eased up until they were eye to eye with her legs wrapped around him. The sheets pooled between them, and her irises threatened to drag him into an abyss filled with crude oil. He bent his head to her naked breast, and the moment he parted his lips to suck, he was jolted awake.

Kellen blinked, rolled onto his side, and cursed the empty room, his dick tenting the sheets. In dreams less erotic, he'd still wake up with a brick-like erection he felt in the veins in his forehead. Work had prevented him from seeing Bailey for the last couple of weeks, so his dreams appeared to be filling in the gaps. It would be like wearing a gasoline suit in hell being around her without those images threatening to ruin what he'd promised—that he would take things slow.

Usually, he could, but he'd never been affected by anyone like this before. He had no idea where to set his limits in order to test them.

His phone screen lit up, and he noticed the missed call from his brother. Apparently, the phone's vibration had woken him up, not his overeager desire to acquaint Bailey's nipple with his tongue. The next time he saw David, he would give him the full extent of his frustration.

He rolled onto his back, pressed the call-back button, and hoped David didn't hear the erection in his voice. However, his sister-in-law's frantic voice knocked out any lingering sleep or desire.

"Kellen? Kellen, it's me."

"Alexis?" He sat up. "What's wrong?"

"It's David. I can't find him." She sniffled, and he could picture her, eyes swollen and red, though he didn't want to. "When I woke up, he was gone. And I think he might have backslid on his sobriety."

Kellen flung his legs over the side of the bed and began searching for a pair of pants in the dark. He located a pair of jeans, stepped into them, and slipped into a shirt while mentally running through the different places his brother could have disappeared to. Hopefully, Alexis was mistaken, and David hadn't thrown thirteen months' worth of sobriety into the wastebasket.

"Why do you think that?" he asked, leaving the bedroom for the dark hallway in search of his keys.

"I found a receipt in the car. I used his car to pick Abbie up from daycare, and she accidentally kicked off one of her shoes. When I went looking for it, I saw the receipt. He bought vodka."

"When was this?"

The keys weren't on the countertop, so he went to the mudroom.

"Two days ago. I know he's been stressed out about work, and his firm's been trying to get that bid for the huge office complex downtown, but I thought things were okay. I never thought..."

He found the keys on the bench in the mudroom, patted his pocket to make sure he had his wallet, and ran out the front door.

"What kind of wife am I if I don't know my husband's been stressed enough to start drinking again?"

The tears restarted, and he heard a thud as she laid the phone down on a solid surface. He didn't hear her voice again until he was speeding down the street, his mind running through the places his brother frequented now and had frequented back in his more troubling days.

"I'm sorry, Kellen. I'm here."

David and Alexis were the fairytale love story of the kids who'd hated each other in middle school, developed an attraction in high school, and married right after college. Their love encompassed passion, understanding, a bit of complexity, and compromise. They'd also had good role models in his parents, and it was something he'd hoped for himself, though his romantic exploits so far had all ended in a massive blaze.

Everyone had their own burdens to bear, their own demons to wrangle, and the free will to deal with them as they pleased.

David had chosen alcohol.

He worked.

Sometimes he worked until his body was both sore and numb, but overworking was now so embedded in him, only a priest could exorcise it. When he worked, the problems slept. The minute he stopped working, they overwhelmed him, and it would be impossible to be the one keeping his family afloat if he was forced to tackle his own shit.

"I'll find him, Alexis." It was a promise he would keep even now, dead tired. "Stay by the phone. Hold Abbie."

"But what if he—"

"He won't." David, no matter how inebriated, would never repeat the tragedy that had driven him to drink in the first place. "He won't, 'Lexis. Now go hold that beautiful baby."

"Call me as soon as you find him?"

He made the promise, hung up the phone, and said a small prayer when he came to a stoplight. His first obstacle was trying to decide whether David had truly backslid. If his brother had, there were a handful of bars he could check. If David hadn't, there was one place he knew David would have gone if caught in the throes of stressful memories.

He went there first.

The entrance to the cemetery was a bit too extravagant for what it held inside, like walking into a mausoleum in ancient Greece with its white stonework and tall columns. The word "cemetery" was curled into an iron gate protecting the dead from the illicit activities of the living, and he breathed a sigh of relief when he saw David's car in the side parking lot.

He pulled up next to it, parked, and checked inside to find it empty. Then he sniffed the air for any traces of alcohol around the vehicle, but there were none.

He continued into the cemetery, walking the path he knew all too well, until he found his brother squatting in front of a tombstone. A fresh bouquet of orange roses rested on top.

"Hey."

David turned around. "Kellen? What are you…did Alexis call you?"

"She's worried." He crouched in the space next to David. "Tell her where you're going if you're going to leave like that."

"She was asleep, and she looked so beautiful, I didn't want to wake her."

He rested a hand on his brother's shoulder. "Have you been drinking?"

"Nah. Thought about it."

"So, where's the vodka?"

David's eyes opened wide, their hazel irises perfectly matched despite their two-year age difference. Seeing a shard of him reflecting in his brother's eyes brought him a sense of peace, especially because of what they'd lost.

"How do you know about that?"

"Alexis."

"How'd she know?" Then David laughed. "I don't even know why I'm asking. She knows everything."

"She found the receipt in the car. Where's the vodka?"

David turned back to the tombstone. "I tossed it. Decided to come out here instead. Can't do that to my ladies."

Kellen took in the dates etched into the concrete pillar. "I do it too, come out here when I feel a little bit lost."

"You talk to him too, or is that just my crazy ass?"

"That's just your crazy ass." He slapped David on the back and stood, David rising with him. "No, I talk to him. I talked to him on my first night out here to tell him I was back."

They stood in a brief shared silence, their gazes bouncing from the stone to the flowers.

"Ready to head back?"

David nodded. "I'm ready."

They headed to the cars.

Their similarities ended at their height and build; David's hair, though dark brown, was shades lighter than his own. David had taken on their mother's features, and even when unkempt, he somehow managed to look like a French aristo-crat. Him, he always looked rugged, like his father's heritage from the barrios of Spain, with thick dark locks and facial hair prone to taking over his face like weeds if he wasn't careful.

"Why don't you want her to know you come out here sometimes?"

"I'll tell her someday," David said. "Right now, I kind of want it to be my thing."

Kellen tipped his head to the side. "Understandable, but at least take your phone. Let her know you're okay."

"You're right. Didn't mean to make you both worry." David slid inside his car, closed the door, and rolled down the window. "Thanks, Kellen. You're a good brother. I'll try to be a better one."

Kellen swatted the air. "Whatever."

They laughed and slapped hands.

David drove off.

Kellen leaned against his car and took a deep breath. Daylight's orange glow colored the sky. According to his phone, it was only a half hour before Starbucks opened, so he got in his car and drove, passing four different locations until he arrived at the one nearest to his office.

A god-awfully long line wound through the front door, across the brick patio, and down the steps leading up to the building. Several people turned away, but he wouldn't be going anywhere.

He hadn't come for coffee.

Someone touched him on the back of his arm. He turned around, and although it had been a couple of weeks since he'd last seen her face, looking at her made him want to skip work and spend the week with her, doing nothing at all.

"I thought that was you," Bailey said, her hair in twists underneath a beanie she'd paired with jeans and a pullover. "Long time no see."

Dawn was breaking, but her eyes were stuck at midnight.

"I'm sorry about that," he said. "The hospital's short-staffed, so I end up—"

"It's okay, Kellen. I'm just messing with you. You're a physician. Doctors are busy. You, at least, make time to text me and call whenever you can. I do have a question, though. How tired are you when you come into the coffee shop?"

"Usually seconds away from passing out." He took her hand, and it was interesting how something so simple could wash away the anguish of the last hour. "But I had to see you. You're not working today?"

"No, I'm off, but I switched my bank, and it messed up my direct deposit, so I came to pick up my check. Boring stuff."

"You look nice." He gave her a quick scan. At least, one more obvious than the last five. "Very cute. Why so early?"

"I couldn't sleep. You're up early yourself."

"Like I said, I came looking for you. Have breakfast with me."

A smile touched her lips. Lips he had to fight not to trace, first with his fingertips and then with his tongue.

"I'd love to," she said. "Be right back."

She ran inside, grabbed her check, and was walking next to him in under five minutes.

"By the way," she craned her neck to look up at him, "would you mind if I chose the spot? There's this breakfast place I go to sometimes, a real Mom and Pop type of place, and honestly, a bit Hole In The Wall."

His brow shot up. "Hole In The Wall? Have you ever seen the movie, *Bridesmaids?*"

"Yeah, I ha—"

She caught herself when she realized what scene from the movie he was hinting at, and she laughed so hard, he glanced across the street at that jewelry store.

"No, no. They're okay. I go there all the time. Trust me, they're okay. I swear."

They'd reached his car, but he took her hand and slid their fingers together.

"You have nice hands," she pointed out. "They're kinda rough. I like that."

"And yours," he stroked the center of her palm with a thumb, "feel like silk."

"Again, with the charm."

He shrugged.

"Are we taking your car?" she asked when she noticed the shiny black sedan. "What is this, a Mercedes?"

"BMW. And my fingers might feel this way because I did some of the work on my house. It was a reno in Morningside."

"Like Morningside Lenox Park? That and a beamer? You must do pretty well for yourself."

"I do all right," he shrugged again, "and yes, we're taking my car. This is technically our second date, so I think we should arrive together. I'll pick you up from your place on the third one."

She looked at him like he'd just told her he'd been secretly filming her, in the shower, for weeks, but she didn't add anything to explain the look.

He opened the passenger door, and she slid inside.

By the time they arrived at her hole in the wall, his stomach had twisted into a surgeon's knot.

They got out and held hands through the diner's front doors, but he sensed something bothering her. Something that had been bothering her since his comment about their third date. As he got ready to comment on it—right after ordering what she'd said were "good ass eggs," hash browns, pancakes, and an extra-crispy waffle for her—she spoke up.

"I have to tell you something." She dipped her tea bag into her cup as if expecting something to bite the other end. "Don't take it the wrong way."

He eased back, giving her silent permission to continue.

"I find you very intimidating," she said. "I'm actually not sure what you see in me."

The statement caught him by surprise, so much so that he mulled over his response before it came out of his mouth.

"Bailey, what do I even say to that?"

She reached for five packets of sugar, tore the tops off all at the same time, and overturned them into her mug. "Kellen, you have a BMW that I'm pretty sure is less than a year old. You went to medical school when I...I didn't finish college. You're so gorgeous, I'm sure even your mirror is grateful. What are you doing here with *me*? If you're looking for sex, you're taking the long way when you don't have to."

He'd thought about the sex. He'd barely been able to stop thinking about the sex. But thinking about sex didn't mean it was exclusively what he wanted, and he got the sense she was offering something she honestly wasn't ready to.

"What did you order again?" Changing the subject seemed easier than confronting what she was hitting him with, head-on. "You got the eggs and the what? I don't think I ordered enough food."

"Kellen, this is important to me. Please. Can we just talk about it for a minute?"

"I, honestly, don't know what to say. Only that you're wrong about me and about you, at the same time."

"I've got demons."

"Who doesn't?"

"What about issues?"

"Again, who doesn't have issues?"

She exhaled, lips puffing up. "Kellen, just tell me. What do you want from me? Everybody wants something."

"I don't want anything *from* you," he clarified. "I just want you."

"In your bed."

"Eventually, but right now, across from me, having breakfast on our second date."

She tossed a few crumpled bills on the table. "Why are you being so persistent?"

"First off, I'm paying," he said. "Two, if you think you're going somewhere, you're not. Not when I've been looking forward to seeing you for weeks. And three, why are you trying so hard to be difficult? To me, you're perfect."

She pushed herself to her feet, palms flat on the tabletop. "Don't do that. Don't call me that. I'll never be able to live up to those standards, and that's not fair to either of us."

She marched toward the doors, and he called out to her, but she didn't stop. Grunting, he followed, grabbing her forearm before she reached the sidewalk.

"Damn it, woman. Would you stop?"

She faced him.

"Was I smothering you or something?" he asked.

"No, I just don't get this." She gestured from him to her. "I don't understand what you expect from me. I don't have much, if anything, to offer you. I asked you if you wanted sex, but you said no."

"Bailey, I never said no. You keep saying I did, but I haven't. At all. Why? Do *you* want sex?"

"Yes."

He stilled, needing a moment to let her answer move through him and to beg his dick to stay down. Now was neither the time nor the place, no matter how much it wanted him to fuck her on the asphalt. If she continued to look at him like she wanted him to, however, the diner patrons might end up getting a show.

"I said not yet," he reiterated. "I want you. Of course, I want you. But I also want to get to know you better."

"Yes, but why?"

"Bailey," he tipped her closer with a hand at the small of her back, "I really don't understand. Break it down for me."

"Kellen, you're successful, tall, kind, sweet, and out-of-this-world attractive. I," her brows pinched in the middle, "struggle with a lot of the things you seem to be good at. There's an imbalance. What if I can't hold intellectual conversations with you? What if—"

"This works, you fall for me, and I wake up one day and decide you're not enough?" he finished. "Am I on the right track?"

"Something like that." She massaged her forehead. "God, you must think I'm so insecure right now. And I am, but you weren't supposed to find out until we were in love with each other."

"You think we'll fall in love?"

"I should be quiet."

He released a chest-deep laugh. "Honestly, Bailey, I have things I'm insecure about too."

Like his recovering brother and an addiction to work that numbed the worst of his grief. Seeing his brother, father, and mother at their lowest points changed him. Someone had needed to be the foundation, and he'd stepped up to the plate. Despite cracks, wear, and tear, he was holding up fairly well.

Somewhat.

"Kellen, we're not equal."

"And I agree," he said. "We're not equal, in any way. All you have to do is look at me, and I can barely get a word out. You smile, and I feel like I'm back in braces. There's something powerful between us, Bailey. It's pointing me to you, and that's the only direction I care about heading right now."

She stared at him, lips slightly parted and her fingers toying with the strings at the neck of her pullover.

"Can I admit to being scared?" she asked. "Scared of not being good enough for you?"

The admission plucked a chord in his chest. He'd failed at this relationship thing so much, he couldn't imagine anyone not being good enough for him. It didn't matter that he'd put his heart into them; the only thing he'd offered was his heart.

And his wallet.

There was much more to him, but those were the parts he'd done his best to tamp down until they gave him insomnia, stomachaches, and indigestion.

"Can you accept that I have the same fear?" he proposed. "Just accept. We don't have to do anything about it right now."

She nodded. "I can agree to that."

"I'm sorry, what? I can't hear you over your stomach growling."

"Boy," she poked his midsection, "you're lucky you're cute."

"Come on." He cupped the back of her neck and kissed her forehead. "Let's go eat, Trouble."

When they returned inside, their waitress was on her way from the back with their breakfast steaming on a tray. She suspiciously eyed them while placing the food on the table but didn't ask any questions.

Before he dug in, Kellen pointed to his plate. "Want some of my pancakes?"

Bailey hesitated, examined her plate, then took a piece of bacon from his.

"Want a turkey sausage?" she asked.

He helped himself to a link.

"Your mother teach you that?" She scooped eggs onto her fork. "Give a girl your food, you might feed her for a day, but teach her how to steal from your plate, and you feed her for a lifetime?"

He smiled, wondering if there was a lifetime in their future. "I guess you could say that. She and my father always order different things when they go out so that they can eat off the other's plates. I guess me and my brother picked it up along the way."

"You have a brother?" She cut into the sausage, and he found it cute that she didn't bite right into it when he swallowed his whole. "Any sisters?"

"Nope. My mother had three boys. Two now. My brother, Connor, died when we were younger."

Her hand closed over her heart. "I'm so, so sorry. Was he younger or older?"

"Younger...by seven minutes."

"A twin? What happened?"

"Accident. It was hard on everybody because we didn't see it coming. My oldest brother, David, was having a hard time with the memory. I was with him before I came here."

She covered his hand with hers. "Rough morning."

"Yes. It's why I came to see you. You smooth out the edges."

She looked down at her plate, but he caught the smile that pulled at her cheek.

"Anyhow," he stabbed his pancake stack with his fork, stuffed the pieces into his mouth, and swallowed the bite with a swig of juice, "my brother and I were the last ones to see

Connor alive. Eventually, David wasn't able to deal with the memories and turned to drinking. Right now, he's thirteen months sober."

Thirteen months, two days, and seven hours.

"Was he drinking tonight?"

"Thankfully, no." He swallowed another bite. "He fights it, hard, for Alexis and Abigail. Alexis is his wife, and Abigail's my niece. She's four months old. Even though he's been sober this long, he said he won't acknowledge any milestones unless his little girl has seen him sober for at least a year since she's been on this earth."

She laced their fingers together.

"*My* vice is that I work like a dog," he went on, the floodgates opening. "Working stops me from thinking, and thinking stops me from feeling."

She pushed aside her waffle and leaned toward him. "So you've never mourned your brother?"

"Can't."

"Why not?"

"My family needs me."

"But," she searched his face, "who supports you when things get too hard?"

"Guess we'll find out when I come to that bridge."

Silence shrouded them, and he held his breath. It was only the tip of the iceberg, but "just the tip" accounted for around ten percent of his patients' births. Just the tip could, very easily, turn into more than planned.

"Thanks for telling me," she said.

"Thanks for listening."

He wasn't ready to go, so he ordered a slice of chocolate sundae pie and requested two extra forks.

"Can I plan one of our dates?" she asked. "Since you've apparently got more planned out already."

"I do, but what about...date number five? You probably wouldn't have liked going out on a boat anyhow."

Her eyes lit up. "Actually, I'd love to go boating. I can't swim, but can we please still go?"

He took her in, his bottom lip passing between his teeth. "We'll get you a life jacket."

"So maybe I can plan date five and a half," she suggested. "Half meaning we maybe go out on a weekday instead of the weekend."

"Weekend? I was thinking we'd get to date ten in the next ten days."

"Dr. Edwards, you don't have ten days to give me."

"*Au contraire*, Bailey. I'd trade sleep for you in a heartbeat."

He leaned back as the waitress placed the pie on the table. She handed him a fork, picked up the other, and he came close to popping a blood vessel, watching a forkful of pie go into her mouth. As she slipped the tines back out between her lips, his thoughts went to explicit places.

"Do you know those couples that sit next to each other in the same booth when they're out to eat?" she asked.

He nodded. "I do."

"Do they annoy you?"

"So much."

"Want to be one of them?"

"Yes."

She came around to his side of the table.

He kissed her, relishing in the taste of her mouth, part her own sweetness and part sugar from the pie. When an erection strong enough to lift the table surfaced, he pulled away.

She settled against his side, leaning into him, and it was like she'd been created for that purpose—to be at his side.

For a while.

CHAPTER NINE

Bailey clicked the "apply online" button for Georgia State University on her old laptop, the second university application she'd be filling out that week. The first had been an application for entry into Emory's English program, and she'd balked the entire time because of her grades from her attempt at Economics at Cornell.

It was what her family had wanted, for her to major in something that would put her on a similar playing field as her prestigious sisters. A Black woman with an Economics degree seemed like the trick, but she'd found herself lost in African folklore and Caribbean folktales, stories from talking "Anansi" spiders to the hidden secrets on sugar plantations. She'd even had dreams about her old house in Barbados, a house she loathed but continuously felt drawn to as if it held its own secrets.

This time around, she was determined to follow her own

path, no matter where it led, both in life and love. Yet, as usual, while she was being pulled in one direction, her past had her by the legs, trying to drag her in the other.

She couldn't explain her childhood to anyone who might've thought it was worth a listen. She had two younger sisters who she adored and hovered over with a fierce, motherly type of protection. Her father was kind and gentle and always there when needed, sometimes before she realized she needed him.

Then there was Alice.

She first realized she was different from her sisters, Noble and Faith, at three years old. She'd been sitting in the middle of their old living room with her mother several yards away. That morning, she'd accidentally called the woman she'd come to know as her mother, "Mom." Then heavily pregnant with Noble, Alice had uttered a single word in correction: "Alice."

She remembered cocking her head to the side, confused even though she'd always called her mother "Alice," but thinking it was odd since all the little kids on her favorite television shows had used a different word.

So she'd tried again, smiling with the eager innocence of a child.

"Mom?"

Seconds later, her nose bled onto the tile floors, the novel her mother had been reading next to her body where it had landed after being hurled at her head. She'd barely felt the pain through her daze, looking from her mother to the book, asking questions that could never be answered with a three-year-old's brain. In that instant, as her mother had hurried from the room without an apology or evidence of regret, she understood that she was different.

That she was Bailey, and this woman was Alice.

Her bedroom door opened.

Erwin poked his head through the door, looking left to right until his eyes landed on her. He smiled, a slow gesture that always came across like a cougar seeing a rabbit, after going without food for several days, trapped in wire.

"What's up, Bailey?" He stepped inside. "It's like three in the morning. What are you still doing up?"

Red streaks lined his eyes, and his butterscotch complexion had been taken over by the flush of inebriation. His hair, loc'd and dark brown, dangled to the center of his back. A missing canine from a soccer incident when he was younger made him appear all the more menacing.

"Reading," she said. "You just getting in?"

He tapped the door, and her heart kicked in her chest. It didn't shut but instead came to a stop, allowing a three-inch gap between the wall and its edge.

"A man's work is never done." He adjusted himself in his jeans. "Get my drift?"

She studied her laptop screen. "When are you going back to Barbados?"

Vodka and Courvoisier steamed from his pores in waves, permeating the room, burrowing into the furniture, the curtains, and her sheets.

"Bailey, look at me."

He reached out to touch her chin, but she backed away, closed the laptop, and left the bed to increase the space between them. She planted her back against the cold east wall, the room constantly frigid because of its location beneath a large oak in the backyard.

"Bailey," his eyes filled, "there's something wrong with the house. The one in Barbados. I think it knows."

She clenched her fists. "Knows what?"

"What I did. What I did…to you."

"Erwin!" Alice's terror-filled voice pierced the air. "Erwin, please come. It's Nigel. Something is happening."

"Daddy?" Bailey rushed from the room and hurried to the master suite. "Daddy, what's wrong? Talk to me."

"Pain," Nigel groaned, baring his teeth, grip tight on his left arm.

"Did you call an ambulance?"

"They said five minutes," Alice answered.

Bailey hurried to the bathroom, sifted through the medicine cabinet, pulled out a bottle of chewable aspirin, and dumped four pills into her palm. When she returned, she offered them to her father, who allowed the pills to dissolve on his tongue.

"What did you give him, aspirin?" Alice crouched next to her husband. "Nigel, are you having a heart attack? You can't leave me, honey. I love you so much. You, Noble, and Faith are all I have."

Bailey sprinted from the room and headed downstairs to wait for the paramedics. When they arrived, she escorted them to the bedroom and didn't fully exhale until their flashing lights, and Alice's car with Erwin in the passenger seat, pulled off.

She had to give it to her mother—the woman was nothing if

not consistent. No matter the situation, Alice always found a way to remind her that she was the family pariah.

It annoyed her that she still felt pain when Alice twisted the knife, and she often wondered if she would have been better off without a mother. It wasn't a fair thought to have, considering the unimaginable hurt those who'd lost their mothers suffered, but they'd lost someone they loved.

To her, Alice was, essentially, a stranger.

The reach inside her that never quite died, the one that desired a mother's love, didn't appear to have anything to do with love. If anything, it felt more like *purpose*. Most people wanted to feel like they'd been born for a reason, that there'd been worth attached to that very first breath they'd taken. Going through the trouble and agony of birthing a child, only to loathe it, seemed…pointless.

However, her father had made life with Alice bearable. He would need her, and she would have to get this time in with him before Noble and Faith flew in, answering Alice's wrangled prayers for her family to comfort her.

Afterward, Bailey Green would be forgotten.

Tangential.

A blip on the outer rim of the family circle.

DOCTORS AND NURSES WHIZZED BY IN STREAKS OF GREEN AND blue, in and out of Nigel's room, talking in hushed whispers and casting furtive glances at her, Erwin, and Alice standing together.

"My daughters are flying in from Boston," Alice babbled to a nurse as the woman nodded, rubbing a reassuring hand up and down Alice's back. "What should I tell them?"

"He's being stabilized, Mrs. Green." The nurse sent Alice a tiny half-smile. "We also have our top cardiologist coming in to attend to your husband."

"When my daughters get here, they can see him, right?"

"Yes, but the maximum is three visitors at a time."

"My nephew's leaving in a few hours." Alice pointed a thumb at Erwin. "Bailey can go back out front when they get here. My daughters will be here tomorrow."

The nurse looked at Bailey.

Bailey shrugged.

They'd both heard her refer to Nigel as "Daddy."

"Actually, Aunt Alice, I have an appointment in the morning," Erwin said. "Bailey can stay with you. Once Noble and Faith get here, she should probably leave to get some shut-eye. We won't be any good to you or Uncle Nigel if we're dead tired."

Alice nodded, slipped away from the nurse's reassuring hand, and wrapped her arms around Erwin. "Thank you, my dear. You are like a son to me."

Bailey glanced down, certain there was a handle sticking out of a wound she would need stitched before the end of the night. Why Alice continued to use knives, she didn't know. A bullet would do the trick, and it would work much quicker.

Erwin left, and an attendant brought two chairs for her and Alice to sit along an empty wall close to Nigel's room. He didn't leave when he was done, and she looked up to find him staring at her.

"Your daughter is beautiful, ma'am," he said.

Alice stared straight ahead.

He lowered his voice. "You're beautiful. What's your name? Can I take you out sometime?"

"I appreciate the compliment," Bailey began, "but I'm seeing someo—"

"Is that my girl?"

She peered around the attendant. Kellen, tall, dark, and handsome, walked toward her in a pair of scrubs beneath a flawless white coat, arms open. She hopped up, met him half-way, and melted into his embrace.

"What are you doing here?" he asked. "Are you okay?"

"It's my father. He's having a heart issue."

"Oh baby, I'm so sorry. Which room is he in?"

Alice cleared her throat to alert them to her presence. Bailey plastered on a smile and gestured to Kellen.

"Dr. Kellen Edwards, this is Alice Green."

"Your mother?"

"Something like that."

He extended a hand.

Alice shot her look and then stilled for a few seconds after studying Kellen's face, as if she'd seen him somewhere before.

"So very nice to meet you," she crooned, placing her hand in his and putting on a display that would have landed her more Academy Awards than Katharine Hepburn. "Friend of Bailey's?"

"Oh, I'm much more than that." Kellen released her hand,

tugged Bailey back close to him, and kissed the very tip of her forehead. "Look, if there's anything you guys need, let me know. I'm good friends with our head of cardiology. Remember Dr. White, Bailey? Cat's husband? You met him on our date at the arena."

Alice cocked her head to the side. "That's who they're putting in there with my Nigel. Can you vouch for him, this Dr. White?"

"With my life, ma'am." He crossed his fingers over his heart. "If that's who'll be in there with your husband, his odds just increased tenfold."

"Thank you, Dr. Edwards."

"No problem." He looked down at Bailey. "Talk to you a second?"

They went further down the hall, and he held her hand while they walked, despite them being in the middle of a decent amount of hospital employees.

"About canceling our last date—"

"Kellen, no apologies necessary. I swear."

Dates three and four had been a cozy Mediterranean dinner, where they'd talked for four hours straight, and a matinee movie. Date number five had pounced upon them, and although he'd had to reschedule the boat ride, she was grateful for the time to think about that date five-and-a-half she'd so readily volunteered herself for.

"Do you work tomorrow?" he asked, stroking the back of her hand with his thumb, making it hard to concentrate.

She nodded. "I work in the morning, but I'm off by two."

"We'll go on the boat tomorrow." He pulled her into him again, held her close. "We can get dinner after. I cleared my schedule, so we should have no interruptions. It'll be just the two of us. Sound good?"

"Mmm." She closed her eyes, imagination running wild. "Sounds perfect."

He kissed her, sweet, hot, and slow, nothing in his body language giving way that he cared who might be watching.

"Holy fuck, my girl's gorgeous. I'm glad I got to see you tonight."

Releasing him was one of the hardest things she'd ever done, in her life, but he had work to do. If she held onto him any longer, she'd never let go, and his patients needed him.

He took a step back.

She smiled at him, and he gripped his chest.

"Aww, you're killing me, B. You really need to stop doing that."

"Doing what?"

"That thing with your face." He gave her a quick peck. "My kryptonite. See you later, Gorgeous."

As he walked away, the floor disappeared beneath her feet. She watched him until he was gone, after he'd turned around three more times to catch her staring at him, a confident swagger in his walk. The man was incredibly sexy, and she knew then that she would never let him go. Fate would have to pry him from her cold, dead fingers.

"Bailey."

A shiver ran up her spine. "Yes, Alice?"

"Nigel's okay. We can see him now."

CHAPTER TEN

Alice kissed the back of her husband's hand and rubbed it along her cheek. Though asleep, he looked much better than he had at the house, his condition downgraded from serious to stable. She couldn't live without him, and ever since they'd met all those years ago, she'd been determined not to. The girl sitting on the other side of the room had almost ruined that.

"You don't have to stay," she told Bailey. "I called Noble and Faith. They're flying in."

"I'll stay until they get here," Bailey insisted.

"I don't think that's wise, child."

"Why name me 'Bailey' if you're only going to call me 'child'?"

"You can leave."

"He's my father, Alice."

"And he's my husband."

"We share DNA…don't we?"

67

She turned away. "You're too stubborn for your own good. The doctor himself said Nigel would be fine, so I don't see why you feel like you have to be here."

As if finally pushed to the end of her rope, Bailey stood and flung her purse strap over her shoulder. "Fine, Alice. You win."

"This was never a competition."

"Trying to convince me or yourself? You act like I'm trying to come between you and your husband."

"Isn't that what you're trying to do?"

"Of course not."

She restrained a shaky sigh.

Bailey pinned her with those familiar dark eyes but then left through the door without saying another word.

The minute she left, Nigel's eyes opened.

"Sweet pea?" He smiled at her and then looked around. "Where's my Sweet pea?"

"Noble and Faith are on their w—"

"I meant Bailey. I thought I heard her voice."

She kissed his palm. "She's not here. Get some more rest, sweetie. You've had a long night."

CHAPTER ELEVEN

He would have preferred to be in Venice, floating on a gondola, navigating the old city's architectural beauty with a man in a striped shirt behind them as their motor and guide. Then, he would say something clever, Bailey would laugh, and she'd fall for him underneath a sky like string lights, a guitar strumming softly somewhere in their imagination and the smell of salt in the air. But all he had was a sailboat and a lake, plus that gray cloud looming not far enough off to the east.

However, the marine weather forecast had predicted fair weather, low seas, winds between ten and fifteen knots, and only a ten percent chance of a thunderstorm.

He'd brought Bailey to Lake Allatoona, which sat a little over an hour northwest of Atlanta. Usually, the lake teemed with activity. Today, the waters were untroubled, the clouds like cotton balls being pulled apart by celestial fingers. There were about three other sails in the distance, which gave him a little bit of comfort. But the sails didn't completely erase the uneasy feeling the fat, gray cloud had given him.

"So, is this your boat?" Bailey asked, swiveling her head to get a full view of their surroundings.

Kellen laughed. "I'm flattered you think I'm that adventurous, but it's a rental. I'd barely have time to use my car if it didn't get me to work, home, and back again."

She smiled at him, and he regretted being too far to lick the outline of her lips. She'd somewhat tamed that coily head of hair, the strands like springs of varying sizes. Today, she wore it pulled back in a thick ponytail and accented by an orange headband that matched her top.

"Do you like working that much?"

"I like what I do," he said. "And right now, I don't have the responsibilities of a family."

"So you can see yourself slowing down if you had a family?"

He'd been trying to set the sails on the nineteen-foot sailboat for the last twenty minutes, but she'd been sitting across from him for the last twenty minutes. It was hard not to get distracted by the stitching in her dark jeans that ran along her thigh and down her leg, ending at ankles to feet he would consider putting in his mouth one day. There were actually several places on her body where he wanted to put his mouth.

"Absolutely."

He made one more round, checking the knots and the lines, surprised he'd remembered any of it as it had been years since his family had last gone sailing. After Connor's death, little by little, family events became nonexistent.

The wind kicked up behind him, blowing east. Luckily, his

angry gray friend looked like it was beginning to move away from the shore. Eventually, the sun would poke out its head, and it would be a beautiful day for sailing. Afterward, they would have lunch at a Mom & Pop he'd spotted not too far from the marina, and damn it, he never asked her if she ate seafood.

He raised the sail, and the boat jerked before slowly easing into the water's black depths. He waited until they reached a comfortable distance before taking a seat next to her.

"There's a life jacket in that compartment there," he said, pointing to a hutch in the center of the vessel.

She moved closer to his side. "I'll get it later."

"By the way, do you like seafood?"

"I love seafood."

They drifted deeper into the lake, into the trees, and into the loud silence interrupted only by the sound of his lips against her forehead and her mouth moving in tandem with his.

It was nearly spring. The orange, brown, and barely there were slowly being replaced with bright green fullness. Tree trunks swelled as branches breathed new life. The birds would soon return, and the lake would fill to capacity.

Once everything was in place, he'd bring her out again. Maybe it would become a regular thing for them, boating on a lazy Sunday before going home or to his parents' house for dinner. Maybe he'd have dinner with her folks.

Speaking of which…

"How's your dad doing?"

She smothered a yawn in a bent elbow. "He's doing really well. Henry said he could go home tomorrow. He's not going to need any surgery or anything like that. Looks like it was just a mild cardiac event. *But* he's going to follow up with Henry at his practice, and then it's going to be healthy eating, low-dose aspirin, and exercise."

Another couple on a boat passed by, frantically waving as they headed back toward the shore. He and Bailey raised their hands to return the greeting.

"Mind if I ask why you're here with me instead of at the hospital with your mother and your sisters? I don't want you to feel like you can't say no to me."

"Noble and Faith haven't seen him in months, and I wanted them to have this time with him."

At the hospital, he'd sensed something between her and her mother. There was usually a certain level of warmth that could be felt between a mother and her child, but he'd almost breathed frost standing between them.

He'd run to the cardiology wing to confer with a colleague. After their meeting, as he was leaving, he'd spotted Bailey next to her mother, a chair separating them like a border wall.

Before he'd called out to her, he'd watched them. They'd been sitting outside a hospital room door where, in a few minutes, they could have received news that they'd lost a family member. Yet, there'd been no touching, no talking, and no eye contact.

"You're important too, you know," he reminded her. "To him…and to me."

A response didn't have time to leave her mouth.

A droplet of water fell onto her cheek. The fat, gray cloud

from before had grown into a dark monstrosity, eating blue from the sky in large chunks.

As though it had been waiting for them to realize the change in the weather, the waters roused into choppy waves, smashing into the boat's hull. The boat rocked, tipping the mast toward the lake's surface.

"Bailey, I'm going to need your help," he yelled, the raindrops pouring down in buckets, deafening him to everything around them. "We have to steady the boat."

Without hesitation, she hopped up.

There was time to steer them north to the nearest shore. He would have to drop the mainsail, but they had enough momentum to make it as long as the waves didn't get any bigger or the gusts any stronger.

Once that was done, he stood looking at her, their faces and clothing soaked. When he noticed the look on her face, he tried to comfort her with a soft, "We'll be okay,"

"What else do you need me to do?" she asked, blinking through the droplets.

So far, he had a pretty good handle on the boat, and they were drifting in the right direction.

"Tether. Harness." He pointed to the box beneath her. "In there. Strap yourself in. You *cannot* get hurt."

She stopped mid-reach. "Me? What about you? Do you think I want you to get hurt?"

"I'll be fine."

They would soon breach the shallow, but the waves were deeper and more turbulent than he'd anticipated, breaking in frothy masses. The storm was also blowing toward them, the waves pitching and roaring as they drew nearer to the shore. When he looked at Bailey again, she was tethered to the boat. She smiled and gave him a thumbs-up.

He returned the smile.

Then a gust slammed into the hull, overturning the boat into the water.

CHAPTER TWELVE

"Easy now, Nigel. Easy."

Alice, a hand against Nigel's back and the other on his chest, helped Nigel sit up in bed. Once situated, she fetched the covered plate of food brought up by the hospital staff and returned to his side, fork poised, ready to take care of her husband.

He accepted a forkful of lettuce and cringed.

She laughed and stroked his arm. "Noble and Faith are about twenty minutes out," she said. "Noble just texted me."

"Is Bailey coming with them?"

She swirled the salad in vinaigrette to make it more appetizing, thinking of ways to continue to make him his favorite dishes without putting too much strain on his heart.

The man had been a beacon of hope in a crisis.

He gave her two wonderful, accomplished daughters, an

MD and a JD, who she cherished with everything she possessed. All the love she was capable of, she poured into those two girls.

"I don't know if you're going to eat this, Nigel." She brought a lettuce leaf to her nose, and the balsamic vinegar could unclog the stuffiest of nostrils. "But I guess you have to. I'll mix it in with the chicken breast."

"Is Bailey coming with them?" he repeated.

"No, I don't think so."

Nigel's brows wrinkled. "My Sweet pea's not coming?"

"Faith is your baby, Nigel. She's the youngest."

"And Bailey's my first."

She grunted and shook her head to clear the image of a little girl in a flower-patterned dress, curls abound, running toward her.

"Did you do something, Alice? Did you start that nonsense again? What you've been doing since Bailey was a baby. You don't think I notice?"

"I was a new, young mother," she argued. "I wasn't my best, but I got it right with Noble and Faith, didn't I?"

"You tried with them. You didn't try with her. You *don't* try with her. I loved her as best as I could, but she needs it from us both." He leaned closer to her face. "Should anything happen to me—"

"Don't say that!"

She took a moment, calmed herself, and cut the chicken into cubes before feeding him a piece.

"Don't say that, Nigel. Especially not so soon after all this."

"We have to talk about it. You can't use me as your backup,

your excuse as to why Bailey didn't turn out as messed up as she could have. She's a wonderful girl, Alice. A wonderful woman. If something happens to me, could you do it? Could you be there for her too?"

Even if she could, at this point, it was too late.

There was no law that said a mother had to love all her children equally, if at all. There was no reason to feel like an aberration if the mysterious love, the one people seemed to think innately developed inside every womb, never came to be.

She never wanted the baby.

Bailey's life, just like her conception, should have never occurred or existed. And she'd tried to do something about it, knowing that if she'd had that baby, if she'd brought that life into the world, she would never successfully bury the past connected to it.

But then she did.

And that baby, regardless of that buried past, had been the most beautiful thing she'd ever seen.

So, she'd done the only thing she'd known to do—she'd detached. She fought every instinct and desire to be its mother so that one day, eventually, she could live without it. One day, she would successfully push Bailey so far away, it would be like her mistake never happened.

"These grapes look delicious, don't they?" She plucked one from the stem and held it toward Nigel's mouth, but he turned away.

"I'm not hungry anymore."

"Nigel, you're making a huge deal out of nothing. Bailey's fine."

"No thanks to you."

"I never wanted her."

"Doesn't matter," he hissed. "She's here, isn't she?"

"So I'm to blame, then?" She popped the grape into her mouth. "The girl is unremarkable, and I'm to blame? She's an adult."

"Harboring wounds from her childhood."

"How is that my fault?"

"She needed a mother." He swallowed, emotion sending his voice a few octaves deeper. "She needed a mother to guide her, show her how to be confident. Show her that she's worth something. Do you know how much a person can accomplish if they feel like they're worth something?"

He closed his eyes and shook his head, his bottom lip clamped between his teeth. When he looked at her again, a tear glistened on his cheekbone.

"You tried with Noble and Faith," he said. "And look how they turned out. Explain to me, then, how a mother's love isn't important? A mother's support? If the only difference between our three girls—"

"Your three girls."

"She's more yours than mine!"

His gaze darted behind her head, and she spun around to find Noble and Faith, somewhere between afraid and relieved, carefully entering the hospital room.

"Oh, Daddy, you're okay," Faith said, running over and flinging her arms around Nigel's neck.

Noble stayed behind, assessing him in a way that said doctor first, daughter second. Once Faith's hug was over, she stepped forward and held him close.

"Where's Bailey?" Faith asked.

Alice folded her girls into a hug. "My babies. I've missed you so much. Want some grapes?"

CHAPTER THIRTEEN

Kellen's nostrils filled.

His ears rumbled.

Brackish water and mud sat bitter on his tongue as he pushed with his arms and legs until he broke through the lake's surface. A wave rushed forward, pulling him back under, and he kicked again until oxygen filled his lungs.

The boat drifted several yards away, heading away from the shore. He tried to search the inky water for Bailey but came up with nothing. Then he remembered she'd said she couldn't swim.

And that she'd been tied to the boat.

He dove beneath the water, barely able to see his hands in front of him, the lake floor a murky mix of sand and plant life. But he was able to make out Bailey's legs, flailing wildly, as she struggled to unhitch herself from the boat.

When she spotted him, she held up the rope.

He swam around to her back, where metal looped through the harness strapped over her shoulders. Had they been on land, it would have been an easy unclip and go, but the water pressure had him bearing down with force to get the latch to unhook. Every second that passed, she lost air, and he'd be damned if she drowned with him *right there.*

They needed more time for Sunday dinners at his family's house. They needed more time to wake up next to each other, her warm body tucked into him while he kissed the rise behind her ear, coaxing out a sleepy smile.

They needed more time to fall in love.

He tugged until the hook depressed and then slipped it from its loop. The second the rope detached, he grabbed her around the middle and raced toward the surface, ignoring panic when she went limp in his arms. He focused only on moving his body until both their heads were above water. Then he listened for coughs, wet and hoarse, between his, and when he heard them, a warm ray of light shot straight through his chest.

"You're okay." He pulled her close and pressed his clammy lips to hers. "Thank God you're okay."

"You came back for me," she said, her voice throaty and mangled.

"Of course I did."

She held onto him as he swam them to shore, the storm raging without an inkling of sympathy for the couple struggling inside its wrath.

She climbed onto the bank and helped him onto the grass next to her. They collapsed onto their backs, panting and huffing, the raindrops pouring from the darkened sky pelting their faces.

She coughed and rolled onto her side. "Did you…get insurance…on the boat?"

He looked at her, looked out at the boat, and then they both burst out laughing.

HOURS LATER, THE STORM CONTINUED TO RAGE, SO HE RENTED A suite at a nearby lake house instead of braving the drive back to Atlanta.

Now, Bailey lay beneath him, his tongue exploring her sweet mouth. He snaked his hand underneath her towel and caressed the soft skin on her stomach, making his way up to her breasts. When he slid his thumb over her nipple, she hissed and trapped his top lip between her teeth.

The mound was so soft and full, his mouth watered as he unhooked the knot on the towel, their clothes downstairs in the lake house's complimentary laundry.

God, his woman was beautiful.

"So lovely." He kissed his way down her neck and over her collarbone until he arrived at the firm bud. "So, so lovely."

Amazing breasts laid before him, the same rich, dark honey of her complexion, capped by areolas the color of brown sugar.

He blew against her nipple while she watched, his hand sliding down that smooth stomach, coming to rest between her thighs. He readied his finger to dip inside but noticed the tenseness in her thigh muscles and leaned back.

"Is everything okay?"

She was uncomfortable, and he could tell she didn't want to mention it and possibly ruin the mood. Yes, he was a steel pole beneath the towel, but…

"I won't do anything to your body that you don't want me to."

"Really?" she asked, brows raised.

"Of course, really."

"It's not that I don't want you. It's just," she closed her eyes, took a deep breath, and reopened them, "can we slow down?"

The single question confirmed what he'd already known—if they'd had sex in his office that night, she would have regretted it and regretted him. She'd offered something back then she wasn't even ready to give now.

"Kellen, I want you. I do. I want you as much as you want me."

Impossible.

"Am I making you uncomfortable?" he asked.

"Not you. This."

"Are you a virgin?"

"No, but you're already doing a lot more than I'm used to."

He angled his head. "Really? Well, I'm completely comfortable going at your pace. I told you I wanted to take my time. I didn't lie about that."

"I can feel how hard you are."

"My dick gets hard when I hear your voice on the phone. He'll be okay."

Laughing, she nudged his hand lower. "I still want you to do that. I've never been pleasured that way before."

He almost burst out laughing, but not at her expense. He wanted to laugh at any man who'd been stupid enough not to take his time reveling in the masterpiece that lay before him, scars and all. There was a particular one across her stomach he wanted to ask her about, but that was something he would reserve for later.

"So, no one has ever done," he parted her with his middle finger, and when he felt how wet she was, moisture trickled from the tip of his dick, "this?"

"No. No one."

"And you're not a virgin." He stroked her clit with his middle and ring finger. "How many other relationships have you been in?"

"Two."

The word came out as a moan, and his steel pole morphed into a diamond rod. Leaning forward, he licked and nibbled her nipple in time to his strokes, dick straining against his inner thigh. If he got any harder, the skin along his shaft would crack.

Her hips lifted from the mattress.

"Can I put them inside?"

He sucked the nipple into his mouth.

This time, they both moaned.

She nodded. *"Yes."*

He slipped his middle finger into pure, tight heat, going slowly to ensure her total comfort with him. At first, she stiffened, but then she grew used to the feeling of his finger stroking her, her hips rocking into the motion.

"What do you want, Bailey?"

"You." She moaned and licked her lips. "I want you, Kellen."

"How?"

The towel fell away, putting her naked body on full display, and he could have never imagined this. His dreams always created her as flawless, but he loved seeing her like this—a mole on her stomach next to her belly button, that scar along her right side, the natural variations in her skin tone, and the fine, barely noticeable vellus hairs.

"Your mouth," she said. "Want...your mouth."

More moisture spilled from his tip, trickling down his shaft, and he descended until his mouth settled right next to his roving hand. Then he licked her clit, and ten fingers were suddenly in his hair.

"Oh, shit."

With a smug, self-satisfied smile, he bent one of her legs and pushed it outward, spreading her gorgeous pussy for him.

After taking a few seconds to admire just how gorgeous it was, he lowered his head and dragged his tongue across her clit.

"Kellen," her grip tightened, "oh, fuck."

He circled her clit, licking slowly, so she felt the depth of every stroke. There was no satisfying this inescapable hunger for her, and having her in front of him, warm and soft and real, buried his dreams six feet under.

He fucked her with his tongue, imagined her riding his face as he licked at her like a bear at a beehive. More than he needed his next breath, he wanted to lose himself in her body and watch her heart-shaped ass slap his pelvis with every thrust. She was his, not only to care for but to protect. That was clear now more so than ever.

"Kellen, please...please..."

Her back arched.

She came, quivering against his lips.

She reached for him, pulling his mouth to hers. While their tongues tangled and curled around each other, he massaged her pulsing, sated clit with two fingers.

"Think you can handle more?" he asked, his voice strained, matching his level of arousal. He kissed her forehead and the bridge of her nose, but a choking cry made him stop short.

"Oh, God." Bailey swiped at her eyes. "Of course, I'd pick now to cry. How do I do this so well? How do I keep ruining everything?"

"Whoa." He grabbed her wrists and gently pinned her to the bed. "Back up a bit. What 'everything' do you keep ruining?"

"Kellen, you're perfect."

"Hardly."

"Well, you're perfect to me."

"I think you mean for. I'm perfect *for* you. And if I'm perfect, you have to accept me telling you the same."

He was only half joking.

"I don't get..." She looked away, bit the inside corner of her mouth, and then her focus slowly drifted back to him. "You're an attractive doctor who's sweet and kind and drives a nice car."

He moved an inch closer. "I'm not following you. You want me to quit my job, trade in my car, and wear a mask?"

"No, you're the type of man who most likely has women falling at his feet."

"What you're referring to is syncope, and I'd honestly be a pretty shitty doctor if all my patients kept passing out."

She managed a tear-filled laugh.

"There's a straight line from you to me, Bailey. Talk to m—"

"Why'd you come back for me?"

He sat at the edge of the bed and dragged her onto his lap. "Come again? Are you seriously asking me why I didn't let you drown? Let you die? You *cannot* be asking me that."

"Let me rephrase. What I'm asking is, what do you see in me? I don't understand why you like me. It's not that I don't understand *that* you like me. I don't understand why." She blinked tears onto her cheeks. "Tell me. Tell me one thing you like."

Was his drool not enough?

"Who told you there was something about you not worth liking?" he half asked, half demanded. "I'm never the guy who stumbles over his words, but it took me weeks to talk to you."

"We talked."

He gave her a look. "You talked. I stared. Every once in a while, I made up a new word."

"Kellen," she cupped his jaw, "I can't see what you see. I want to see what you see in me, but I'm not sure how to look for it."

"Who did it?"

"Did what?"

"We're not born thinking we're not good enough," he said. "You do realize that's what you're really saying, right? That you don't think you're good enough for me. That you don't think you were worth saving. It's the same thing you were saying at the hole in the wall, and I'd laugh if I wasn't so pissed."

That had to be the rift he'd felt between her and her mother. It had been the oddest thing, standing between them and feeling as though he was standing between rivals.

"She's never come right out and said it," she mumbled. "But it was definitely heavily implied. And I want to ignore it. I swear to God, I want to wake up one day and just be over it. But, no matter how hard I try, it's always kind of just *there*."

"Your mother?"

"Something like that."

It was the same way she'd answered the other night.

"That's enough of her for now," he said. "Things have been going really well, and I'm not going to let her ruin that for you or us."

She circled her arms around his neck. "Thank you for coming back for me."

"Bailey," he kissed her nose, "if I couldn't save you, neither one of us was coming up for air. I'm here for you. I want you. I want this. I fully intend for you and me to be a long-term thing, so buckle up. We're in this for the long haul. And if you ever need anything, anything at all, come to me, baby."

"What if I want the moon?" she teased.

"Then I'd google 'biggest damn lasso in the world' and get it for you."

She burst out laughing.

"What? If my girl says she wants the moon, then my girl gets the moon."

The storm continued to rage outside, but with the way the room lit, like sunlight breaking through clouds, when she smiled at him, he'd had to check to be sure.

"I love it when you call me your girl," she said. "Thank you for being a part of my life."

No one had ever said anything to him like that before. His

friends, his family—he knew they cared about him and that he played an important role in their lives, but he'd never *heard* those words.

His family had lost an entire person, his twin, and he'd sacrificed physical and emotional health to keep them relatively stable. Yet, it was like no one noticed him unless he was fixing something, propping someone up, or chasing his brother down in the dead of night.

"So you're buckled up?" he asked, brushing the tip of his nose over hers. "Ready to do this thing for a while?"

She nodded. "Buckled up, ready, and excited to 'do this thing for a while' with you."

He smiled so big, it hurt the corners of his eyes, and slowly eased her onto her back, his tongue sliding past her lips.

CHAPTER FOURTEEN

On Bailey's left, the "Rocky" theme song blasted from Noble's phone. Faith jogged in place, striking the air like a punching bag.

"Come on, Daddy," Faith called. "You can do this. Noble, turn that up."

Noble turned up the phone.

Their father, with a tired smile on his face and sweat on his brow, jogged the rest of the short distance to the house. It had been four weeks since his episode at the hospital, and since then, he went for a walk every single evening. Today, he'd upgraded to a jog.

"We're almost there, Daddy," Faith yelled.

"You can do this, Nigel," Bailey screamed.

"That's *Dad* or *Daddy* to you, ma'am," Nigel huffed with a wink. "Always."

Noble clapped and Faith hollered, neither stopping until he

was in the driveway, bent over with his hands on his knees, struggling to catch a breath.

Bailey danced like she'd scored a touchdown. "You did it! I'm so proud of you. And you said you'd never finish."

"Me too," Faith chimed in.

Noble patted him on the back. "Me three."

Nigel straightened and rested his hands at his waist. "I think I'm ready for dinner. Has your mother finished yet?"

Bailey, Faith, and Noble doubled over in laughter.

"You accomplish something huge, and the first thing you think about is food," Noble said. "Sounds about right."

He tried to throw his arms around them, and they wriggled away from the large sweat stain on his gray sweatshirt.

Finding his second wind, he chased them around the yard. Bailey grabbed Faith and used her body as a shield. Noble jumped in to save Faith, or so Faith thought; Noble ended up using their sister as a shield as well.

They ran around the yard for a few minutes, pretending Nigel was fast enough to catch them like he'd been when they were children.

Bailey could feel Alice watching them from one of the large living room windows, but she didn't look up. Every once in a while, she caught her mother staring whenever they interacted with Nigel. But, if she turned to look at her, Alice would slowly slink away.

"Whew." Nigel bent over again. "I think I'm done for the day. You girls win."

"*Boo*, you didn't even try." Faith, smiling, walked over and looped an arm around his neck.

"You girls are faster than you used to be. At least, you and Bailey. Noble still has those two left feet."

Noble scooped up a few blades of grass and tossed them at him. "A quick pick-up game, me and you, after you get a clean bill of health. These two left feet will mop the floor with you, old man."

"Old man?" Nigel acted like he was going to grab her but then pulled her in for a kiss on top of her head. Then he looked at all three of them, and Bailey watched him in that faraway moment, wondering what he was thinking. She could see that he was proud, but he also seemed grateful. It was as though his life had turned out exactly the way he'd hoped.

His phone rang, and he yanked it from his pocket and raised it to his ear. They followed him toward the house but stopped when he reached the door and turned around.

"Wait, you're coming today? When did you get in town? How long are you staying?" He covered the speaker. "Your grandparents are, apparently, in town. They said they're on their way over."

Faith and Noble cheered.

Bailey's stomach dropped.

Her father's parents treated her no differently than Alice did, and they always came with gifts for Faith and Noble. Eventually, Nigel mentioned something to them, so they started bringing her small trinkets—a pencil, a pen, a button. For Faith and Noble, they brought decorated, handmade European journals, expensive clothing and jewelry, and rare antiques, all gift-wrapped.

Nigel ended the call.

They all went inside, cleaned up, and were setting the dinner table by the time Jacquelyn and Amos Green rushed into the house, wrapping everyone up in tight, too-eager hugs. Bailey stood off to the side to avoid that awkward moment where they paused in front of her before giving her a conciliatory tap on the back—a classic "church hug."

"We've got presents!" Jacquelyn announced, clapping while Amos retrieved bags and boxes that had been sitting on the front stoop. "You know we'd never come empty-handed."

Noble unwrapped an expensive pair of Chanel sunglasses. Faith pulled an Hermès blanket out of an ornate gift bag. Then Jacquelyn turned to Bailey, a yellow envelope held to her chest and a broad smile on her face.

"And *this* is for you, Bailey."

Bailey took the envelope and started to rip the top off, but Jacqueline's hand jutted out.

"Wait until after dinner. I smell fried fish and macaroni pie. Did you know we were coming, Alice? You had to know we were coming. You have it smelling like a Bajan kitchen up in here."

Jacqueline linked elbows with Faith and Noble, and the trio headed to the kitchen. Amos and Nigel went to the dining room to wait for their food. Even when everyone was seated, eating, and the stories had begun, Bailey's fingers itched to open the envelope.

When her mother's parents, Thomasina and Cecil Wright, passed away, she'd assumed Jackie and Amos would have closed the wound their deaths had left. Thomasina and Cecil had loved her like they'd raised her. They'd cherished her, and the only relief she'd known in her younger days had been the times she'd spent at their house.

However, Amos and Jacqueline never stepped into the roles they'd vacated. In fact, they'd done the opposite, and now that she watched them, Jacqueline regal and poised compared to Thomasina, who'd been preserve-making sweet and homely, she realized they never could. Her father's family was about appearances, while her mother's family had been about warmth and love. It was like each couple had raised the wrong child.

"This is delightful, Alice," Amos raved, dabbing his mouth with a folded white handkerchief. "You know, Jackie and I were afraid we'd miss out on good Bajan food on our trip here to see an old church friend of hers, but you brought us right back. What's for dessert? Tell me something good."

Alice beamed. "I think inside I must have known you were coming because I made a fresh batch of coconut bread."

"Watch out, now!" Amos set his hand on his stomach. "Nigel, be careful. I might steal your wife."

Nigel grinned. "Not fair. I can't take yours."

Bailey waited on pins and needles as dishes were taken up, bread was brought out, more stories were told, and then they all retreated to the back patio to let the day wear off.

"Oh, Bailey, your gift," Jacqueline said. "It's time. Open it."

Bailey eagerly tore through the envelope and pulled out a document written in so much legalese, merely looking at it gave her sinus pressure.

"Somebody left me something in Barbados?" she asked, looking up. "Was it you, Amos?"

Amos shook his head. "No, not me and Jackie."

"But we do have everything set up so that all you'll need to do is go down and sign some papers," Jackie added.

"Yes, but what is it?"

Faith held out a hand. "Bailey, let me see that."

Bailey handed it over.

"Who are Ada and Walter Bailey?" Faith asked, brows narrowed.

Amos and Jacqueline shrugged.

Several seconds later, so did Nigel and Alice.

"One of you has to know," Faith insisted. "Why would two random strangers leave a whole piece of what looks like personal property to Bailey unless they knew one of you in some way?"

"Ada and Walter were friends of your grandparents," Amos offered. "They were there when you were born, Bailey, and they loved Thomasina and Cecil so much, they gave you this gift, as a gift to them."

Thomasina and Cecil had been well-liked. It was believable that friends of theirs would want to carry out such a generous act, but something didn't feel right.

Jacqueline leaned back, hands clasped, as Alice placed another slice of coconut bread on her plate. "So, Bailey, when are you leaving?"

Faith handed over the deed.

"I don't know," Bailey said. "I'll have to request time off and—"

"We only have things set up for thirty days," Amos cut in. "It's not that your trust will be forfeited in that time, but we'd have to go through this process again, and Bailey," he reached across the table, hand stopping short of touching hers, "you don't want to wait an entire year for this."

Bailey looked at Alice, who was staring at her as if seeing someone else. As if she had transformed right in front of the woman's eyes.

"I'll talk to my manager and see what we can work out," she resigned, rising from her chair. There was someone else she wanted to talk to as well. "If you guys will excuse me, I'm picking up a shift tonight. Thanks for dinner, Alice."

She didn't wait around to hear whether Alice would reply and hurried upstairs to change into her work uniform. Before leaving, she planted a kiss on her father's cheek and waved goodbye to her sisters.

ALICE ENTERED THE KITCHEN, WHERE JACQUELYN STOOD BY THE stove, heating water for tea.

"Jackie, why are you doing this?"

"To release you," Jacquelyn said, staring at the blue-orange fire underneath the teapot. "You've shouldered the burden of that child for much too long. She's not blood, and I'm tired of pretending that she is for her sake. She's a grown woman now. She can handle it."

Alice folded her arms and leaned against the counter. "But Bailey *is* blood, Jackie. Mine. Regardless of what you think, feel, or want to believe, she's mine. I gave birth to her. She's part of me too."

Snorting, Jacquelyn searched through a cupboard and

retrieved a box of lemongrass tea. "Your parents did you a disservice, Alice. If you were my daughter, I would have taken you to a clinic to get rid of it myself."

"Don't say that."

"I mean it."

"Jackie, don't do this. Don't make Bailey go there."

Jacquelyn shrugged and added sugar to the tea. "It's already done. Secrets want to be seen, Alice. It's not fair to you to keep this one buried, all alone. People need to know the truth about what happened thirty years ago. Bailey is a kind of enough girl, but she's not my granddaughter, and I'm tired of pretending that she is."

"But she's *my daughter*."

"I know. Not Nigel's. And Nigel is my son."

"Jackie," she swallowed a groan, "you and Amos visibly resent her. You don't pretend a thing."

"And you don't do that same?"

She remained silent.

"Alice, she's a child of sin. It's time for the truth to come out."

That was precisely what she was afraid of.

The truth.

Because what she'd told them, what she'd told everyone, was markedly different from "the truth" that had actually happened.

CHAPTER FIFTEEN

Kellen stood in front of another one of his places of employment, and Bailey wondered where he found time to do it all. According to him, he worked to stay sane, but his eyes, which otherwise blazed like a broken horizon, were barely brighter than the sky at midnight.

He was there when she parked, pulling her into his arms the minute she got out. She'd lied to her family about going to work to avoid their questions; she didn't want to risk anything, no matter how slight, ruining what she and Kellen were building.

They walked, hand in hand, and he gave her a brief overview of how he'd arrived there, a young professor at the Emory School of Medicine.

He was nothing like her old Cornell professors with their gray hair, bow ties, and plaid jackets. To have accomplished as much as he had, and before forty, was an amazing feat, adding weight to her fear that they were mismatched for one another.

It was the thing with insecurities—they hung around, waiting for an inopportune moment to pounce as a reminder that they truly never went anywhere.

But when he kissed her, she felt like he was taking a vacation in her lips rather than caring what the people around him thought or said. He'd also come back for her at the lake, something she didn't think her own mother would have done. As a matter of fact, Alice would have probably rejoiced behind closed doors, then pretended to be a grieving mother whenever in the public eye.

"So, yes? No?"

She looked up to Kellen's eyes on her, his head cocked to one side.

"Oh, I'm sorry. I didn't catch that."

"I was asking if you wanted to see where I teach before we head to my office."

She nodded. "I'd love to."

He took her first to an auditorium-sized lecture hall, and she made her way up the steps to sit in the middle while he gave a brief, impromptu lecture on neonatal pathology. He taught first-year medical students in a pediatrics, application of medical sciences course where they also did some hands-on work at Grady Memorial Hospital. He also taught another course for those seeking dual degrees in medicine and public health.

She raised her hand.

"Go ahead, Miss Green."

"So you're saying that, although we've come a long way in this country with reducing premature babies' deaths, we're still the number one developed country in the world for infant mortality?"

His smile warmed her body, the sensation simultaneously innocent and erotic.

"Yes, Miss Green. I see you paid attention to the articles I assigned last class."

"Well, I want to make sure I pass your class, Dr. Edwards." She moistened her lips with her tongue. "In *any* way I can."

He bound up the steps, placed both palms on her desk, and leaned in. "I've got some extra credit I think you might be interested in."

"Can I *come* during your office hours?"

A wolfish grin curved his lips. "I think I can manage that."

Their lips met, and she hoped he found himself thinking about their kiss in the middle of his lectures.

"Now," he took her hand, "to my office."

His office was more upscale than expected, nearly as modern as his office at the hospital. His degrees and certifications lined a wall painted in a calm, bluish-gray color with white trim. A massive desk sat in the middle, mostly empty except for a flat-screened monitor and a few desk accessories. The shelves on the wall held volumes of medical texts.

"You like?" He motioned around. "I know it's not much, but—"

"It's lovely." She released his hand and went to sniff the

books. There was something about the smell of old books. "I like it. If I had an office like this, I'd probably write every day."

"You write? I didn't know that."

Probably because she'd had zero intentions of telling an accomplished physician that she penned manuscripts no one would ever read.

"I do. As a hobby. Obviously, the real money's in my gig at Starbucks."

He laughed, and her body's reaction to the sound reminded her of the pleasure he'd brought her at the lake house.

"Well, I'm pretty sure those high on the Starbucks corporate ladder do pretty well for themselves," he said. "Many writers do too."

"Like you. Doing well for yourself, I mean."

"I guess." He cleared his throat. "Does that bother you?"

"That you're successful? Oh God, no."

"But it makes you feel...some kind of way."

She spotted his medical degree in an expensive-looking wooden frame. At first, the old English letters written at the top were blurred.

"Johns Hopkins?" She spun around. "You went to *the* Johns Hopkins University School of Medicine?"

"I went there for undergrad and medical school."

She squeezed her forehead, her insecurities bulldozing their way in.

Would Faith and Noble be more his speed?

They'd gotten their degrees from Harvard and the University of Pennsylvania; she wasn't sure she could get into community college. Moreover, her university grades had been so awful that her advisor had suggested she take a semester off before trying to return to the classroom.

She never went back.

"You okay, Bailey?"

He'd leaned against the edge of the desk, his blue shirt and gray slacks tailored, his shoes expensive, and his tie a perfect match to both, with one of those bars across it whose purpose she'd never learned. He didn't look smug, and he never looked at her like he was better than she was.

Like her mother's rebuffs, it wasn't clear why their differences remained so difficult to shake.

"You said you wanted to talk to me about something you got from your grandparents?"

"Oh, right." She reached into her bag and retrieved the envelope. "It's something about a trust that friends of my mother's parents left me. I had my sister, Faith, look at it. She's an attorney," she searched his face for any flicker of interest, "but it doesn't say much other than I have to go to Barbados to sign some documents."

He took the envelope, poured out the papers, and sifted through them. "When do you want to go? We can get these papers signed and a vacation in at the same time."

"Kellen, I don't even know if I can get time off for this. Plus, have you seen the price of tickets to Barbados right now? It's technically still peak season."

"What kind of 'boyfriend,'" he made air quotes, "would I be if I'm this guy who, as you put it, does so well for himself but doesn't take his lady on vacation when the opportunity presents itself?"

She mimicked the air quotes. "'Boyfriend'?"

"Not a fan of the word. I'm your man."

"Ah, I see." She stepped forward and circled her arms around him. "And what a mighty good man…"

"What a mighty, *mighty* good man," he added.

Laughing, she drank in the spicy scent of his cologne. "Okay. I'll talk to my manager and let you know."

Fingers meandered into her Starbucks cap.

She leaned back.

"Wait, hold on," he said, reaching forward. "I want that thing off."

"Why?" She backed away further. "Do you know what's under there?"

"This is just a guess, but your hair?"

She hadn't moisturized in days, and there hadn't been a drop of gel at home. She didn't even get the chance to style twists that she could have passed off as decent looking. The Starbucks cap hid a frizzy, fuzzy ball of mess.

"Wait." She stretched an arm between them. "You're white. You don't understand."

He shook with a laugh. "I don't understand…what?"

"My hair. You take off this cap, you don't know what you're going to get."

He laughed again, and she was trying very hard to be serious, but the amusement on his face turned her into a puddle of melted wax.

"All right." He held up his hands in defeat. "You win."

She sighed. "Okay. So, about this trip to Barbad—"

One of his arms locked her in place while the other tugged

off the cap. Then he ran his hand over her head, smoothing her hair.

"They won't lie down," she said, defeated. "The frizz, it won't lay down."

He continued to stroke, and it was pretty damn soothing. She even eased into it. At least, until he went for her hair tie.

"Kellen, no. Don't take that out."

He slipped a finger between her hair and the band. "Why not?"

"Why do you want to? Are you trying to run your fingers through my hair? You can't. And I don't mean I don't want you to. You literally can't. The way my hair is set up—"

There was no use in talking.

He unraveled the elastic, a headband she'd looped over and over to fit her kinks, coils, and curls. The strap on the Starbucks cap had been holding on for its dear life. It was her fourth hat, and it kept its hold like it knew what had happened to the other three and was determined not to fall to the same fate.

The elastic snapped in the middle of his removing it, and her hair expanded like lungs filling with air. The sensation relieved a tension headache that had been bugging her all evening.

"Hmm."

"I'm going to need more than that from you, Dr. Edwards." She closed her eyes as his fingers meandered into her hair and over her scalp. "You've released Medusa. I'm afraid that if I look at you now, you'll turn into stone."

She looked up.

His fingers stopped moving, and he went completely still.

She swatted his chest. "I'll give it to you. That was good."

"What if I'd said I didn't like your hair?" he asked, grinning. "Or that it made you less attractive this way, in its natural state?"

His fingers moved to the base of her skull, massaging in small, tight circles. She almost had to remind the space between her legs, now throbbing with heat, that he wasn't touching her there.

"I'd be hurt, but not because I hate my hair."

She'd be hurt because she liked him. In liking him, she wanted him to like all of her. Over time, they'd find minor annoyances, but the big things? Those that revolved around how she looked, bare and unaltered? Those, she wanted him to find beautiful.

"I love your hair, by the way." He gently pressed against the curve of her neck. "But I'm supposed to, Bailey."

"I'm not following you."

She almost moaned the words.

"Feel good?"

Apparently, she *had* moaned the words.

"It feels amazing," she said.

"Do you feel like my accomplishments somehow translate to us and our relationship?" he added. "Like because I went to Johns Hopkins and you, I don't know, work at Starbucks, we're unsuited for each other?"

Yes.

"Why?"

Damn it, she'd said that out loud too. She was losing herself to his magic fingers, which had journeyed to the space behind her ears.

"What if you want to invite me to fancy dinners with your colleagues, and I can't jump in during the conversations about the latest developments in medicine?"

When he didn't respond, she opened her eyes.

"Bailey, fuck my colleagues. You won't be there to talk to them anyhow."

His fingers moved south, and he tipped her forward so that her forehead pressed against him while he massaged her spinal column. The kneading and pressure felt so good, if he'd asked her to have his children right then, she would have ended the night pregnant.

"So I'd be there to, what? Look pretty on your arm?"

He grunted. "Pretty's as easy for you as breathing, Bailey. And you'd be there to support me, share in the experience, and be with me because you're in my life. You're part of my life. Of course, I want to share all those aspects of it with you."

"Then I'm sorry," she said. "I won't bring it up again."

"You will."

He raised her head, lowered his, and gently sucked and nibbled on her lips. Her mind dropped her right back into the lake house memory.

"You will until you stop believing it. Until I've convinced you it's not true, show you that it's bullshit and that you're perfect like this."

He gripped her scalp and walked until her back pressed into something solid.

A wall, she guessed.

She might as well have been up against the steel grates of a cage. Only instinct existed—the thuds in her chest, her grip on his body, the movement of her mouth as his came down on hers, hard and possessive. He kissed her like he'd created her.

"Kellen, I want you," she croaked between swollen, tender lips.

"I'm not making love to you in my office." He pressed into her, moving his mouth to her neck. "Not our first time."

His phone vibrated on his desk.

"If not sex," she fiddled with his belt, "let me return the favor from the lake house."

The right man could get a woman to do things she'd never done or only dreamed about doing. Kellen made her feel cared for, treasured, and supported, which was more than enough to bring her to her knees.

Literally.

The phone went off again.

She reached inside his waistband and wrapped her fingers around him. Not only was he hard, but he was also thick.

Fingers-struggling-to-touch thick.

The thickest she'd ever held.

Girth like this stretched walls and tapped nerve endings. She almost climaxed, thinking about it moving inside her, her wet walls gripping him as he moaned, gritting his jaw, trying to hold out because he wanted nothing more than to come inside her.

The phone buzzed a third time.

"You've got to be shitting me," he grated out. "I'll be right back."

He released her and stormed across the office. After reading the name on the phone screen, his anger receded.

"David?" he answered. "Everything okay?"

It took her a few moments to realize she was still against the wall, holding onto the position he'd left her in. She straightened, then busied herself by looking at what else he had in his office, pretending she wasn't eavesdropping on his conversation with his brother.

"I'm at the office with Bailey," he said. Then he sighed, and his face fell into his palm. "Okay. Where are you?"

After a quick nod, he hung up the phone.

"We can pick this up later," she offered. "I won't pretend I wasn't listening. Sounds like your brother needs you."

"He and Alexis got into a fight, which I get is important. But, if I'm being honest, I'm not ready to let you go. So…do you want to come with me? Or is this too much? Yeah, it's probably too much."

He went around his office, picking things up here and there —his blazer, his laptop case, a yellow folder. Then he mumbled something about losing his keys, but she'd felt them in his pocket earlier. She was surprised she'd noticed them; she'd been wholly captivated by how heavy he'd felt in her hand.

"Kel."

"Yeah?" He stopped moving and turned her way. "Yeah, babe?"

"One," she pointed to his pants, "your keys are in your pocket. Two, I need to stop at my car for another hair tie, and I'll need help getting my cap back on. And three, I'm coming with you, even if it might be too much."

He crossed the room in three strides, lifted her off her feet, and held her close, rocking them from side to side. She wrapped her arms around his neck and buried her face in his collar.

"Thank you, B."

"Oh, baby." She held him tighter. "Anytime."

CHAPTER SIXTEEN

Instead of a receipt, this time, Alexis found a bottle of alcohol, the cap unsealed. She'd confronted David, who'd immediately denied drinking it, claiming it had probably been left over from before.

She didn't believe him.

They argued.

She threatened to leave.

So, David barricaded her and Abigail inside the upstairs owner's suite.

Kellen had secretly hoped that Bailey would have declined to come with him, as he didn't really want her privy to this part of his life. He wanted her to think of them as a normal, ugly Christmas sweater-wearing, social media *cringe*-level couple. Unfortunately, this was part of him, and he'd just given her an entire speech about his acceptance of her.

Still in his car, they sat staring at a two-story brick house with a sweeping gable accentuated by a three-car garage. Every last light in the house was on, and with the massive lake behind them, it stood out like a lighthouse. He half-expected one light to be flickering, Alexis signaling in Morse code in hopes of someone coming to rescue her.

"You can stay in the car if you'd like," he said, unbuckling his seatbelt. "I'm not really sure what I'm going to get on the inside."

She shook her head. "I'll come in. That time we had breakfast, I could tell things with your brother can get pretty tough. If I can help it, I don't want you to face that alone."

Just like that, she became several times more beautiful right before his eyes.

They exited the car, walked up to the front door, and he held his breath as he tried the handle.

Unlocked.

Inside, a long hallway led into an open living space on one side and a staircase on the other. Upstairs, they found David sitting in front of the owner's suite with his back pressed against the door and his head down, his forearms on his knees.

At times like these, he wondered whether this was the end for his brother and Alexis. There was no way they could continue to survive through turmoil like this, especially with a young child to raise.

"Is Alexis in there?" Kellen asked.

David, startled, looked up. He started to respond, but then his eyes landed on Bailey.

"Bailey, I presume?"

She waved. "Nice to meet you, David."

"Nice going, Kel. This isn't exactly how I wanted my first time meeting her to be."

Kellen crouched in front of him. "You brought this on yourself. Now, move."

"Did you forget who the older one is?"

"Hard to tell right now."

"I haven't had anything to drink. Now please, could you tell my wife that? I haven't picked up a bottle since I started AA. I know how much this means to her. I wouldn't mess it up, not for me or my family."

Kellen tilted his head at the door. "Okay. Move."

David stood and poked something flat between the door handle crevice. A handful of pennies hit the ground.

"You locked her in with the penny trick?"

"Could you think of another way?"

"Yeah. *Don't* lock her in." Kellen reached behind him, taking Bailey's hand. "Bailey Green, this is my brother, David. He's an engineer, and apparently, a psychopath."

David extended a hand.

Kellen blocked the hand with his body and ushered Bailey past it.

Inside the large suite, they found Alexis sitting calmly in the middle of the bed, Abigail strewn across her lap. Abigail was asleep, her hair in three curly ponytails. Alexis had a fourth separated from the rest, braiding a third plait to match two others already in the section.

She looked up, and her warm brown eyes failed to hide her sadness. Her skin was a dull, yet beautiful ebony, and she'd pulled her hair up into a topknot bun, wisps falling out of their tendrils.

"'Lexis, what happened here today?"

She tipped her chin at the door. "He's drinking."

"I haven't been drinking," David bellowed from the entry-way. "Kellen, talk to her."

Kellen glanced over his shoulder. "If you'd let me."

He didn't have this in him today. He barely had it in him any day, but especially not today. He'd wanted to spend the evening with Bailey, have dinner, and then maybe find a park bench to sit and chat on. He wanted to decompress with her, shrugging off the effects of a long day that, though he was used to, ran him ragged by the time the sun set.

"I know I'm not crazy, Kellen," Alexis went on. "I've known that man since I was thirteen. He keeps telling me the receipt was nothing. That the bottle was old. Does he think I'm stupid? I tossed out every bottle of liquor in this house, so if I missed one, why would I have found it somewhere I already checked?"

Not this shit again.

David didn't smell like alcohol, but one of his favorite activities, back when he'd been drinking heavily, had been lying. He could have been standing underneath a blue sky and would still try to convince the entire world it was purple, eyes so bleary they crossed.

Tonight, he looked normal. A bit tired from fighting with his wife, but normal. He wore a T-shirt and shorts. His attitude was borderline, but then again, it could have been because of the fight.

"Where's the bottle you found?"

"Got rid of it like I did with all the others." Alexis, finally noticing Bailey, straightened her back. "Oh, I'm so sorry. You must be...Corrine?"

Kellen narrowed his eyes.

Alexis rubbed her chin. "Not Corrine? How about Jennifer? Stasia? Let's see, what day is tod—"

"You're not funny, 'Lex. She knows who you are, Bailey."

"Of course, I do." Alexis twirled the end of Abigail's braid around her index finger. "I was just messing with you. Kel can't stop talking about you. Pretty sure he hasn't shut up about you since the first time he saw you."

He prayed the flush he felt crawling up his neck didn't show on his face.

"If you'd like, I can step outside," Bailey offered.

Alexis started another section. "Oh, no, you're fine. Like I said, he talks about you. Actually, didn't you say something to the effect of that she's your future wif—"

He coughed into his fist.

Alexis winked at him, but he knew she could sense the slow burn of his manhood as it died at her feet.

He talked about Bailey.

Some could even argue that he talked about her a lot, and had done so before they'd met when she was just the "insanely cute girl at Starbucks." The mistake had been in mentioning her to his family and friends, who regularly used every opportunity to embarrass him.

"Ignore her, Bailey," he said. "Now, what do you want me to do, Alexis? I can take David back to my place to cool off."

"Actually, if you could keep him there for a couple of days, that would be best."

"Will you be here when I get back?" David entered the room, eyes wide. "Because the last time you told me you needed some space, when I came back to tell you I'd joined AA, your stuff was gone."

Alexis, focused on the braid, shrugged. "I can't make any promises."

"Baby, I have *not* been drinking."

"Where'd that bottle come from?"

David tossed up his hands. "I don't know! That's what I'm trying to tell you. You have to believe me, Alexis. What do I have to do?"

Kellen glanced at Bailey. Who she believed he wasn't sure. He'd been more prone to siding with his brother, even through all the bullshit. At the end of the day, in his opinion, David and Alexis belonged together. However, belonging together and being good together, he'd eventually learned, weren't the same.

"David," Alexis finally looked up, eyes locking with David's, "look me in the eyes and tell me you're not drinking."

David leaned over the edge of the bed, inches from her face. "Baby, I'm not drinking."

A tear trickled down her cheek.

"'Lexis, don't cry. I'm sorry. I know I've put you through hell, and you have every right not to trust me. But I'm not just doing this for me. This is about us. Our family. Our little girl."

Kellen eyed his brother, searching for any sign of a lie. "So, leaving or staying?" he asked.

"He can stay," Alexis said. "I'm sorry we had to meet like this,

Bailey. I promise we're a lot more normal under different circumstances."

"So we're good here?" He grabbed Bailey's hand and kissed it. "I can put my cape away?"

Bailey moved behind his back and pretended to remove a cape.

"Roll it up, baby," he said. "It doesn't fold well."

"I've got you, boo."

David's mouth fell open. "I never thought I'd see the day. A woman who not only can live with Kellen's weirdness, but gets it."

Kellen groaned, reached in for departing hugs, and kissed his niece's hair. As they made their way out, he promised that he and Bailey would be back on better terms and when Abigail was awake. Bailey had been looking forward to holding and playing with her.

It was late, but he was hungry. Then Bailey's stomach growled loud enough to nearly drown out the car stereo, and she suggested picking up a burger and fries.

He said nothing short of a "Hallelujah."

They took the greasy bags back to campus and ate while sitting beside each other on the curb near her parked car.

"Your brother's wife is Black," she said, shoving a handful of French fries into her mouth, and he swore he was falling in love.

"I think I told you that."

"Nope. Never mentioned it."

"Is that surprising?"

"Not surprising, *per se*." She reached for another handful of fries. "Just not something you see everyday, both you *and* your brother."

"Maybe it should be."

He'd ordered onion rings, and it was impossible to define the mix of comfort and delight he felt when she reached into his carton and popped one into her mouth.

"Is that what attracted you to me?" she asked. "My brown skin?"

"I think we already hashed out this question." He grabbed several of her fries. "I was initially attracted to you because you're gorgeous. Now, there are too many reasons to count. Maybe you just want to hear me say you're beautiful again."

She sent him a teasing look. "Wouldn't hurt."

They relished in an easy silence he'd assumed wouldn't have come for months into their relationship. He offered her a bite of his burger because she'd never had one with a fried egg on top, and she moaned and fluttered her eyelids, making him jealous of the burger.

"Did your parents have a hard time accepting Alexis?" she asked.

"Because of her race?" He shook his head. "No."

"Do they 'not see color'?"

"You're hitting me with the hard questions tonight, aren't you?"

"Personally, I'm curious."

"Maybe you should have asked before we became exclusive. What if you don't like my answer?"

She shrugged and took a long sip of her soda. "I can always back out."

"You can try, but I'll go from Kellen the Gentleman to Kellen the Stalker pretty damn quick. That's how gone you've got me."

Smiling, she nudged him in the side.

"But to answer your *questions*," he went on, "David and Alexis are one of those middle school enemies turned high school sweetheart couples. She's been in our lives since she was thirteen. My mother would have probably keeled over if Alexis didn't become her daughter-in-law. So, no. No problems with her, and they won't have any with you. I was raised by good people."

He'd been raised by exceptional people.

"Are you asking because of your situation?" he added. "Growing up mixed, did you have any conflicting feelings about coming from two different races? Alexis used to worry about that for Abigail, but—"

"I'm not mixed."

It wasn't exactly as apparent as someone with skin on the lighter side, looser curls, and light eyes, but something about her screamed *blended*.

"I mean, I met your mother, but I assumed your father was something other than Black."

She remained silent.

He took another study of her features. "I could have sworn...has anybody else ever made that mistake?"

"Yep."

"Do you at least look like your father? Your sisters?"

She left the curb and went to lean against the side of her car. He also stood but kept his distance.

"My mother used to tell me I wasn't her daughter," she said, staring at her cup. "It was sort of a punishment type of thing. Something she said to hurt my feelings or whatever. Thing is, I have her face. Where I look like my sisters is where I look like her, but I look nothing like Nigel."

"And Nigel's your father?"

She pushed the ice in her cup around with her straw. "Something like that."

"You've said that a few times now. What does it mean?"

"That I hope I'm wrong about something. It would explain a lot, but with every fiber of my being, I don't want it to be true."

"What is it?"

"Not..." She shook her head. "Not now."

The streetlamp highlighted every line of sadness etched into her lovely face, and he felt like someone had torn his heart down the middle like a flimsy sheet of paper. Mother or not, this woman was on his shit list. If he could help it, Bailey wouldn't ever need her again.

None of them.

Sure, she lived with them, but he had a house. Home could be with him, if she wanted. If they helped with any of her bills, fuck that too. He'd pay them. He'd take care of her. All she had to do was say the word, and if he had his way, she wouldn't even go back there tonight.

"Babe," he carefully moved toward her, "I'm really sorry you've had to deal with that."

She swiped the back of her hand across her cheek. "God, why am I tearing up about this? I *hate* crying about this."

He drew her into his chest. "You cry because a mother's love teaches us how to love. Hell, a mother's love physically affects the development of our brains. When something that strong is instead given as hate, neglect, or apathy, it's a pain that those who've never experienced it can't so much as fathom. That piece of you is simply missing, so you cry for the little girl who searches for something she's too young to understand she may never find."

She grabbed fistfuls of his shirt, sobbing quietly into the fabric. There was more to that story, and it was something he would unearth in due time.

After a while, she quieted. Then they stood there, her arms tightening and relaxing around him.

"I'm sorry—"

"No need for that." He stepped back. "I knew that was coming."

She laughed, the sound hollow.

"You walked into the La Brea Tar Pit known as my family, all because you wanted to support me." He kissed her, a swift touch of their lips. "You didn't think I wasn't about to do the same for you, did you?"

She looped her hands behind his neck and pulled his lips down to hers. At the same time he slid his tongue into her mouth, he picked her up and settled her on the trunk of her car. Then he lodged himself between her legs, close enough to smell the rosy scent of her hair and skin.

He wanted every last bit of her, from head to toe and everything in between, and because it was Bailey, he would wait for her. It meant difficult, *hard* nights and mornings, but she was well damn worth it.

Their lips separated, and she pressed her forehead into his chest.

"I *really* like you," she said.

He felt it again, that schoolboy embarrassment, and saw the images of those cartoon buck teeth. He had no response for that and knew he wouldn't find one if he tried. Instead, he searched for her lips, traced them with his tongue, and then kissed her with every ounce of what coursed through him, for her, as his response.

DAVID STOOD OVER HIS DAUGHTER'S CRIB, PRIDE SWELLING IN HIS chest. Alexis had finished her hair, and he loved the way the pattern of braids showed off the natural cuteness of her face. She was his life, his breath, and he would do anything for her. Anything for them both.

He kissed Abigail's plaited head, turned out the light, and left her room.

Alexis had already turned in, more than likely waiting for him. Usually, a fight like this would lead to unbelievably hot rounds of makeup sex. He was thinking about it now, creeping beneath the covers, pulling down her panties—if she was wearing any—and sliding inside her. Finding home over and over again.

Yet, he made his rounds around the house instead, locking all the doors and checking the windows. He then took a backward glance up the stairs before leaving through the front door and walking around the side of the house toward the lake out back.

The one thing he didn't understand, and possibly never would, was that he had an unquantifiable amount of love for the two most important women in his life.

He would do anything for them.

Anything.

So why couldn't he do *this?*

He looked around, as if anyone would actually be on the lake that late, and used his hands to dig into the soft dirt. Usually, he would grab a small shovel from the shed, but Alexis would hear that.

Glass appeared between the loose brown soil. White paper followed, a red emblem on the label. Then the name showed itself, and he felt both a knife in his chest and an insatiable thirst on the back of his tongue.

Jim Beam.

The taste was already in his mouth, pulling at his palate. Like with the bottle of Jose Cuervo Alexis had found hidden in the house, he would only have a sip. It would be enough to hold him over, but not enough to send him back over the edge. Then he'd start up his AA meetings again, let his sponsor know he'd fallen off the horse, and try harder for his wife and little girl.

Now, however, he needed a drink.

He sat along the edge of the lake, opened the bottle, brought the spout to his lips, and tipped it back.

CHAPTER SEVENTEEN

It was as simple as a "Have fun, Bailey," and she was off for two weeks. When she called Kellen to let him know, there'd been a loud cheer in the background, and Catalina had yelled, "Bailey, thank you for getting Kellen to take a vacation for the first time in his life. *Pásalo bien!*"

That had led to a first-class trip followed by a Caribbean villa.

A freakin' *villa*.

They had actual staff, and the place was gorgeous with its multiple stories, glass walls, infinity pool, and oceanfront views.

Views.

Despite growing up in Barbados, she'd never seen anything like it.

After unpacking, they had lunch at a local seafood spot within walking distance, near the beach. Then she'd suggested a taxi, but Kellen had hired a private driver—a stocky, middle-aged man with rich, black skin who went only by the name Leo —for their stay. She'd known physicians made good money, but damn.

"So you're a physician, a professor, and you own part of a practice," she said, the car bumping and ambling through the narrow streets. "Is that all?"

"You and my money." Kellen shook his head and rested a hand just above her knee. "Don't think about it so much."

She nodded.

Ten seconds later, she asked, anyhow, "Can I ask one question?"

"I also had a modeling gig in college," he said. "Paid for medical school for myself and my two good friends, Tayler and Ethan. I invested some, spent some. I do well for myself."

She grasped her forehead. Of course, he modeled. Of course, a man this sexy modeled. That question, she could have answered herself.

"Kellen, how are you single?"

He frowned. "How...what?"

"Sorry." She suppressed a smile. "I mean, how *were* you single?"

"Good. One more time, and I'm doling out," he dropped his voice, "punishments."

"And that's supposed to make me behave?"

He traced a line from her knee to the middle of her thigh. "I used to be attracted to projects. Despite all of my exes' accomplishments, they all had the same thing in common—brokenness. My worth was attached to what I could do for them, so I couldn't see myself in any other role but as an emotional handyman. The problem with that is, fixing brokenness is not a partner's job."

"And now?"

"Now?" He cast a lustful gaze down her body. "Now, I'm addicted to you."

"But I've got aspects of that brokenness."

"Regardless, Bailey, you put a lot of energy into making me feel supported. Being in my corner. Being my girl."

Doves released in her belly.

"You don't expect me to fix you. It's like all you want from me, is me. If I never bought you expensive jewelry or purses or took you on five-figure trips, I feel like you'd still want me."

"I would, Kel. I do."

His hand moved up her thigh, his large palm and long fingers palming the flesh there. He stared at her, devilish intent in those blazing eyes of his, and she glanced at where Leo sat behind a not-thick-enough partition.

"Don't worry about him," Kellen warned. "Worry about what I want to do to you. Spread your legs."

She parted her legs, and he slipped his fingers into her panties. Thank goodness all the windows were down, and there was a partition, because she was soaking wet.

"I can't do to you what I want right now," he began, "so tell me what you want."

"I'm not sure—"

He pinched her clit.

She swallowed a moan.

"Kel, I didn't bring an extra pair of panties, and these are about done for."

"I'll find a dark corner and lick you clean."

With how he looked at her, if it had been left up to him, his head would have been trapped between her thighs right there on the seat.

"Want me to play with your clit," he entered her with two fingers, "or do you want to go on a ride?"

"Both."

She barely got the word out, legs spreading wider as her hips sank, taking his fingers deeper. He grinned, wicked and sexy, and she tried to reach for the bulge in his pants, but he grabbed her wrist.

"Wait, you weren't trying to touch my dick, were you?" he growled. "You aren't thinking about riding me, are you? Is that what you're thinking of? Riding me, my dick inside you while I fuck you from below?"

Whatever Leo heard or picked up on, he would simply have to. It probably wouldn't be his first time.

"Bailey?"

Her eyes had closed at some point, and they slowly fluttered open, searching until she found Kellen next to her, as though he hadn't been there the entire time.

"I remember how you taste," he said, fingers stroking in concert with the movement of her hips. "Do you remember that? How it felt with my tongue on your clit? How I licked you..."

She went warm all over.

"...and fucked you with my tongue?"

She'd worn a dress with spaghetti straps because of the weather. Now, those straps worked to his advantage as he coaxed one down over her shoulder, tugged on one side of her strapless bra, and his mouth, like a furnace, closed over her areola.

He sucked.

And she came instantly.

She bit down on her bottom lip to squelch what would have been an extremely loud moan, grabbing onto his forearm to stabilize herself as she throbbed and shuddered through the strongest climax she'd had to date. He continued to move his fingers in and out of her until she caught herself, then he sucked the fingers clean, eyes never leaving hers.

"Leo," she knocked on the partition, "are we almost there? How much more time do we have?"

She *sounded* like she'd come, hard, seconds ago.

"Um, we have about twenty minutes," Leo replied. "You know, I can't see a thing. Can't hear when the speaker is off, neither. If that helps."

They'd reached the point where it both helped and didn't matter.

She unclasped the button on Kellen's waistband, yanked down his zipper, and a whimper leached from her throat when she saw him—firm, smooth, and with beads of liquid pleasure dripping from his tip. With an almost uncontrollable urge, she lowered her head and lapped it up.

He hissed, the muscles in his thighs tensing.

She closed her mouth around his head and sucked, and he sank further into the seat, fingers closing around her ponytail.

But then, he released.

"Kellen the Gentleman?" she said, looking up at him as she

licked at his head with only the tip of her tongue. "Right now, be Kellen the Nasty."

"Are you sure?" he grated out. "Say yes."

In answer, she took him to the back of her throat. He guided her head and pivoted his hips, thrusting up into her mouth. Every thrust sent the pulsing veins of his heavy dick over the surface of her tongue, straining the corners of her mouth.

He tossed his head back, eyes closed, but reopened them and looked down as if he couldn't decide which was better, watching or feeling.

"I want to come in that pretty mouth."

Technically, he could, but he'd been giving her solo pleasure since the lake house. It was time for him to reap the rewards of his good service to her lady parts.

"I'm close, Bailey, so if you don't want a mouthful of cum, you should probably...*mmm.*"

At some point, between his opening and closing eyes, she'd snatched off her panties, certain he never noticed.

"B," he thrust faster, "I'm right there, baby. I'm-right-there..."

She climbed over him, sank down onto his length, and she'd heard about eyes rolling back to the whites, but it was her first time witnessing it as he came with her walls clamped tight around him.

"Holy shit." He held onto her, pushing deeper into her body. "Holy, holy shit."

The tighter he held her, the deeper he went, and the more amazing it felt—for them both if his grunts and groans were any indication. The sensation of Kellen coming inside her, breathing hard and spasming, nearly snatched another climax from her body.

Once his breathing returned to some semblance of normalcy, she leaned back and searched his face. "We need to head back to the villa, don't we?"

He stared at her, looking from one eye to the other.

"'Cat' got your tongue?" she teased.

He blinked, slowly, and switched from looking into one eye at a time to directly holding her gaze, head on.

"Everything okay, Kel?"

"Yeah." He nodded and looked down, breaking their eye contact and whatever trance he'd fallen into. "Yeah, everything's okay."

"Are you surprised that I didn't wait until we were in a bedroom? Technically, we still have the full-blown thing to look forward to. I mean, we talked about it before we flew out. We both know what's going to happen on this trip."

"No, not that," he said.

She threaded her arms under his, closed him into a hug, and laid her head on his shoulder with a sigh of utter contentment.

"Bailey, *je crois que je tombe amoureux de toi.*"

"That's French, right?"

"Mm-hmm. It means," he exhaled and kissed her frizzy hairline, "that I'm glad you're in my life too."

Leo's voice surrounded them. "We're heading back to the villa for now, I take it?"

Kellen laughed, a deep rumble that massaged her chest, and held her closer.

"Yeah, Leo. Thanks."

LATER THAT AFTERNOON, ON THEIR SECOND ATTEMPT AT exploring the island, Bailey looked around, taking in what eventually became familiar rows of houses. New structures had gone up over time, and trees had been chopped down or had grown to towering heights. However, mostly everything else was the same.

There was Ms. Yardley's white house with the columns out front, Ms. Yardley actually sitting on the porch in the same spot where she'd always remembered her sitting. It had been twenty years, but the woman had barely aged.

She wanted to wave, but Ms. Yardley wouldn't remember her. No one around these parts would remember the once outgoing, outspoken, full-fledged tomboy who'd regressed into a shy, meek vestige of the girl she'd once been.

Then came the two-story house with the outdoor staircase where Mr. Paul and Miss Robison used to live, on separate floors. Alice and her father would always gossip about Miss Robison's constant refusals of Mr. Paul's offers of marriage. Now that she was older, she believed Miss Robison's good friend, Claudette, had probably had something to do with those refusals.

"We're in Bridgetown," she said.

Kellen's eyes lit up. "Where you grew up?"

If memory served her correctly, once they rounded the corner, it would be there on the right—the house where she'd spent nine years of her life after Nigel and Alice left their smaller home closer to town. But twenty years was a long time, and there'd been hurricanes, emigration, and weathering. All of which could have leveled the structure to the ground.

The house had been an always-pristine, single-story structure painted white with glorious roof paneling, surrounded by a large yard. It had boasted wood floors inside, expensive window trim, and a ductless air conditioning system. It had been the envy of all of St. Michael Parish.

Or so Alice would claim.

"Did you live anywhere near here?" Kellen asked.

As they drove over a small hill, Bailey's stomach rose with the car. Then, partially hidden deep in the green, there it was, as beautiful as the day she'd last seen it. The landscape appeared well-kept, but even from a distance, she could tell no one lived there.

"There it is. That's the house."

Kellen stared at it, frowned, and reached for her hand.

"Leo, can we stop?" she asked. "That house right there, can we stop?"

Leo's eyes met hers in the rearview mirror, the partition lowered to prevent her and Kellen from getting caught up a second time.

"You want to stop at *that* house?" Leo asked.

"Yes."

He sighed, long and heavy. "Okay, but I am staying at the end of the driveway."

"Why is that?" Kellen asked.

Leo slowed to prepare for the turn. "They say that when bad things happen in a place, the energy, it *stay* there."

Kellen's grip tightened on her hand. "What bad things happened in the house?"

"Not the house. On the land."

"Okay, so what bad thing happened on the land?"

"Just rumors." Leo shook his head. "Only stories."

True to his word, Leo parked at the very end of the long driveway, shut off the car engine, rolled down his window, and pulled out a book. She and Kellen exchanged glances, stepped out of the car, and made their way up to the front.

The house stood high off the ground, and a stairway that wrapped around the side led to the entry. The roof's pitch reminded her of a gnome's hat, and beneath the house was an open space they'd once used as a double carport.

Shielding her eyes from the sun, she took in her former prison. The mango tree she'd climbed once, and almost fell out of after reaching for a mango that hadn't even been ripe, was still there. That stump of stone she'd accidentally kicked, injuring three of her toes, had grown more ominous. There wasn't a weed or dry petal to be found in the rose garden her mother had once tended. If no one lived there, who was in charge of the upkeep?

"Something doesn't feel right," Kellen said, stretching the muscles in his neck and rolling his shoulders.

She felt it too, but that same something compelled her inside.

"Bailey, did something happen here? Because those haven't stopped shaking since you saw the place."

She glanced down, noticing for the first time the way her hands trembled, and clasped them together.

"We can go in," she insisted.

"Or we can leave."

"I need to go in."

"Bailey—"

She reached for the doorknob, and a jolt of electricity sparked in her hand and tingled down the length of her forearm. It wasn't a painful jolt, more like a bee whose sting had left something behind underneath her skin. Then she smelled the roses as fresh as if she held a bouquet in her hand.

Kellen grabbed her wrist. "What just happened?"

"Nothing serious." She shook out her fingers. "A little sting or jolt or something."

"Let me look at it."

"No, babe. It's fine."

"Bailey, I swear to God if you—"

She turned the knob and headed inside.

The house was just like she remembered it—those same wooden floors, that oaky, just-painted smell, the buzz of the mesh screen covering the windows whenever the wind blew.

It was all the same, which meant...

She faced the hall, faced her old room. Like her room in Atlanta, it hid behind the last door at the end of the corridor.

"Bailey?" Kellen's voice came through muffled and distant, like they were back underneath the water at the lake. "Bailey, you're shaking."

The middle of her palm, where she'd felt the tiny shock, tingled, and an unknown force propelled her legs down the hallway.

Kellen tugged on her arm.

On any other day, he would have been more than strong enough to stop her. But she continued past the double doors of the owner's suite, past the white wood of Noble's old room door that still had where she'd etched an "N" with a nail file, and past Faith's door that had been painted cornflower blue because she'd wanted to stand out. Her door, white wood with white trim, stared back at her.

"This is my old room." She ran her fingers over the trim her father had put up. "It's crazy how much it looks the same."

Kellen grabbed her shoulders and spun her to face him. "We're leaving."

"I can't."

"I don't fucking care what you *can't* do right now."

"Kel, I assumed that if I ever saw this place again, I'd want to stay clear away from it."

"Tell me why."

"Because…bad things happened here."

She sounded five, felt five all over again.

"What kind of bad things?"

She tried to pull away from his grasp, but this time, he held her firm.

"Bailey, *what kind of bad things?*" Then he looked down at his watch and cursed. "Shit, we're late. Let's go."

It was as though someone had attached manacles to her feet, closing them tight around her ankles. In her mind, she was "going," but she'd yet to move.

"Fuck this."

Kellen picked her up and stalked back to the front door,

descending the steps outside in three long strides. Leo, partially reclined, set away his book when he noticed them coming.

"All set?" he asked.

"All set," Kellen barked. "And don't ever bring us back here again."

THE ROOM THEY MET IN WAS FAIRLY SMALL.

The wooden desk Bailey and Kellen sat behind spanned nearly the full width of the room, with just enough space along one edge for the younger man across from them to pass through.

Despite the cool air blowing onto their heads, the man looked hot in his slim, navy blue suit and colorful dress shirt, the shirt's sleeves peeking fashionably from beneath the edge of the blazer. His hair was close-cropped with a razor-sharp part on one side, and the name "Stephen Murrain" was engraved on his nameplate.

"Well, Miss Green," Stephen said, looking up, "I don't have anything like this here for you to sign."

Bailey and Kellen exchanged glances.

"Come again?" she asked. "My grandparents specifically said they'd arranged everything for me, and the only thing I had left to do was sign some papers."

"Mm-hmm, yes, I understand. It seems they spoke with our Chief of Operations, Vincent D'enard."

"Well, can I speak to him?"

"Of course. He's on vacation for the next few days, however. How long did you say you were in town?"

"A couple weeks."

"How about this?" Stephen reached for a pen and sticky pad. "I'll send this to his desk so he can sit with you when he gets back, first thing."

"Is there someone else we can see in the meantime?" she asked.

"Not on this matter." When the pen failed to write, he scratched the tip against the wooden desktop, then tossed it in a trash bin on the other side of the room. "This document is, in particular, handled by Mr. D'enard."

Kellen squeezed her hand, gave her a look that told her to take a breather, and took over the questioning. "Mr. Murrain, can you give us some clarification as to what it is, exactly?"

Stephen finished scribbling and stuck the pink paper to the form. "I'll leave that up to Mr. D'enard. But," he quickly added, when Bailey started to protest, "you're in Barbados. Vacation while you wait."

She stared at him, first with poorly hidden contempt and then in resignation. Every word that left his mouth felt like steel blades on ice. More than once since they'd sat down, she'd envisioned circling his slim neck with both hands and bearing down.

"Have you visited before?" he asked.

Her molars grated against each other. "I was born here."

"Really?" His orbs lit up a few notches, and he leaned back in his chair and folded his arms. "Where?"

"Bridgetown."

138

"Small world! That's where I'm from. My family is Murrain, and you are, what, Green?" He stroked his chin. "Green... Green...do I know any Greens?" As though suddenly struck by an epiphany, he popped up and squeezed between his desk and the wall. "I'll be right back."

He hurried from the office.

Kellen placed an index finger under her chin. "Are you okay?"

She wasn't sure whether she replied. In her mind, Stephen Murrain gulped and gasped for air as her fingers crushed his windpipe.

Stephen returned, followed by a stout, older woman whose hair was pulled back in a tight ponytail ending in a faux bun piece.

"This is Inez Clifford," Stephen introduced. "She says she might know a Green."

It was a common thing, being of Caribbean descent and spending nearly hours trying to figure out if someone was related or knew a member of another person's family. Especially if they were from the same island.

"Alice and Nigel Green," Bailey said. "Those are my parents."

"From Bridgetown?" Inez's eyes rolled around in their sockets. "Did they used to live in a house over there near Massiah street?"

"I believe so. I was too young to remember that house. They eventually moved to a white one close to Brighton Beach."

Both Inez and Stephen went still.

"A white house?" Inez asked. "Not the one that's still standing?"

"That's the one."

"What is your name, dearie?"

"Bailey."

"Your full name."

"Bailey Danielle. I'm still Green at the moment."

She felt Kellen look at her, but she didn't face him. Technically, she did want to be his wife; the realization bulldozed over her the night they'd had the burgers at his campus after leaving David and Alexis' house. Yet, even a man like Kellen could get spooked if she started expecting too much, too soon.

"And you are Alice Green's first daughter?" Inez continued to prod. "The Alice who *did marry* Nigel? My Lord, my Lord. Wicked, wicked."

Kellen stood. "Why do I get the feeling that there's something nobody's telling us? First the house and now Bailey's name."

Inez looked up at him, eyes softening. "And you are, dearie?"

"A problem if someone doesn't start explaining."

"Not my place to explain." Inez shook her head. "There is something around you, my child. My dear, Bailey Danielle. Secret. Lie. Evil. Evil is like energy, you know? *It carry, it carry.*"

"Can everybody stop speaking in code and just tell us what's going on?" Kellen snapped.

Inez held out her hand. "Come, Stephen."

Before they had a chance to leave, Bailey reached out and grabbed Stephen's wrist.

"Talk," she hissed. "Now."

He looked from Inez to Kellen, then back to her. "I don't know what you mean."

"Inez," she shifted her budding rage to the old woman, "are you saying I'm evil?"

Stephen cried out.

Bailey removed her hand, and an imprint of her fingers remained behind on his skin, as if she'd burned them into him with a cattle prod.

"Go now," Inez ordered. "Now, Stephen. Go."

They hurried out.

Bailey stared at her cold, unscarred palm.

"B," Kellen tilted her chin up, and their eyes met, "you know that's bullshit, right? There's nothing evil about you, so don't let them get in your head. When this Mr. D'enard gets back from his vacation, we'll meet with him and get all of this over with. Until then, we're going to have ourselves a much-needed vacation because these are some of the bluest damn waters I've ever seen in my life."

She laughed, but it felt dark and hollow. "I agree. We're on vacation. Let's act like it."

Kellen reached for her hand, but she pretended not to see it and walked ahead of him out of the tiny room. Burning Stephen had left her confused. Scorching Kellen would rip a hole in her heart.

CHAPTER EIGHTEEN

Date number five and a half, though well overdue, had them lying on large, colorful beach towels on the beach adjacent to their villa, the sun directly above them.

Breezes passing through cooled their sun-beaten skin. Salt licked the air, and as best as she could, Bailey shoved what had happened at the house to the back of her mind. Everything was going well between her and Kellen, and she wanted to keep things that way.

"What do you write about?" he asked, out of the blue, turning his head to look into her eyes. "You mentioned that you write at my office."

She paused, needing a moment to finish taking in his gorgeous features. "I haven't really written anything in several years."

"Well," he took her hand and coaxed her until she straddled his midsection, "tell me about what you would *like* to write. If you had all the free time and the fastest computer processor in the world, what would you write?"

Interestingly enough, she couldn't wait to share this part of her with him.

"Well, I have this one story in my head. One of the most interesting characters from Caribbean folklore, at least to me, is *la diablesse.*"

He frowned. "Say that again?"

"La diablesse."

"That's French." A broad smile replaced his frown. "Female devil. I'm interested already."

"Really? Okay, here's how I see it in my head. There's a scandal in this small Caribbean town of...well, I haven't pegged down the place or decade yet, but it's a fictional town. The scandal is that something forbidden has happened." She took her voice a few octaves lower. "A baby is born to a clergyman and the town diablesse. This is where you gasp."

He spread his long fingers across his chest. *"Gasp."*

"Perfect. Now, the townsfolk, after hearing of the abomination, storm the devil woman's house, demanding that she show the baby. She refuses, and even after a thorough search of the house," she waved her arms, demonstrating the search, "no baby is found."

"No baby?"

She shook her head. "Nope."

"Where'd it go?"

"They never find it. So, the townspeople take her to the gallows where, right before she's hanged, she promises that twenty-five years from that day, the town will know ruin because of what happened on that night."

She ended the story, staring at him with her hands steadied on either side of his chest. This close, his body was even more impressive, hard and with the masculine roughness that made him irresistible.

"So?" he asked.

"So…what?"

"What happened to the baby?"

"That's the central part of the story. I can't give that away."

"Oh, come on."

Mischief gleamed in his eyes.

He was so handsome, it was hard for her to look away. Kellen Edwards was magnificent, smiling up at her the way he was, eager to hear the rest of her story, showing interest in something she loved. There was virtually nothing more attractive.

If this was what falling in love felt like, she saw why it was the subject of so many works of art. Why, for some, it became an addiction.

"You've got to write that, Bailey. You've got a talent for storytelling."

"I'm planning to…after I get into a creative writing program somewhere. If I don't, it doesn't mean I'll stop trying. But I'd like to at least have that under my belt, maybe get into a college in the Greater Atlanta area. I mean, my job's there." She leaned forward, kissed the space between his brows, then placed a kiss on his lips. "You're there."

A solid ridge rose underneath her, pressing into the middle of her bikini bottoms.

"I like when you say things like that to me," he tilted his hips, adding more pressure, "but I'm a physician. I can practice almost anywhere, and I'm already licensed in three states."

"What about if I got into a school in Oregon? You'd come with me?"

"Of course," he said, without hesitation. "Actually, have you ever thought about quitting your job? Maybe going to school and writing full-time?"

"*All the time.* If I get into a program somewhere, I'll see if it's something I can budget with my stipend. If not, I don't mind the hard work."

He chewed on the inside of his bottom lip. "Hmm."

"But, we have to go."

She stood and held out a hand to help him up, fully aware he didn't need it, but he indulged her by letting her believe her strength got him to his feet.

"I was distracting you while I had dinner arranged for us at The Cliff," she said. "It's this really nice restaurant on the island's West End that overlooks the beach, and it's got great food and a magical sunset. Perfect for date five and a half."

"I thought date five and a half was supposed to be simple?"

"It was, but this is my first chance to take my man out. Show him a good time. Whose money we're using is not important."

In spite of her protests, he picked her up and raced them toward the water's edge. She screamed as he jumped in, partially submerging them beneath the water, this experience a far cry from their time at the lake. No matter what, he would always come back for her, and he'd promised to always be there for her.

"Might have to push that reservation back a few hours," she said, injecting a bit of huskiness into her tone. "There are other things I'd prefer to be doing right now. Specifically, to you."

The firmness returned, poking her in her belly, and he licked his lips, staring at hers.

"Well, I've heard about The Cliff, and the reviews said they serve really good lobster ravioli."

"Really, Kellen?"

"B, be honest. Am I better than lobster ravioli?"

She nibbled on her top lip.

"What about steak? Red snapper?"

"Am I?" she countered, attempting to look serious.

"To be honest," he scanned her face, "I don't know if you're better than an expired can of green beans right now with how hungry I am."

She burst out laughing.

Joining her, he ducked them under the water.

ON DATE FIVE AND A HALF, BAILEY LEARNED THAT HER MAN looked remarkable, even with slightly damp, unruly hair that still fell with stylish grace as they walked into the restaurant. They'd brought "just in case we leave the bedroom at some point" clothes, so tonight, she wore a floral, ankle-length dress and wedge sandals. He wore a lightweight collared shirt, the sleeves rolled up to expose his forearms, with a pair of shorts and low-top leather sneakers.

She got a taste of his Spanish blood when he took her hand and guided her to the dance floor. No one had been more excited than Kellen when he found out how similar Caribbean and Spanish music were, just "with less horns" as he'd put it.

After a dinner of outstanding prime beef tenderloin, vegetables, and chocolate mousse for dessert, they downed a bottle of wine and twirled until the band announced they were playing the last song of the night, the sky chock-full of stars.

They sauntered, hand in hand, out of the restaurant and into the car where Leo waited, probably sick of their antics, but they were too drunk to offer any realistic apologies.

Kellen's curious hand snuck up her dress, and she giggled in part due to his touch and them sharing a second bottle of expensive red wine they'd taken to go.

The minute they pulled up to the villa, wedge sandals in hand, she ran up the slight hill to the front door. Kellen, hands curled around the wine bottle's neck, started after her, but Leo called out to him. Leo then said something to him that made him touch the tip of his nose with an index finger. Although he managed to do so, he exchanged the half-empty bottle for a satchel Leo handed over, and returned to his initial pursuit.

She watched that pursuit, back plastered against the door, nipples tight.

He turned her around and pinned her to the solid oak, her breasts so sensitive, the wood felt like fingertips.

"God, you're so fucking sexy, *mon chou*," he growled, lips brushing her neck.

He slipped his hands beneath her dress and caressed her skin, running his large palms over her hips and down the curve of her ass. He smelled like ginger and spice, and when she tried to face him, he held her more firmly in place.

They'd talked about sex. They'd specifically talked about having sex on this trip. Unless a surprise hurricane popped up after being missed on every weather center's radar, sex would happen on this trip.

Him being ever the doctor, they'd talked about birth control, which she'd already been on, and he'd made a joke about her getting pregnant so quickly into their relationship. She'd realized that a child with him, at some point, wasn't something she was at all opposed to.

She tilted her head, exposing more of her neck, and he traced the arc, his tongue hot, before finding a spot to suck.

The pull of his mouth wrenched a moan from her throat that she was sure the entire island heard.

He made a noise, like the midway line between a laugh and a groan, turned her around, and planted his hands high on either side of her head. Playful wickedness gleamed in his eyes, and it didn't come across as terrifying. In fact, it spoke directly to her, disrupting her heartbeat until her pulse drowned out everything around them but his breathing.

"You're so beautiful," he said, again looking from one eye to the other. "My girl. My Bailey."

She'd *never* felt like this.

Kellen made everything she'd ever endured, every difficulty and pain she'd ever been put through, completely worth it if they'd all driven her to him.

He slipped his finger beneath the strap of her dress, drew it down, and kissed her bare shoulder.

The man was actually seducing her.

She'd been touched, teased, and kissed, but seduction, she now understood, was a different concept altogether.

He teased the strap from her other shoulder and kissed her bare skin there, allowing his lips to linger for a moment. Then he kissed a trail across her chest to the hollow at the base of her throat. While he kissed, his finger found the line of her jaw and stroked, a smooth, slow, unexpectedly erotic movement.

She sunk her fingers into the fabric of his shirt and pulled him closer when there was barely enough space for air to squeeze between them. He kissed his way up the curve of her neck, to her lips, and expertly glided his tongue into her mouth.

The oak against her back felt like feathers as he pushed her further up against it, taking the kiss deeper but keeping the movement of his finger along her jaw very, *very* light.

They parted for air, but the distance was minimal, their breaths mingling, harsh and loud against the quiet night.

"Mine," he whispered, their lips brushing.

"All yours," she said.

He picked her up, pushed the door open, and carried her inside to the private patio next to the master bedroom, where he set her on her feet. A strong gust of wind curled the hem of her dress around her calves, and even the moonlight had gotten caught up in their sensual night, its glow timidly caressing her skin.

"Take this off." He fingered the straps that fell about her arm. "Strip for me."

Holding his gaze, she slowly removed the slinky fabric, growing wetter at the sight of his pupils enlarging with each inch of skin she revealed. The dress fell, pooling at her feet, and she stood before him in nothing but a teeny, red lace thong.

He sucked in a breath, stepped forward, and snapped the panties against her skin with a flick of his wrist.

When she moaned, his brow lifted.

"I'll keep that in mind," he said. "Now, turn around and bend forward."

She turned.

The black ocean formed a seam with the sky, and as she waited for the pleasurable sting of his palm, she felt his hand wedge between her thighs instead, jimmying them apart. His breath followed, swirling over her inner thighs.

He pulled the thong to the side.

And licked.

Although no one was around for miles, the night was so tranquil, she fought the urge to scream.

Grunting, he spread her wider and went from gentle flicks to engulfing her pussy. Then, with another grunt, this one in obvious frustration, he stood, urged her to bend further, and growled a low, "Just like that" before plunging his tongue inside her.

"Kel…" The humid night air curled around her hard nipples. "Oh, baby."

She came with a cry that slapped against the quiet. Before she had the chance to completely descend, his voice sounded.

"Turn around, Bailey."

Legs barely functioning, she turned around to him studying

her as if deciding, from a million different things, what to do next.

"Now, you strip," she commanded. "I want all of you, Kellen. Including the good parts."

The side of his mouth tilted into a wry smile, and he took his time removing his shirt, revealing that magnificent body. He played with his belt, and she almost had a fit from waiting.

When everything fell, she couldn't help but moan. A thick shaft led up to a soft, succulent tip gleaming with moisture. She reached out, needing to touch him, and stroked his hard, velvety skin until his eyes closed and a guttural sound vibrated in his throat.

"You keep doing that, and it won't end well for you," he warned.

"On the contrary," she lowered her head and licked his tip, "I think it would end very well."

Rather than tease, which would be agony for them both, she sucked him into her mouth. The sound he made this time she could only classify as a growl as she crouched and wrapped both hands around his length.

"No, ma'am." He pulled away. "Tonight, I'm coming inside you."

He picked her up, walked them inside, and set her down on the bed. She spread her legs, and when he slid inside her, the same word resonated through her head.

Mine.

The room shattered.

He gave her every inch her body could take, even when she didn't think it could, his thrusts deep, steady, and powerful. Her requisite to remain quiet tumbled off the edge of the hill, and every moan and cry she released, he answered with a groan and hiss.

"*Fuck*, Bailey."

"Fuck, Bailey?" She managed a throaty, hedonistic laugh. "Fuck, *Kellen*."

She felt every vein, every ridge, and her pleasure surpassed any semblance of inebriation from the wine. Needy pressure built in her clit, drawing her to the edge, and she chased the sensation with her fingers, stroking and circling in time to his thrusts until her back bowed and his name tore from her lips.

"That's my girl," he forced out.

And, like a wave breaking against the shore, he moaned and came inside her.

She wasn't ready to be separated from him, so when he went to pull out, she asked him to stay in. For as long as he could, she wanted him inside her, wanted every drop he spilled.

At the moment, she had no words, so she reveled in the kisses he placed against the side of her face, feeling safe and secure.

Feeling loved.

CHAPTER NINETEEN

He was having another one of those dreams again—Bailey straddling him, pinning him beneath eyes so dark they altered the atmosphere of the room. Her skin was smooth and hot against his palms, and his dick probed where she was so damn wet.

He wanted to take his time with her, to mentally sketch the details of her brown areolas, imbibe on the scent of her desire, and nudge her forward until her thighs straddled his face. But he also wanted to be selfish, to plunge into her this first time, choosing to savor her later and whet a thirst that would never be satisfied.

"Kellen? Is everything okay?"

He tried to open his eyes, only to find they were already open. It was dark outside, and Bailey was actually on top of him, naked, with the sheets wrapped around her middle. He squeezed real hips, traced real variations in her skin up to her face, briefly cupping her cheek before moving back to the scar on her stomach.

The raised, marbled skin was a sign of embarrassment to many. To physicians, it was one of the telltale signs of health and healing. Whatever had hurt her had happened long ago, but the gash was much too long to be an appendectomy. Yet, it had definitely needed a doctor's suture.

"Everything's okay," he said.

She leaned forward, as best as she could with his dick trying to drill through her belly button, and rested her chin on top of clasped hands. "I like watching you sleep. You look so hand-some and peaceful."

He sat up and situated himself between her thighs, the sheets bunched between them. He couldn't keep his hands off her, dipping his fingers in the crooks of her elbows, the groove of her neck, over her shoulders and down her sides.

"That thing you call me." Her eyes closed. "*Mon chou*. What does it mean?"

"Sweetie," he said. "Actually, it's 'my sweet bun.'"

"Do you speak French at home?"

"Sometimes. With my father, we speak English exclusively, unless family visits."

"Does your mother speak any Spanish?"

"A little. She learned from my dad."

"So, what would you call me in Spanish?"

"Mi querida, corazón, bebe…mi vida y una dia, mi esposa."

"And what do those mean?"

My darling, love, baby…my life and one day, my wife.

"They all mean relatively the same thing as mon chou." He could only imagine how awkward it would have been to get dumped halfway into their first vacation together because he already knew she would be his wife one day.

"How do you say 'I want you' in French?"

His brow popped up. With the way she twitched, it wasn't the only thing that had.

"Je te veux."

She tapped her chin, searched the sheets, and then he felt her grip around the base of his dick. Blood engorged his shaft, already familiar with the grooves of her palms and the shape of her fingers. He wouldn't speak, wouldn't ask her what she planned to do as the look in her eyes told him everything he needed to know. Then she bent and wrapped her lips around his head, confirming that look.

The tip was the most sensitive.

Extremely sensitive.

As she sucked it into her warm mouth, he wasn't about to bitch out with a full-on moan, but his toes had curled in all sorts of directions.

"Mmm…Bailey."

So, maybe he would moan.

It was difficult not to, as she first wet his shaft with her mouth, then stroked him with both hands. She took him to the back of her throat, raising and lowering her head, keeping that tight suction in one smooth motion. It felt so good, jealousy crept in—his crazy, smitten, completely-in-love ass wanted to know how she'd gotten this good.

The jealousy didn't last long, however. After all, he was

crazy, smitten, and in love.

And his dick was in her mouth.

"Kel," she ran her tongue the full length of his erection, "you taste amazing. Why is that? Actually, taste and feel."

A weak voice in the back of his mind wanted to know what she meant. If he was the best she'd ever tasted and felt. However, it died a very rapid death because *his-dick-was-in-her-mouth.*

She returned to working her hands and mouth in tandem, those beguiling eyes imprisoning him in their hollows much like they'd done the first time they'd met. He tried to relax, to ease into the moment, but it was coming in fast and hot. If she kept this up, they wouldn't wake until five the next evening.

Then she moaned.

And he came in her mouth.

Her hot, *hot* mouth.

She didn't look away, never looked away, and once his body was devoid of all its bones, she ran the tip of her tongue over his head in an easy checkmate.

"I know how this is going to sound," he prefaced, "but I swear it's not that. Could you get me a glass of water?"

She nodded, easing off the bed. "Sure, but I don't get it. How else is it supposed to sound?"

"I don't want it to seem like I'm asking you to fix me a sandwich."

"Do you want a sandwich?"

He eyed her. "No?"

"Okay." She headed for the kitchen. "I might be a minute, though. I want one."

"Then I change my m—"

"Too late."

His second wind came in sooner than anticipated, so he followed her to the kitchen and found her, perfectly bent over, searching a low cabinet.

"Glasses are up top," he said.

Before she could right herself, he grabbed her hips and entered her in a single slow thrust. She gripped the edge of the counter, her walls tightening around him, and pleasure nearly bowled him over.

"Bailey, Bailey," he eased out, sank in, "you should have never let me get a taste. This is my pussy now. I'm addicted now. *Good luck trying to get rid of me now.*"

"Kel," she shook her head, "I—"

"You...what? I know you're not about to tell me it's too much." He fucked her harder, their bodies slapping together, echoing through the villa. "I know you're not about to tell me you can't take it. You just sucked my dick and made my toes curl, so whatever you were about to tell me, swallow it like you swallowed my cum."

He wet his thumb, reached around, and massaged her nipple.

"Take it, Bailey. Say yes."

"Yes." She gripped his wrist with one hand, back arching. The other hand stroked feverish circles between her legs. "Oh, God...yes."

A rush of heat coated his shaft.

A slippery, sticky sensation followed.

Then came the tugs from her climax, in waves, and he saw white as he came for what he knew wouldn't be the last time that night.

CHAPTER TWENTY

Body weary, Bailey slipped into her sandals, quietly grabbed her purse, and left the bedroom, but not before placing a kiss on Kellen's forehead.

Their first time together had been nothing short of outstanding.

Exquisite.

Amazing.

Magnificent.

All the synonyms.

In the past, sex would usually end once her partner achieved orgasm, even if from foreplay to the finish line, the entire thing lasted only thirty seconds. She'd then convince herself that "being close to him" had been good enough, no climaxes necessary.

Bullshit.

Kellen made love to her with her pleasure as his goal,

masterful and powerful, yet tender. And, when it was over—and over meant they'd tapped each other's well dry—he'd pulled her close and held onto her like he'd needed her to sleep. Like he'd needed her to *breathe*. It was why walking away from him now was suffocating, but she had to go back to that house.

She had no other choice.

Leo stood waiting at the end of the driveway, leaning against the car, arms crossed and his expression absent any evidence that he'd been asleep when she'd called. She'd had to beg him to pick her up, and he'd agreed only after revealing her intended destination.

"When we get there, I'm giving you twenty minutes," he said, holding the door open.

She climbed inside. "Or else, what? You'll come in after me?"

"Not stepping foot inside that house."

"Then why'd you agree to take me?"

"Can tell you have unfinished business there. Now move your feet so I can close this door."

As he drove, her fingers twitched.

Her toes tapped.

Her stomach stirred with either excitement or fear, perhaps a combination of both. The sensation grew as the landscape became more and more familiar.

The house came into view.

Dark clouds shadowed the moon, the sky like an ink spill on black paper. In the distance, if she listened hard enough, she could hear the quiet roar of an angry sea slamming against rock, wearing it down, subtly winning the battle of nature.

Leo stopped at the end of the driveway and lowered the partition. "Twenty minutes, Miss ma'am."

"Twenty minutes," she echoed.

He kept the engine running.

The island couldn't have been cooler than eighty degrees, but the air around the house felt thirty degrees lower.

She crossed the threshold, shivering and rubbing her arms, opening her mouth to exhale what should have been a frosty breath. The room at the end of the hall called to her, so loudly she could have argued she heard a voice, but she didn't immediately follow the urge. Instead, she walked to the back porch, lifted the notch locking the sliding doors, and wedged her fingers into the groove to slide it open.

Wind slapped her in the face, bringing granules of sand, some of which settled on her eyelashes. The coconut tree was missing, she noticed, stepping out onto the wooden floor. There'd been a coconut tree about a quarter mile down the hill, next to the road on the path to the beach. Whenever they'd walked to the beach, she would look up at it, the large green fruit dangling, and wonder at what point they would fall. She would sometimes shield her head, Noble and Faith giggling and following suit.

They would walk like that, hands clasped like *teepees,* all the way to the beach. The tree was gone, but it had, at least, offered her a gentle memory.

A grip on her shoulder yanked her out of her reverie, turning her until she faced the inside hallway.

A man's silhouette stood watching her.

He tipped his head toward the dark corridor. Before she

could react, she found herself a few steps away from the door with no recollection of walking or moving. This close, she could see the door was slightly ajar. Earlier, it had been shut so tight, it had looked fused to the doorjamb.

She nudged it open.

In this room, when she opened her mouth, her breaths dispersed in clouds of white. The man stood by the window, fully formed yet translucent—like wax crayons on tracing paper.

He had dark hair, dark eyes.

Like Kellen.

He smiled, and she half-expected his mouth to open and for his voice to resonate across the room. But then the tingle in her arm returned, at first as cold as the room; however, heat quickly seeped its way in.

Intense heat.

As quickly as the temperature had dropped, it rose, so hot there should have been flames. Sweat trickled down on her temple, her neck, and along her inner thighs. There was no wound, but she felt one open and swore she felt something slither inside.

She turned to the door to escape but stopped abruptly when she spotted Kellen standing in the doorway. Then a single command resonated through her head.

Kill him.

CHAPTER TWENTY-ONE

Kellen opened his arms, expecting an embrace, but Bailey's body unceremoniously collided with his. She clawed at him, trying to climb his torso, a shard of a broken mirror in her hand. It was how he'd found her—on her knees in front of the mirror he'd watched her tear from the wall and punching the glass with her fist.

With much more power than she should have been capable of, she aimed the shard at the large vein in his neck.

He squeezed her wrist until the shard fell, picked her up, carried her outside until they were several feet from the entrance, and sat in the middle of the grass. She thrashed and snarled, doing everything except foaming at the mouth. He held her, using one hand to secure her wrists and the other to squeeze her to him.

This was his woman.

She was the woman he wanted.

More than anything, he wanted her to be his, in sickness and in health, one day. But this, whatever *this* was, pinpointed the exact reason he'd told her never to come back to this place.

The deed, her mother, and the way the island folk spoke about the house—some shit had gone down here. Though he wasn't sure what, he knew it involved Bailey, and it involved her in a significant way.

Eyes closed, between pressing kisses into her hair, he recited one of the first things his mother had made him memorize in French.

"Par sa vie, sa mort et sa résurrection, nous a mérité, les recompenses du salut eternal, faites que—"

"Mr. Edwards!"

He looked up.

Leo, waving, hurried over and kneeled next to him in the grass. "Is everything okay? What's going on? Is that a prayer?"

"I didn't know what else to do." He pulled Bailey closer. "Bailey? Come back to me, baby. I don't know what's happening, but please...come back to me. I need you."

"I know I shouldn't have brought her back here. I'm sorry."

"It's okay, Leo. She asked you to."

"Look at her. How is it okay?"

A few minutes later, Bailey's wriggling subsided. As quickly as she'd morphed, she fell asleep, her face a peaceful opposite of the one that had looked up at him from the mirror.

"She'd been in there an hour," Leo said, repeating what he'd relayed on his frantic phone call. "I called out for her, even tried to go in, but the door wouldn't open. Where did you find her?"

Kellen ticked his head at the house. "In one of the back bedrooms. Can you tell me what they say about the house?"

"Do you know what they call *duppy?*"

Kellen shook his head.

"A ghost. A spirit." Leo shrugged. "It's just tales. A man disappeared from the island long ago. Some people think he was killed and buried around where the house sits now. Because he was killed, they say his soul is unsettled and full of anger. Some people, they are more...*open* than others. Those people, they say, should stay away from places like this."

"Open? Like susceptible?"

"Mmm."

"Do you believe any of it?"

"I have never seen a spirit. Still, I don't go looking, either. But come on, son. Let's go. You all need to rest."

Kellen stood, lifting Bailey with him. "Yeah, you're right. And thanks again for calling me, Leo."

"Kellen, the way you look at that girl, you would have run here if you had to."

He followed Leo to the car and kept Bailey close on the ride back—in his arms, on his lap, her head in the crook of his neck. Once at the villa, he undressed her to her bra and panties, placed her on the bed, and climbed in next to her. And he didn't sleep a wink and instead lay watching her, mentally searching PubMed articles and medical texts and coming up with nothing.

The "duppy" story was what it was, but he was thinking along different lines. More plausible and logical lines. Granted, he'd only done a rotation in psychiatry in med school. Still, he'd never seen anything like what had happened to Bailey. He couldn't wrap his head around it. She'd had no discernible signs of mental illness up to this point, especially not any psychoses. It didn't rule them out, but the person he'd watched break that mirror in that room wasn't his Bailey.

Even as morning streamed through the bedroom windows, bathing them in faint daylight, he watched her, their half-naked bodies fitted together. The coastal island trade winds sent the curtains draped around the four-poster bed flying into the air, one caressing Bailey's cheek. Like this, with the morning rays dancing off her skin, she was mesmerizing. Her hair shimmered, every frizzy coil and fuzzy ringlet on display, each one a star of its own show.

"Good morning, beautiful."

She stretched and rolled onto her side, facing him, resting her head on her clasped hands on the pillow. "Knew it," she said. "I knew you'd look sexy in the mornings. Have you been up long?"

"You don't remember."

"Remember what?" Her eyebrows, mussed from sleep, squished together. "Oh, I left last night. You must have found out. I'm so sorry. It's not because I didn't enjoy myself."

He grinned. "Oh, I know you did. 'Kellen, mmm, right there. Yes, baby, please don't stop…'"

She grabbed the only throw pillow that had made it through their lovemaking and swatted him.

"Don't act like you're not happy I can make you make those noises," he teased. "But…what all do you remember from last night? After the phenomenal sex."

She rolled her eyes, smiling. "After the phenomenal sex, I went to my old house."

"And why'd you go back to the house?"

"I don't know. I just felt like I had to. Like I needed to. I can't really explain it."

"Did you find what you were looking for?"

She opened her mouth to respond but then closed it and sat cross-legged on the bed. "It's the…it's the weirdest thing. I can't remember. The last thing I remember is walking into the house and going out on the porch. Then I, at least I *think* I saw someone and followed them down the hallway into my old bedroom."

"What happened after you got to the room?"

"I," she frowned, "wait, how did I get back here? Where's Leo?"

He tossed the decision on whether to tell her he was the one who'd found her back and forth in his head. However, he'd expected his friends to tell him what he'd done during his liquor-induced stupors in college and thereafter. This was similar.

"I found you," he said.

"You? How'd you know where I…oh. Leo. But why'd he call you? He told me I had twenty minutes. I couldn't have been in there longer than that."

"An hour."

Her eyes opened wide. "An *hour?*"

"You'd been gone an hour before he called me. It took me about twenty minutes to get there, and it would have been longer if Leo hadn't found me a ride that late."

She deserved to know everything, but looking at her, her dark eyes eager and more innocent than he'd ever seen them, it seemed unfair to tell her she'd charged at him like a woman possessed.

Possessed.

The word resonated, but he shook his head to cast it away.

"When I found you," he cleared his throat, "you were punching a mirror. A mirror you ripped clear from the wall."

"Punching a mirror?" Her brows dipped into another frown. "That makes no sense."

"Well, it didn't at first, but then you took a piece of the mirror and came at me with it. You tried to stick it into my neck."

At the same time she choked on a gasp, she backed away from him.

"Bailey, don't freak out."

"Don't freak out?" She unfolded her legs, left the bed, and went to pace in front of the windows. "You just told me I tried to stab you, my boyfriend, who I…have strong feelings for, and you think I'm not going to freak out? Why would I do that? How could I do something like…"

Her body went stiff.

"Bailey, don't go there."

"Miss Inez was right," she said.

He went to her, but she wouldn't let him touch her. "Bailey, come on. You're not evil, for one, and all that stuff is nonsense."

"Then how would you explain it?"

He had no answer for that.

"Kellen, I tried to hurt you."

"Do you feel like hurting me now?"

"No, but who's to say it's not in here somewhere, waiting and lurking? Did you sleep last night? Of course, you didn't. Is that why?"

She tried to charge past him, but he hooked her around the waist.

"Calm down, B—"

"How'd you get me to stop?" She took a step back and examined his bare torso. "Did I get you? Did I hurt you?"

"I'm fine, baby." Sighing, he sat along the edge of the bed. "You're like half my size. I just restrained you until you calmed down. After that, you went right to sleep, and I stayed up, not because I was worried about me, but because I was worried about you."

She settled next to him. "So what, do I need to see a psychiatrist? Do you think I might have some sort of mental—"

"I don't know."

"Then what—"

"I don't know that, either."

"Just so you know," she placed a hand on his shoulder, "I can't explain what happened, but I'd never hurt you. You're the best boyfriend in the universe."

"Man," he said. And, if she hadn't already realized it, their first date had officially been her last first date.

"I like boyfriend here, better. Anyone can be a best man, but only you can be the best 'mine.'"

He kissed her temple, and they sat in silence until the chime of the villa's phone system brought them back to reality.

She walked to the phone like she wore shoes made of lead

and picked up the receiver. "This is she," she said. "Oh, Mr. D'enard's back? He'd like to see me today? Great, we'll be there."

She ended the call and came back to him, stepping right into his arms, and he coaxed her onto the bed before pulling her close.

"Everything okay with you?" she asked, the question muffled by his collarbone.

Virtually nothing was.

"Yeah, I'm fine," he said.

"You pretend you're okay with everyone else, Kel. Don't pretend with me. I…care about you."

She'd paused twice now before mentioning she cared about and had strong feelings for him. If he learned she was trying not to say she loved him—or, even better, that she'd fallen *in love* with him—the entire night would be forgotten.

Forever.

His entire world would become consumed by the fact that she loved him.

"Honestly, Bailey?" He glided his fingers over her stubborn frizz. "Something happened last night that scared the hell out of me. I don't understand it. It's like you were a completely different person."

"If you had to explain it in one word, what would that word be?"

Although he'd instantly come up with a word, he didn't want to use that particular one.

"Rabid."

"Like possessed?"

"No…like rabid."

She backed away. "Like *possessed.*"

"Bailey—"

"Things are a little bit different, culturally, here in the Caribbean. Here, spirits and possessions aren't considered left field. They're accepted as a part of life. Here, so many things we do are steeped in African culture, and spirituality is a big part of African culture."

She returned to the windows.

"I understand that," he said. "It's the same in French and Spanish culture. We have a lot of similar ideologies, stories, myths, legends, and folktales. But I grew up in Western society, so I can't help if logic is battling against what happened last night."

"What did you do when you found me?"

"What do you mean?"

"I mean, what did you do? Did you just hold me down until I calmed?"

He looked away, but she moved into his line of sight.

"What did you do, Kellen?"

"I held you down, yes. But I also…okay, so when we were kids, my mother made me, Connor, and David memorize…it's a Catholic, uh—"

"Prayer?"

"Yeah."

"So, you prayed."

"Only because I didn't know what else to do. Not because I thought you were…that word."

"Kellen, science is based on multiple layers of proof," she said. "Spirituality is based on belief. However, beliefs and experiments all start with the same thing: a question limited by our knowledge."

He stared at her, feeling his eyes glaze over.

She sighed and folded her arms underneath her breasts. "I started writing when I was very young as a way to cope with life. My interests were spirits and spirituality, folktales and folklore. I even used to write about my house when I was a kid. When things got really bad, sometimes it would feel like somebody crawled into bed with me while I was sleeping. And it wasn't a creepy feeling. It felt more like they were trying to soothe me, even though no one was there whenever I opened my eyes."

He wanted to believe her, indulge a little, but logic batted away every word that left her mouth. She'd probably had a momentary lapse in something, maybe oxygen, that had sent her into a crazed stupor. He'd never heard of something like it happening before, at least not without help from a narcotic or hallucinogen, but anything was possible.

"There's a story my father used to tell me and my brothers," he said instead. "It's about *La Llorona,* or 'the weeping woman,' who's supposedly this mysterious woman in white. In life, she drowned her children in a river to get back at her cheating husband, only to end up committing suicide in the same river because she couldn't live with the agony. Because of her crime in life, she gets stuck between life and death, crying at night for the loss of her children. Some people even think that, if you hear her crying, it means someone close to you is going to die."

She eyed him, squinted, and then looked away. "You're right. I'm being ridiculous."

"I never said that." He walked over and stood next to her, close enough for their sides to touch. "Look, you mentioned not finishing college. Did you study writing back then?"

"Economics, and it was a complete fail. I hated it. I've only ever wanted to study writing. It's why I recently applied to GSU and Emory."

This close, it was impossible not to hold her, so he drew her into his arms. "Emory?" he asked. "Why didn't you tell me you applied? You know I have connections there in the faculty."

"I didn't tell you because my grades from my first attempt at college are horrendous. I'm sure even you couldn't get me in."

Not if he had anything to say about it. It wasn't the moon, but he could get her in. She deserved it, and he would do anything to make her happy.

"Don't lose *faith*," he said, wiggling his brows.

She groaned. "Don't tease me. It's been a long night for us both."

"I know. I'm sorry." He kissed her forehead. "We should get some breakfast before we go see D'enard. Want to have breakfast here or go somewhere?"

"Here. I think Leo needs a break from us. If it's not raunchy backseat sex, it's twilight insanity."

He laughed. "I wonder what we have next in store for him?"

As she looked up at him, he reminded himself to breathe. This woman was, without a doubt, the one for him.

And he loved her.

He loved her so damn much.

CHAPTER TWENTY-TWO

Mr. Thomas D'enard was the color of an orange, a telling sign of the vacation he'd just returned from. His office, much larger than Stephen's, spilled over with books on bookshelves that took up most of two walls. Though the a/c unit in his office blared loudly, whenever he pivoted, Bailey caught a glimpse of the patch of sweat printing through the white dress shirt underneath his blazer.

He'd had a confident handshake but now rummaged through the files on his desk as nervous as The White Rabbit.

"It's not in a file?" she asked, pointing to the flat-screened monitor across from him. Kellen had her other hand trapped in his. He'd barely let more than a two-foot gap of space get between them all morning.

"No, this wouldn't be," D'enard said. A wisp of hair jumped free from his man bun. "I'm looking for a letter. The document before the document. I remember when the couple came in.

They mentioned leaving something for their granddaughter, Bailey. A house and the land it sits on. It was very important to Ada that I included the land."

Kellen flicked a thumb toward the single office window. "What house? Not that creepy ass white one on the stilts? That's a hard no, D'enard."

She squeezed his hand. "Kel, I've got it, babe. And, Mr. D'enard, you said my grandparents left me that house, but I don't think that's right."

"I remember them saying grandparents," D'enard continued, "but it's like that down here. Maybe they were so close to your grandparents, they felt like your own."

"But I've never met them."

He frowned. "Really? Ada and Walter Bailey? Elderly couple? The man had white hair, and the woman was blonde with—"

"*Blonde?* Are we talking dyed blonde, yaki blonde, or a white woman?"

"White woman. A white couple."

She glanced at Kellen, not surprised to find him staring at her, the look in his eyes saying, *I told you so.*

"A white couple who you thought could be *my* grandparents?"

D'enard nodded. "Yes. Ah, here it is."

He pulled a folder from beneath the clutter on his desk, one that looked like it had been sitting there for decades, and slid it over to her. Her fingers trembled as she opened it, delicately lifting the flap and pushing it back. But, as she read, the anticipation died.

"A safe deposit box? I came all the way here for a safe deposit box? There better be a million dollars in there."

"That box was left directly in your care by Ada only," D'enard explained. "So they both left you the 'white house on the stilts,' but Ada specifically told me that only you could access the contents of that box. Not even her husband knew about it."

"Didn't you say you grew up in that house?" Kellen asked her. "If that's the case, why did Ada and Walter have possession of it? And if they're giving it back to its natural owner, why Bailey and not her parents?"

"It never belonged to anyone else," D'enard said. "The property ownership report shows it always belonged to the Baileys."

She'd never so much as heard of an Ada or Walter Bailey, and that last name concerned her.

Worried the hell out of her.

"My father built that house," she argued, hand tingling. "Look, none of this is making sense. You're trying to tell me the house I grew up in didn't belong to my parents?"

"According to our records, not officially, no."

"And what's this about a fucking safe deposit box?"

"Um," D'enard glanced at Kellen, "well, uh, I can give you its location and everything you need to access it."

"What about the house?" Kellen asked. "She doesn't want that house."

"I'm sorry, since when do you speak for me?" she spat. Every word that left either man's mouth dripped acid onto her skin.

"Yeah, not doing this." Kellen led her away from the desk, out the door, and down the hallway. "Take a minute."

The room whirled, like she was standing, on tiptoe, on a spinning top. She looked up into what she'd assumed would have been Kellen's angry eyes, but all she saw was concern.

"Kellen, I—"

"I said take a minute. Breathe. Deep inhales."

She inhaled, exhaled, and waited while he checked her eyes, inside her mouth, and felt around on her neck.

"You're warm."

"Warmer here." She held up her hand. "What does it mean? Can fevers be isolated to one body part?"

"With a fever, you'd be hot in more than just your hand, and you'd have more symptoms. How do you feel?"

"Dizzy."

"Lean back against the wall."

She leaned.

"Anything else?" he asked. "Pain, sore throat, headache? Fatigue?"

"I'm a little bit tired, but nothing else."

"Maybe we should go home. We only have a few days left here, but I think we should spend the rest of our vacation in Atlanta. I'd like to get you in for a full workup at the practice and an MRI, as soon as possible."

She half-smiled and hung her head. "Only I could make Atlanta look better than an island in the Caribbean."

"That's not what I meant."

"I know. I know." She flexed her fingers, the hand finally cooling off. "Honestly, I don't know what happened in there. All I know is, I felt very hot, and then my outburst."

"Did you feel hot last night? When you were in the house, right before I found you."

She closed her eyes and tried to recount her steps through the house, but everything went blank after she saw the translucent man.

"The room you found me in was pretty warm," she said.

He scanned her, eyes golden in the light coming through the open area at the end of the hallway. "Bailey, that room was freezing."

"To me, it was boiling."

"Is there anything else? Anything else at all that you're not telling me? Did you hear, smell...*see* anything?"

"There was a m—"

"Ahem." D'enard stood in the doorway, folder and pen outstretched. "I was hoping you two hadn't left. Here's all the paperwork you'll need to access the safe deposit box. All I need for you to do is sign a couple of forms, and both that and the house are yours."

Kellen stared at her, challenging her with his eyes. He obviously didn't want her to accept the house. He'd felt something in there, just like she had. But like going back there, despite his justified warnings, she had no other choice but to do this.

"I'll sign," she said, clicking the pen. "For both the box *and* the house."

CHAPTER TWENTY-THREE

The clock ticked past the forty-five-minute mark since they'd been waiting to speak to a representative at the Scotiabank downtown.

Kellen opened his hand, palm facing up. Bailey slid their fingers together.

Ever since they walked through the establishment's glass doors, he'd been on edge, keeping it masked to avoid bringing out whatever had come roaring out of her before. She'd looked at D'enard like she'd looked at him, and he'd pulled her away to prevent the same rage to fall on D'enard.

But then, just like that, she'd become his Bailey again. And again, just like last time, she'd felt feverish.

"You think I'm crazy, don't you?" she asked.

He shrugged. "Would it matter?"

"What do you mean?"

He was in love with her. It would change nothing.

A woman who'd been in the teller line turned around, head down as she placed her wallet in her purse.

"Hey, B?" he called. "I'll be right back."

He stood and headed over. The woman raised her head, their eyes met, and she lowered it again, trying to avoid his gaze, but he blocked her path to the door.

"You know something," he said.

"I'm sorry, but I have to—"

"What are you hiding? Tell me *something*, Miss Inez. Bailey's not doing well. She went to the house, by herself, in the middle of the night. When I found her, let's just say she wasn't acting like herself."

"How was she acting?"

"I don't know how to explain it." He squeezed the back of his neck. "Wild? Feral?"

"Possessed?"

There was that damn word again.

"I don't know what that even means," he half-lied. "Look, I've heard stories. My parents have told me stories and folk-tales, but I've never been inclined to believe them. I like to err on the side of logic, but sometimes a baby comes across my table with a five percent chance at life and not only lives, but thrives. Or a brain defect shows up on an ultrasound that vanishes at birth."

Inez shook her head. "You are talking about miracles, sweet-heart. This is not that."

"Then tell me what *this* is."

"I already *tell* you." She touched his stomach. "She *have* something in her."

"Are you saying you think she's pregnant? That's impossible. We only just recently had se…" He paused. "That's impossible."

"Bailey Danielle, she has secrets."

"That she's keeping from me?"

"She's channeling, but she doesn't know. Don't be too hard on her. Now, you said she went back to that house?"

He nodded. "Yeah, and two people who she never met, who claim they were her grandparents, left it for her."

"Ada and Walter."

"So, you know them."

"I did."

"Are they actually related to Bailey?"

"It's not for me to say."

He took a steadying breath, inhaling so hard he had to stifle a cough with the crook of his elbow.

"Miss Inez, please, I don't even know what I'm asking you, but if you know anything, about Bailey's family, about that house…tell me. I've wanted her ever since the first time I saw her. Whatever's going on with her, I don't know how, but I'm supposed to fix it."

"You are not supposed to fix it," she said. "You are not supposed to fix everything. Are you a doctor?"

"Yes, ma'am."

"I see." She scanned his chest as though looking for something. "You fix everything for everybody? Everybody but yourself?"

"I don't care about me."

"You need to."

"Not when it comes to making things better for her."

"My dear," she took his hand, gripping and releasing, "listen to me. This is Bailey's puzzle to solve. You can't do it for her."

"I have to."

"Why?"

"Because…"

Because he couldn't ignore it like he ignored all his other problems. Because, apparently, he still felt worthless if he wasn't proffering someone's foundation or making everything all right in the world for everyone but himself.

But this was different.

This was Bailey.

"I had a friend like you," Inez said. "Thought she was supposed to take on everybody's burdens. But she took so much, it made her sick. When she got sick, all the people she helped disappeared. Learn to let people fall sometimes, my dear, or else they will end up begging on your grave."

He understood that, but he always failed to execute it.

"Then what do I do?" he asked. "Miss Inez, I'm in love with her. I've never loved anybody like I love her."

"Bailey's strong, sweetie. For her, that love will be enough."

"Somebody help her! Jesus!"

They both turned toward a woman shrieking from inside the bank. Everyone was staring out the window, and he didn't have to search to find what they were looking at. There was Bailey, completely nude, standing in the middle of afternoon traffic.

"She's channeling him," Inez called after him as he headed for the doors. "Channeling the truth. And she will until it's uncovered."

He pushed through the crowd of bystanders slowly forming, many with their phones out, taking pictures.

Not a single one helped.

Articles of Bailey's clothing trailed her like breadcrumbs to where she stood in the center of the narrow street.

Drivers pressed on horns. Others hurled insults. A select few nearly collided with pedestrians, gawking at her naked body.

He barely glanced to make sure no cars were coming and made his way to her, picking up the articles of clothing and folding them into his fist. When he reached her side, she turned to him and cocked her head, studying him like it was the first time she'd seen another human being.

He dragged his T-shirt off over his head, covered her nakedness, picked her up, and walked to the other side of the road. When he turned around, Miss Inez stood looking at them.

The crowd parted, and he found a nearby bench at a bus stop and sat, cradling Bailey in his arms. Blank eyes stared up at him, her pupils like shiny black pearls, and he felt sick watching her. She was slipping away from him, and he had no clue how to pull her back. It was like the lake all over again, except that this time, he didn't get to her.

"Bailey, what's going on?" He wasn't sure she'd be capable of an answer, yet he asked. "What's happening? Is there something you're not telling me?"

She was thirty, right around the age when episodes of schizophrenia peaked. It wasn't impossible, and it was a better explanation than absolutely nothing at all.

"I saw a man," she said.

"Where?"

"My old room. He was white. Dark hair, dark eyes."

"Did he hurt you?"

"He couldn't. He wasn't real."

"Is this your first time seeing people who aren't real?"

"I'm not sure."

Tightness built behind his sternum. "That night in the hospital parking lot, did something happen that led you there? Did you see someone?"

"No. I came looking for the doctor from the coffee shop."

"You were different, though," he said. "You seemed…distant."

"I was actually kind of scared."

"Of what?"

"That you would say yes if I came on to you."

"And why would that be something to be afraid of?"

"Because I wanted you to be different. I wanted you to take me to breakfast instead of only wanting to take me to bed. I wanted to mean something to you. So when you turned me down in your office," she cupped his jaw, "I freaked out. I couldn't tell if it was because you *were* different, or I'd mistaken your smiles and kindness for flirting. I was so embarrassed, I couldn't look you in the face for a while."

"Do you get a lot of those offers at the coffee shop?"

"Several per shift."

In short, she was quitting that fucking job. He would lose his shit if he ever walked in and heard another man propositioning her.

"You kept hiding from me," he pointed out. "What made you stop?"

She smiled. "You kept coming back. Then I realized that if you liked me as much as I liked you, it could change everything. And you're the only man I've ever considered taking that chance with."

Leo's car appeared in the distance.

"Kellen, do I need medication?"

"I," he sighed, and it felt like he'd been sighing their entire trip, "don't know."

Leo pulled up to the curb, and he stood, carrying Bailey and her clothing in his arms. Even her feet were bare from where she'd kicked off her sandals in the middle of the street, but those hadn't fared well in the traffic.

Leo didn't ask about his bare chest or her oversized attire. And as they pulled off, he realized he had more questions he was certain wouldn't help him better understand the situation.

"B, what happened that made you walk out into the street?"

She'd settled next to him, her head against the window. "I wanted to die."

He schooled his features, consciously avoiding any expressions of surprise or shock.

"Tell me about that. Why'd you want to die?"

"I didn't *want* to, but I started feeling this heavy, heavy sadness. Like...like ultimate betrayal."

He thought back to what Miss Inez had said.

"Miss Inez said you have secrets."

She nodded. "Technically, I do."

"Will you tell me?"

She nodded again. "Yes."

"Okay."

They remained silent for the rest of the trip.

Once at the villa, he headed to the main bathroom and started the faucet over the large garden tub. Next, he closed the blinds to make the room as dark as possible, although it was early afternoon, and lit several white pillar candles he found beneath the sink. Then he poured the organic, fancy bubble bath that had come with the villa into the tub, and it rippled and frothed as the tub filled.

"Bailey," he called.

She joined him in the bathroom.

He ran his hand over her hair and kissed her forehead before brushing a kiss over her lips. Without breaking the kiss, he stretched his shirt down over her shoulders and hips and shrugged out of his shorts.

"Come on."

He stepped into the bathtub.

She followed.

"We've both had a hell of a day," he said. "I figured that if you're about to tell me something you've never told anyone else, it should be where you feel as safe as possible."

She relaxed against him, her back against his chest, and remained silent for a few minutes.

"Kel, what I'm about to tell you...it's not what you think."

He kissed her hair. "It's okay. I'm listening."

Bridgetown, Barbados
June 1994

THE NIGHT WAS SO HOT.

The air conditioner had broken, and the repairman wouldn't be out to fix it until morning.

So, for now, Alice suffered.

Her nightgown, which had been made of the thinnest material she could find, stuck to her skin like plaster. Moisture sprinkled her arms, legs, and face, and yet next to her, Nigel slept, comfortably with a thin flat sheet thrown over his body.

She flung her legs over the side of the bed, tormented. Everything seemed so peaceful and unbothered when she felt like someone had placed a candle inside her uterus. It burned continuously, the flame and hot wax bathing her womb. But when she placed her hands there, the area was as cool as skin could get.

She trudged to the living area and nearly punched out the screened netting covering the open windows, not caring about lizards or mosquitoes. Through the window in the distance, she saw Mrs. Clifford squatting in her garden and tugging at something with a shawl thrown over her shoulders.

A shawl!

The nerve of that woman to be covered by even a sliver of additional fabric when summer tore through the island like they'd been dropped into hell.

She walked, her steps light, to Faith's room. Inside, her daughter was sound asleep, also covered by a flat sheet, and curled into a ball. The open bedroom window brought in a cool breeze that appeared to be too much for her little girl, but she couldn't bring herself to close it. She needed as much circulation throughout the house as she could get.

However, because her baby was cold, she fished another sheet from the linen closet and draped it over her. A few seconds later, Faith's limbs relaxed.

Perhaps she was the only one suffering on this tortuous night.

She moved directly across the hall to Noble's room, but Noble, her tiny warrior, was already huddled beneath extra covers. Noble had also piled her mountains of stuffed animals around her body, creating a barrier.

Alice smiled and sat on the edge of Noble's bed. She stroked her little girl's hair and wondered how both girls would fare when she and Nigel moved the family to the States. His number of business contacts there had grown significantly, and she was tired of the island. It would always be home to her, but this home wasn't a sanctuary.

A noise creaked in the hallway.

She waited to see if it followed its familiar pattern—a cascade of squeaky floorboards, muffled footsteps, a sound like fingers being dragged along a wall.

It didn't happen every night, but on the nights it did, the sound of the floorboards always woke her. It could be the slightest noise; she'd still be riveted out of her sleep. Also, every night the floorboards creaked, she boiled in sweat.

She rose, peered through the crack in the door, and caught Erwin's ribbed tank-covered back as he stepped, one toe at a time, down the hallway past Faith's door. Oblivious to the pair of eyes on him, he twisted the handle to Bailey's door and walked inside.

The kerosene fire turned into gasoline and dynamite.

No.

Not this.

Not Bailey.

She lifted Noble into her arms and went next to Faith's room. A girl on each hip, she carried them to her and Nigel's bedroom, situated them on the bed next to their father, and patted them until they drifted back to sleep. Then she spread a bedsheet on the floor where she huddled, clutching her stomach, waiting for the pain to subside.

Not this.

Not her little girl.

Not when she could do nothing about it.

Hopefully, Bailey's father's spirit had found a way to rest in peace. Because if he ever found out what was happening to the girl he'd wanted more than anything, they would never know the end of his wrath.

CHAPTER TWENTY-FOUR

Every muscle in Kellen's body tightened.

He was angry.

Pissed.

Almost unable to contain himself from flying off the fucking handle.

"Did anybody know this was going on?"

"I didn't think so at first," Bailey said. "But that night, I saw my mother. I don't think she knows I saw her, but she was outside my bedroom door."

"And what happened?"

She released a long breath, and her head rocked to the side, pushing her cheek into his chest. The water sloshed, the bathroom pin-drop silent in the seconds before her response. Even his breathing had come to an abrupt stop.

"Nothing."

"What?" His anger punched and kicked, trying to force its

way through the steel gates of his control. "What do you mean, nothing happened?"

"She didn't do anything."

"You mean she left you there? She let it continue?"

"Kellen—"

"Oh, no. No, no, no. Fuck that. You're not going back home. I stood in front of you and that woman at the hospital when you thought your father was *dying*, and she didn't seek you out for comfort. She never touched you. I watched you."

"I understand, Kel. Trust me, I do. But I just can't—"

"You're staying with me. Case closed."

He wouldn't ever forget the name Erwin.

"Bailey, how did you get that scar?"

"The one on my stomach?" He felt her trail a finger across the cicatrix. "When I was a kid, me, my mother, and my sisters went to visit my father at one of his work sites. He was in charge of building a mid-sized office complex downtown. Forever the wanderer, I went off in search of 'buried treasure.' Noble and Faith wanted to follow me, but my mother made them stay with her."

He closed his eyes, already not liking where the story was headed.

"The rooms were mostly finished at the time, so I walked through them, pretending I was the boss of the office. As I was rounding a corner from a narrow hallway, somebody had left a broken piece of glass lying on a workbench. I was so wrapped up in my imagination, I didn't see it, and I ended up walking too close to it."

He held his breath.

"I screamed for my mother, and she came running down the hallway, rushing around the corner almost like she couldn't help herself. But when she saw me, she stopped. I was on the floor, clutching my stomach, bleeding, but she just stood there, frozen. Trembling. Then I heard my father's voice. He ran over, picked me up, and rushed me to the hospital. I couldn't tell you how many stitches I got. I had to stay in the hospital for like a week."

Keeping his anger intact had officially become a physical struggle.

"Do you believe she froze out of fear?" he asked.

He had an opinion, but this wasn't about him.

"It doesn't matter anymore," she said. "But one reason I got into spirits and folklore is because when I was in the hospital, one of my father's coworkers came to check on me. I heard my father ask him if he knew who'd called his name and told him I was hurt, and the coworker said nobody knew I'd even gone down to that room. But my father swore, and still swears to this day, he heard a man's voice call his name."

"Or he heard you calling for your mother."

"With multiple floors between us? And I heard a man's voice too. He told me he would be there for me, no matter what."

"Bailey—"

"Hear me out, Kellen." She turned around, sat on her legs, and stared into his eyes, the soapy water turning her nipples into dark jewels. "Every time Erwin crept into my room, I heard that voice after he left. Some nights, I even felt a stroke of my hair or a kiss on my forehead, only to open my eyes to an empty room. During some of my darkest moments, that voice was there. Now, when things get to their hardest...I hear yours."

Anger and love spilled out of him like a gaping wound.

"Then Erwin began to have accidents," she continued. "Falling down stairs, tripping on the bare floor and landing on a pair of scissors, nearly severing his femoral artery. Each time he came into my room, something worse would happen."

"And where is Erwin now?"

"He's...around."

"Where is around, Bailey?"

"At my parents' house."

"Listen," he cradled her chin and looked into her eyes, "you-are-not-going-back-there. You and I will be shacking up from here on out."

"What about your Catholic mother?" she teased.

"I'll shoulder the guilt."

He nudged her close, kissed her softly. Recovery from that kind of trauma could, and usually did, span years. A lifetime for some. It was incredible she'd found the bravery to let him into her life.

"I'm starting to prune, babe," she said. "Plus, I'm getting hungry. We should get out."

He wanted to push her. This wasn't something to sweep beneath the rug, but he was the first person she'd ever told. He would have to give her time.

"Want to eat out?" he asked. "Maybe go to a fancy restaurant?"

She reached for a towel, stood, and wrapped it around her dripping-wet body. "And wear a fancy dress?"

"Anything for my Bailey."

She sent him a tired smile. "I'll go get ready."

After she left, after he'd spent several moments staring at the bathroom door, he let out the words he'd been holding in for days.

"I love you, Bailey. Jesus, do I love you."

CHAPTER TWENTY-FIVE

They left paradise three days early.

True to his word, the minute the plane landed, Kellen set up for her mail to be forwarded to his house, and they went to his house straight from the airport. The following day, he arranged for her to get bloodwork done, all of which had returned within normal limits.

His house was gorgeous, a two-story craftsman with original wood floors, four bedrooms, three bathrooms, magazine-worthy interior design, and a cozy back deck. Now, they were on his living room sofa, watching something on TV she hadn't been paying attention to. She'd coaxed him into making love that morning, several times, and then went out for a walk while he'd slept.

His neighborhood was even more gorgeous.

There were large yards with gardens whose sprouts she'd

spotted towering above wooden fences, as well as treehouses and children's play equipment. She'd been there less than a week, but his place and his neighborhood felt more like home than anywhere else she'd ever lived.

His head currently rested on her stomach, his long arms draped on either side of her. She began playing with his hair, running her fingers over his scalp. Groaning, he turned his head to place a kiss on her stomach. He swirled his tongue inside her belly button before creating a wet trail down her middle.

Sex was effective at taking his mind off the events in Barbados. Whenever he tried to talk about it, all she'd had to do was get naked, and the conversation would be tabled for later. Hell, she'd yet to tell him she'd accessed the contents of the safe deposit box while he'd been off talking to Miss Inez, and those contents were sitting, unopened, in her bag.

After her walk and a shower, she'd changed into one of his T-shirts, and he raised it until the ends pooled underneath her breasts. She'd decided to forego panties in the event of an uncomfortable conversation, so it was only seconds after pushing up her shirt that she felt his soft tongue where she was softer.

Her legs fell apart, and she reached for her breasts, squeezing and stroking her nipples, doubling the pleasure brought on by each flick of his tongue. He speared her with two fingers, groaning and grunting like she was the most delectable thing he'd ever had the pleasure of having in his mouth.

"Shit, Bailey." He gently nipped at her clit. *"Fucking* pretty pussy."

Soon, her moans overtook his grunts of appreciation. She was close and knew the minute her climax subsided, her body would be ready for him to lodge himself deep inside her.

The doorbell rang and was immediately followed by three loud, successive knocks.

"Kellen, c'est Maman et Papa!"

He stopped.

"Wait, baby," she wheezed. "Don't stop."

The doorbell and knock combination came again.

"Shit." His head popped up. "Um, Bailey? My mother's at the door."

That knocked the pleasure right out of her.

"Your...what?"

"That voice, that's my mother, and she's at my door. I've been so preoccupied with you and work that, of course, she'd drop by. Unannounced."

"She doesn't have a key, does she?"

"No, she doesn't."

"Crap." She sniffed the air. "Does it smell like sex in here? Think she'll be able to tell? Of course, she'll be able to tell. She's a mother. Oh, God."

"You run upstairs. I'll use the bathroom down here and straighten up. Spray some Febreze or something."

He started to retreat, but she pulled him back by his shirt and kissed him, sucking his lips into her mouth. He returned the kiss and began to ease her back onto the couch, but she shook her head.

"Baby, we don't have time. Your lips were wet. I was helping out."

He stared at her, then closed his eyes.

"What are you doing?"

"Praying for my dick to stay down. Wear something that hides your breasts, hips, ass, face, stomach, hair..."

She laughed and hurried up the stairs to clean up, change into something more presentable, and check her hair and face in the bathroom mirror.

When she emerged from the bathroom, she peered around the wall that opened up to the stairs. Unfortunately, Kellen and his guests weren't in the living room. She contemplated climbing through the bedroom window and running until she crossed the state line into Florida, but she loved him. She would have to face his mother head-on, and she prayed the woman liked her.

Carefully, almost stealthily, she crept down the stairs and heard chatter coming from the kitchen, way more voices than she'd been prepared for. Kellen suddenly came walking around the corner, nearly bumping into her. He grabbed her by the shoulders and gently pushed her backward.

"It's not just your mother, is it?"

"No. And I might have forgotten that it's my birthday."

She tilted her head to the side. "How do you forget that it's your birthday?"

"Because I always work through it. My family usually has something at my parents' house in memory of Connor, but I kinda just—"

"Skip it," she finished.

"Yeah. But when they heard we got back from Barbados, I

guess they decided, since I finally wasn't working, to have it here this year."

They'd been so preoccupied with her crazy ass that she had completely forgotten he had his own crap to deal with. Her man was a work addict, his older brother had substance abuse issues, and from what she could tell, he never truly mourned the loss of his twin brother. And there she was, his "girl," standing in front of him on his birthday without a clue or a gift.

"So, is it a celebration of you *and* Connor going on in there right now?"

He pulled her close. "We use this day to remember Connor. It feels better than using the day he passed away."

"But what about you? Kellen, baby…who celebrates you?"

A woman appeared behind him in the entryway to the kitchen with eyes like denim, and light brown hair etched with notes of gray. She had a round face and motherly plumpness that made her look like she gave terrific hugs, and she wore a long dress whose print mirrored Moroccan textiles.

Before Bailey knew it, she was in the woman's arms, the hug tight and genuine. And Mrs. Edwards smelled like heaven. She almost burst into tears when it dawned on her how much she'd yearned for this very thing.

Mrs. Edwards stepped back and held her at arm's length, then started spewing something in French. She looked to Kellen for help, but his mother's mouth moved so rapidly, he looked like he couldn't keep up himself.

"Oh, shoot." Mrs. Edwards tapped herself on the forehead. "I am so sorry. English, Anouk, English. I'm Kellen's mother, Anouk, and I was starting to wonder if you were real, *cherie*. A woman that can make my Kellen take a vacation? Witchcraft, I said. And then look at you. So beautiful. So, so beautiful. I love her eyes. I love your eyes, Bailey. So dark, so wise. Don't you love her eyes, Kellen?"

"Yes, Maman." He looked directly into her eyes. "I love her..."

Then he winked and walked into the kitchen.

Bailey followed him with her eyes, visually dragging him back by the casual shirt he'd slipped into at some point. Was he trying to tell her he loved her? If so, he needed to come on out and say it.

She'd been trying not to for weeks.

There could be a wrong time. It might be too soon. She'd fallen in love with him after the boat accident, and without realizing it, he'd shown her what she'd been looking for. One thing she could see in herself that made her worth everything he'd done for her.

But she was currently trapped, though she didn't mind. She wouldn't mind another hug, either.

Mrs. Edwards pulled her close, responding to her thoughts. It was a simple gesture, yet it was glorious to be lovingly embraced by a mother.

"So, I understand you have met David, Alexis, and little Abbie," Anouk said, holding her hand as they walked to the kitchen.

Even Sariyah, Catalina, Marcus, and Henry had shown up. They all stood around, waiting while the food was set up in the large kitchen.

Alexis released a loud exhale. "*Whew*. Thank goodness. I

thought you'd run off after you came to your senses about who you were dating."

Laughter rippled around the room, and Bailey was rushed with hugs and questions she couldn't possibly answer, not with how fast they were thrown at her.

"How have you been?"

"Are you feeling better?"

"How was Barbados?"

"Has Kellen been a gentleman?"

"Can you tell me that story you told Kellen? The one about the diablesse."

She'd then found herself standing in a line of people waiting for food with a man who *had* to be Kellen's father on the other side of the counter, serving. He had the same dark hair, rugged handsomeness, and those charming eyes that reminded her of dusk.

"Welcome to the family, beautiful," the man said, placing something called *chorizo* on her plate that she'd later come to know as *lord-have-mercy-this-is-magic-sausage.*

He had virtually no accent, unlike Anouk, who when she spoke, had a cute lilt similar to Juliette Binoche.

"Are you Mr. Edwards?" she asked, leaning forward so he could place a kiss on each cheek.

"I am." He bowed. "Or Master Chef Desí, whichever you prefer."

"You made all of this?"

"Stayed up all night."

"Thank you, Master Chef Desí."

She grinned so wide, it pained her cheeks. Desí reminded her of Nigel, warmhearted and playful.

"Actually, I think I want *you* to call me Papa," he said.

She didn't have to do much talking or socializing; enough chatter went around the room to liven up the celebration. Kellen, in front of his family and friends, kissed her several times whenever their paths crossed. Over the fray, he asked, "You doing okay, baby?" and her face burned hotter than the food being passed around. He cherished her openly, and that, along with the energy of the festivities, left her feeling so loved that she had to escape to the backyard, needing a breather.

Thankfully, the yard was empty. However, she kept one eye on the sliding doors to make sure she didn't miss when they announced it was time for cake.

Movement from one of the upstairs windows, a guest bathroom if she remembered correctly, caught her eye.

David.

She studied him, amazed at how much each son looked like either parent. Had Connor not been Kellen's twin, she wondered if he would have been split somewhere down the middle.

At first, David's head fell, but then he looked up into the mirror over the bathroom sink. He passed his fingers through his hair, dropped his shoulders, lifted something to his mouth—

one of the small paper cups Kellen supplied for guests—and tilted his head back. She'd assumed he was gargling with mouthwash.

Until he swallowed.

"Bailey?" Kellen poked his head outside from the sliding doors. "Oh, there you are."

David looked out the window, then down, and locked eyes with her. He shook his head, an obvious warning, and closed the blinds.

"Hey, we're getting ready to cut the cake, even though I already know what it is. Marble with buttercream icing. Connor's favorite."

"What's yours?" she asked.

"Italian cream." He walked over, grabbed her hands, and kissed a palm. "What are you doing out here? My family over-whelm you?"

"Yes, but in a good way."

"So you're doing okay? After hearing about all that stuff with your mother, this wasn't the way I wanted you to meet mine. I figured that, at this point, mothers probably terrify you."

"I was at first. But now, not so much."

They started for the doors, hands clasped.

"By the way," she looked up at him, "what was that earlier? That little 'I love her' moment with your mother?"

He remained silent all the way across the yard and through the doors. "I'm not sure what you're referring to," he said. "What 'I love you' moment with my mother?"

"I love 'her," she clarified.

"That's what I said. I love you." Then he winked again and left her standing alone.

So, they had cake.

They ate, they talked, they laughed.

For most of the afternoon and evening, if Abigail was on someone's hip or lap, it was usually hers.

Life had cornered her with the experience of holding Abigail while Kellen played with the little cutie over her shoulder. Then she'd sat on the sofa, and he'd eased down next to them, draped an arm behind her neck, and kissed her temple. Now, he watched her from across the room, Abigail's sleepy head on her shoulder.

Alexis crept up behind her. "I see you, girl."

"God, he's beautiful," she said. "I can't stop staring."

Alexis pretended to give Kellen a once-over. "Meh. He's okay. Me, I'm partial to the bourgeois edition of the Edwards brothers seated over there."

Bailey and David's eyes briefly connected before he looked away.

As the evening drew to a close, guests filtered out, leaving behind well-wishes for their relationship. Bailey, after giving Abigail a bottle, a bath, combing her curls, dressing her in her pajamas, and setting her to sleep, *finally* handed her back to her mother in the entryway.

"Hey, Kel, can you help 'Lexis with the car seat?" David asked. "I want to talk to Bailey real quick, if that's okay."

Bailey's stomach dropped.

"You want to talk to Bailey?" Kellen asked. "Why?"

"Everyone else got to talk to her."

"I know. What do *you* want to talk to her about, though?"

"It's okay, Kel," she reassured him. "It's fine."

Kellen eyed him and then left with Alexis to secure the car seat.

David's gaze settled on her. "I could lose my daughter, my wife, my whole family. Do you understand? Don't, and I repeat, *do not* say anything to Kellen about what you saw. Keep in mind that I'm his brother. His blood. You're just another girlfriend."

She hadn't planned to say anything; the last thing she wanted was to create a wedge between Kellen and his last living brother. Despite knowing how Kellen felt about her, David's statement left a pang.

"I wasn't going to say anything."

"I'm getting help, you know," he added. "Don't look at me like that."

"Like what?"

"Like I'm pitiful. I'll have you know I didn't have anything to drink all month until today. Today's Connor's birthday. Did Kellen tell you about Connor?"

She nodded. "Yeah, he did."

"Really?" He sighed, as if coming to grips with two distinct sides of himself. "Jesus, what am I doing? Bailey, I'm sorry. I didn't mean to snap at you, and trust me, you're not just another girlfriend of Kellen's. No one makes him happier than you do. I can't believe I said that to you. My brother, who never stops working, took a day off to try to *talk* to you. You're in his heart."

"And he's in mine," she said. "But I do appreciate your apology."

"Look, if there's anything I can do for you, just let me know. I'm putting a lot on you. Now I'm yelling at you when you make my brother happy and gave me and my wife the first real break we've had in months with Abbie."

"You mean that?"

"Of course."

"What about right now?"

LATER THAT NIGHT, BAILEY WALKED UP THE STAIRS, CAREFUL NOT to lose her balance. She entered the bedroom, and when Kellen looked up, he smiled in such a way that, had she not already been in love with him, she would have fallen right then.

"Happy birthday to you," she sang. "Happy birthday to you. Happy birthday, my Kellen, happy birthday to you."

Even more carefully, she climbed onto the bed, balancing an Italian cream cupcake on her palm with a single candle planted in the middle.

"Make a wish."

"What do I do if it's already come true?" he asked.

"Make a wish, Casanova."

He looked to the ceiling, closed his eyes for a second, and blew out the candle. She fished the candle out of the cupcake and set it aside.

After peeling the paper down one side, she held it up to his mouth, and watching him take a huge bite was a massive turn-on.

"*Mmm.*" His eyelids fluttered. "Bai...ley, you did *not* get me Italian cream cupcakes."

"Bai...ley sure did." She wiped frosting from the corner of his mouth, licked it from her finger, and then took a bite. "I called them in earlier. Well, it was more like I begged the bakery to see if they could make them today on such short notice, and then I had David pick them up. I know you were a twin, so you have to share a birthday, but you deserve to have your favorite cake on your day. So, happy birthday, Kellen. You are the best thing that has ever happened to me. You make me deliriously happy, and I feel like the luckiest woman in the world because I get to call you mine."

Tears sprang in her eyes.

"And I love you. I love you so much."

He pushed her back on the bed, the cupcake still in her hand, and hovered over her. A half smile curled on his lips as he stared at her, through her. Using her cupcake-free hand, she cupped the side of his face.

"I love you too, Bailey."

No matter how long she lived, she would remember this moment for the rest of her life.

He moved toward her mouth but diverted at the last moment to take another bite of the cupcake. She laughed, popped the last piece into her mouth, and wrapped her arms around his neck. This time, when he moved forward, their lips connected.

Playfulness turned into lust, lust into hunger.

How he could be so gentle and rough at the same time, she didn't know, but she welcomed it, wrapping her legs around his waist as he entered her. He gave her everything, all of him, and she felt it in each thrust, in each droplet of sweat that formed on his forehead, taking his dark hair shades lower.

And, as she threaded her fingers through that hair, the world split apart. He held her quivering body close, reaching his orgasm in the flurry of her own, and whispered in her ear how much he loved her, in every language he knew.

CHAPTER TWENTY-SIX

He loved her.

And, because he loved her, he was up in the dead of night with her wrists in his grip, blood running down his biceps while he straddled her.

What had happened in Barbados hadn't stayed there.

It was probably only because she'd sneezed, waking him up, that he'd dodged—narrowly—the ceramic knife she'd brought toward the center of his back.

The knife struck his biceps before he'd gripped her wrist until she dropped it and pinned her beneath him. They were still naked, as they'd been too wrapped up in each other the night before to stop making love until they passed out from fatigue.

"Bailey, listen to me. Listen to my voice. It's Kellen."

Her skin felt like it was going to burn through his.

If he were a crying man, he would have been in tears. This

could not be happening. Not when everything had been going so perfectly. Not when she'd turned out to be everything he wanted and needed. He wanted to do everything in his power to make her okay again but had no idea what was wrong in the first place.

The cut on his arm throbbed, but he gritted his teeth through the pain. "Bailey, you're okay. You're with me. You're safe."

What the hell was he dealing with here?

Was she mental?

Was she that *other* word?

Suddenly, she exhaled, dots of sweat covering her skin. He didn't release her until he was positive she was somewhere in this realm. It seemed to take forever, but when her eyes widened and darted around the room, he knew she was back.

"Kellen?" She spotted the blood on his arm, then his position on top of her. "What happened? Did I do that? Did I do that to you? I did that to you, didn't I?"

"Bailey, it's okay."

It was no use.

She was already in tears, mumbling how sorry she was and wished she could somehow stop something she clearly didn't know was happening.

"Bailey," he removed his hold and pulled her into a one-arm embrace, "it's okay. We'll figure this out."

"But how? How can we figure something out when we don't know what's happening? What's wrong with me, Kellen? How could I hurt you?" Her mouth fell open. "What if Abbie had still been here? What if she'd spent the night with us?"

"You wouldn't have hurt her."

"Please, just walk away, Kellen." She pressed her forehead into his shoulder. "I'm not worth all this."

"You're worth everything," he whispered directly into her ear. "I love you. We'll get through this. For now," a wave of dizziness washed over him, "do you think you can drive?"

"Oh God, we have to go."

She sprang up from the bed, ran into the bathroom, and reappeared with a towel. He showed her how to fold it before he pressed it against his arm.

In under a minute, she was fully dressed and helped him into his clothes, holding him carefully on the way to the car. She was unnaturally calm all the way to the emergency room, periodically asking him questions, especially when he closed his eyes to try to ease the pain.

When they pulled up to the emergency room, he was immediately taken back. She chose not to go with him. Right before he disappeared through the double doors, he glanced over his shoulder and found her watching him, biting the nail on her thumb.

It didn't take long to patch him up, mainly because he was good friends with Dr. Samir Shah, an ER physician currently on shift. But once he was fully sutured, Samir pulled up a stool and looked him dead in the eyes.

"That gash was pretty deep, Kel. That had force behind it. How'd it happen?"

He squeezed the space between his brows. "Honestly, I don't want to get into that right now, Samir. If that's okay. But I do need a favor. Do you know if anybody in psych is working tonight?"

"You mean like George or Renee? No, they're not here. Why?"

"Because I need somebody in psych."

Samir studied him. "Did your girlfriend do this?"

"Look, is anybody here tonight who can sit with her for a few minutes?"

"We have a psych nurse that can probably do a quick assessment, if she's willing. What are you thinking, mood disorder? Psychosis? Both?"

"I'm not thinking anything. She just...she needs somebody to talk to right now. Have the psych nurse go out there and talk to her, have a conversation. She's wound up, so make it casual."

Samir sighed. "Okay, but Kel, if this is something that might have been intentional, I have to call the police."

"Come on, Samir. As your friend, I'm *telling* you what happened. She's been through enough. So fucking much. Have somebody talk to her and help her calm down while I figure some shit out. Please."

Samir nodded, stood, and they shook hands.

Kellen double-checked his bandage and headed back to the double doors. He peered out and could see Bailey sitting alone despite the moderately packed waiting room. Her head was in her lap, and she lifted it only when a nurse walked up, said a few words, pointed to the chair next to her and sat down.

While they talked, he searched until he found an empty computer, took a seat, and opened up a search engine.

Atypical Symptoms of Psychosis in Young Women

After staring at the blinker for an eternity, he deleted the search, gripped his hair, and typed again.

Mysterious Disappearances, Barbados

When the search results popped up, the first was about a twenty-three-year-old woman named Amy Bradley, who'd gone missing in 1974. However, a second article about a young man's mysterious disappearance caught his attention.

He wasn't sure if it was the man's features—dark hair, dark eyes—or something else, but he printed the information as something he wanted to further look into. For some reason, he felt as though this article held one of the missing pieces he was looking for.

CHAPTER TWENTY-SEVEN

"Hi, are you feeling okay? I noticed you were over here by yourself. Do you need to see a doctor?"

Bailey raised her head.

A nurse stood over her, looking at her first with surprise before it softened into a welcoming smile. She knew she looked like a mess; she hadn't been able to stop crying since they took Kellen back. She'd hurt him. Just last night, she'd told him she loved him, and a few hours later, she'd seriously hurt him.

"No, I'm here with my boyfriend," she said. "He's already gone back. I'm just worried about him."

The nurse pointed to the chair next to her. "Mind if I sit?"

"No. Go ahead."

The nurse sat quietly for a while, and it was an unsteady quiet. Like she was gearing up for a question.

"I don't want to sit here with you under false pretenses," she said, turning slightly in the chair. "I'm Mellie, a psych nurse, and I'm worried about you. Anything you want to talk about? Maybe what happened with your boyfriend?"

She didn't want to talk.

She *really* didn't want to talk.

But the dark-haired, brown-eyed woman with the bouncy ponytail looked at her like she actually cared. And she might not have wanted to talk to someone, but she needed to. Hopefully, what she shared wouldn't wind up getting her committed.

"I love him," she began. "He's the first person I've loved that I didn't have to. I love my father and my sisters, but they're family. He's not. I choose to love him because we mesh well together, and he's a wonderful person. But I can't shake this feeling that he's too good for me, and that I'm eventually going to mess up, someway or somehow, and force him away. I think I'm doing that already."

"Is Dr. Edwards your boyfriend?"

More tears wanted to fall, but she barely had any left to give.

"Of course, you'd know him."

"And his injury, did you do that?"

"Yes."

"Intentionally?"

"No. Oh God, no."

"Why did you do it?"

"I don't know. I would never hurt him. Not on purpose. Never in a million years. But look at where my accident got us. What if it had been more serious? Doesn't it make more sense to walk out of his life before he has no choice but to leave?"

"So hurt him before he hurts you," Mellie said. "Why are you so sure he'll eventually hurt you?"

"Nurse Mellie, my own mother never loved me. She doesn't love me. Yet, I've never hurt her, even accidentally. Kellen, on the other hand, is amazing. So amazing. I want to treat him better than I treated her. I want to treat him better than I've ever treated anyone. I want him happy, even if it's not with me."

"But would you rather a life without him, or a life where you try to work on your accidents to avoid hurting him again?"

"Honestly?" She smiled. "I want to marry him. I like my last name and all, but I'll gladly burn it to ash to be Mrs. Kellen Edwards. I want to start a family with him. I met his niece for the first time, and I realized that I want it to be us sitting together, on the couch, with our baby one day."

The nurse looked up.

Kellen was standing over them, his arm bandaged and a smile on his face that gave no hint of what had happened.

"Ready, B?"

"Yeah." She stood and turned to the nurse. "Thanks for the talk."

"Of course. Anytime."

They headed for the parking lot.

Before they entered the car, she squeezed him tight around the midsection. "Kel, I know this isn't enough, but I'm truly, very sorry about what happened tonight. I think it would be best if maybe I got my things and went home."

He shook his head. "No."

"Then I'll get a hotel. Kellen, I tried to kill you. Twice."

"I know, and I still want you to come home."

"Then I'll sleep in a different bedroom. Lock me in. Do that thing with the pennies David did."

"Not doing that, either." He sighed like he carried the world on his shoulders, reached into his back pocket, and pulled out a folded sheet of paper.

The paper turned out to be a year-old article from the Barbados Advocate commemorating thirty years since one of the nation's most savage criminals went missing. Someone named Daniel Bailey.

Daniel Bailey.

Bailey Danielle.

A shiver tickled her spinal cord.

"Have you ever heard of this man?" he asked. "His name was Daniel Bailey, an American serial killer who flew to the islands to escape conviction. Then, he went missing."

Like Ada and Walter—more Baileys—she started to tell him she had no idea who the man was, but when she saw the face, she nearly screamed.

"That's him. That's who I saw at the house."

"This man? You sure?"

"Positive."

Kellen paused for what felt like an eternity. "Let's go home and see what else we can find. I have a feeling this man's disappearance is going to matter to you, and it's going to matter in a big way."

CHAPTER TWENTY-EIGHT

"I looked this up on a whim," Kellen prefaced, subtly reminding Bailey, and himself, that everything so far was pretty circumstantial. "Daniel Bailey's disappearance was one of the biggest stories to hit the island in decades."

They sat in the middle of the living room, flipping through the article, their backs against the front of the sofa.

"But, at the same time, why would he be at my parents' old house?" she asked. "Spirits inhabit places well known to them. As far as I know, even though it belonged to Ada and Walter, only my family lived there."

"And you're still sure this is him?"

"That's the face I saw. You guys have similar features, so I'd remember."

"Could it have been me in the mirror?"

"Kellen, I know what I saw. Yes, I've been acting a bit strange lately, but that doesn't mean I've gone completely insane."

The evidence supporting her explanation was pretty damning. There was no other reason she should have recognized the man in the picture, as he'd disappeared right around the time she was born. If they chose to believe Miss Inez's theory—which he wasn't sold on—it would have created the perfect atmosphere for negative energy to be attracted to and possibly attach to her.

Negative energy.

He'd officially gone insane.

"Maybe if we find out who his victims were, we can start making sense of some of this," he suggested.

She gazed off in the distance at something only she could see. He hoped it wasn't another figure. He wasn't in a position to deal with a second episode so soon.

"He's related to them." She held the printout close to her face, skimming, tracing lines across the page with an index finger. "Ada and Walter Bailey. He's related to them. What if they left me the property because they wanted me to, I don't know, find something? Does that sound crazy?"

"Tonight, crazy is sane," he said. "But we've already gone through these a million times. I don't remember seeing anything other than he was staying with his parents—"

"Ada and Walter Bailey." She turned the page toward him. "There it is, plain as day. Ada and Walter, the couple who knew my grandparents and left me an entire property, were this man's parents. Now we just need to figure out why he chose to enter me."

"How about we find a different way to say that?"

She laughed. "Can't believe you're jealous of a little ghost."

All this talk of ghosts left him feeling a little off. Like soon, they'd be talking about witches and who should be burned at the stake. There were French and Spanish folktales his parents had told him, cultural things that encouraged this sort of "paranormal" talk, but he'd barely given them a second thought.

After their stint at the hospital, the nurse had sent him a text declaring that she thought Bailey was perfectly lucid, with no overt signs of psychosis. She suggested Bailey follow up with a psychiatrist, but all she saw was a woman under extreme stress. So, something else was going on. Something he had no way of explaining in a way he was used to.

"Now I really wish we'd gotten the contents of the safe deposit box," he said.

Bailey went back to reading the article, a little too intently.

"You did, didn't you?" he asked. "When?"

"When you were talking to Miss Inez."

"Well?"

"I haven't actually gone through any of it. Everything's in my bag."

She rose to get it, and his focus helplessly lingered on her shapely legs and ass. Knowing he wasn't supposed to hear her declaration didn't change the fact that she'd said, with her own magnificent mouth, that she wanted to marry him and have his babies.

He grabbed his laptop from the coffee table in front of him and began his search for Daniel Bailey's victims.

Bailey appeared with an armful of papers and envelopes that she dropped in the space between them. "This is everything. Actually, one of these I can already tell is the blueprints for the house. They were drawn up by my father, which is why I don't understand why D'enard kept saying it wasn't his house."

The U.S. victims came up first, and Kellen tapped each one, reading every blurb.

They were all women.

From what he could tell, Daniel Bailey had been more than sick. He would abduct women under the guise of different personalities. As a widower, he abducted his thirteen-year-old neighbor; as a drifter—an unsuspecting college student; as a musician—an aspiring singer; and he did a stint as a high school girls' basketball coach where teammates, Rebecca Waverly and Amanda Johnson, never made it home one afternoon after practice. Their bodies were discovered a few miles from the high school.

"Are you hungry?" Bailey asked.

He shook his head. "Not really."

"What about coffee?"

"Maybe later."

"Tea?"

He looked up into dark, hopeful, apologetic eyes. "On second thought, I *am* a little bit hungry."

"You are? Okay." She clapped her hands together. "I'll be right back."

For the second time that night, he studied her as she disappeared into the kitchen. Before any proposals could happen, he needed to ask her if she was willing to quit her job. That way, he could help her pursue her dreams. She was helping him pursue his by admitting she wanted to be his wife and have children with him. His favorite part was when she'd said she would gladly take on his last name. He wouldn't have cared either way. All he cared about was her saying yes—yes to him and yes to a future he'd pictured even before their first date. That part, however, he'd tell her later. Years down the road.

Her phone rang, and lost in his thoughts, he raised it to his ear. "Hello?"

"Who is this?"

"This is Kellen."

"I'm looking for my sister."

He checked the phone screen—Noble Green. Bailey hadn't mentioned it outright, but he knew having a lawyer and doctor as siblings had probably made not succeeding at that Economics major attempt sting harder.

"Bailey's busy."

"I'm sorry, *who* are you?"

"Kellen. Bailey's boyfriend."

"Since when does Bailey have a man?"

"Since me."

"I need to talk to her. It's an emergency."

He rose and headed for the kitchen. "What's the emergency?"

"I want to talk to my sister."

"Bailey," he called. "It's Noble. She says it's an emergency."

"Put it on speaker," Bailey said, re-twisting the tie on a bag of sliced bread. "Hi, Noble. I'm here."

"Am I on speaker?"

"Noble, *what's the emergency?*" they both asked.

"It's our father. He had a heart attack."

GIVEN HE WAS MORE FAMILIAR WITH THE BUILDING AND therefore quicker, Kellen led Bailey through the wide, polished hallways to the room number her sister had given them for where her father had been assigned. He'd reassured her that although a heart attack wasn't good news, it was a good sign they weren't headed straight for the ICU.

Inside, Alice and Bailey's sisters sat around her father's bedside. Alice held the sleeping man's hand, one sister was reading, and the other napped upright in a chair.

The minute Bailey entered the room, Alice looked up. When she and Bailey locked eyes, a silent explosion resounded through the room. Alice stood, her eyes steady on Bailey, taking in every detail of her face as though she'd never seen her own daughter. Kellen placed himself on full protective alert.

He could see traces of Bailey in the sisters' faces, a reflection of the similarities they shared with their mother. From the photos Bailey had shown him, the one glaring at him with the brown skin like something sweet he'd get at a Spanish sidewalk café, kissed with a drop of milk, was Noble.

"Where were you?" Noble demanded.

Faith yawned, arms stretching over her head. "Bailey, you're here! We kept trying to reach you in Barbados. Mom said she called you at the villa, but I guess you were having too good of a time."

"What do you mean, Barbados?" Bailey asked. "How long has my *father* been in the hospital, and why am I only just now hearing about it?"

"Your mother never called us in Barbados," Kellen cut in. "If that had been the case, we would have been here long ago."

Faith and Noble's focus shifted to him.

"Kellen, I presume?" Noble asked. "The piece of work I talked to on the phone?"

"That's me."

"At least you're gorgeous. A dick, but gorgeous."

"He seems all right to me," Faith argued. "And a dick could be good for Bailey." She snorted. "A little dick could be good for us all."

"Noble, Faith, be quiet," Alice spat.

Alice's chest heaved, and her teeth worked the inside portion of her mouth. "Bailey, you don't need to be here."

"At my father's bedside?" Bailey asked.

"He's not...never mind."

"He's not what, Alice? Say what you have to say. Air it all out."

"What is wrong with you, child?"

"I've had it up to here," Bailey leveled a hand above her head, "with the way you've treated me. I tried to be the perfect daughter for you. I never gave you any trouble, and yet, you continued to treat me like I wasn't even worth the ground you walked on."

"Do you really think this is the time or place for this?"

"When is the time or place, Alice? Every single day I spent with you, looking at you, loving you, and wishing, just once, for the mother I deserved was always the time and place. But no, out of obligation to you, out of respect for the fact that you're my mother, I didn't. I bit my tongue. I tried to be perfect. I tried to force you to love me. Children shouldn't have to beg for their mother's love. They should be overwhelmed with it!"

Alice shook her head. "I knew it was a mistake. I knew I shouldn't have listened to my mother. I should have never gone through with the pregnancy. This is a mess. It's all a mess."

Bailey didn't flinch.

Kellen watched her, the cap loosening on his fury, then turned to Alice. Based on Bailey's reaction, or lack thereof, this was something she'd heard before. Something she was used to hearing.

"It's Alice, right?" he asked.

Bailey's hands curled around his biceps. "Babe, you don't have to—"

"I'm off the leash, B. Don't bother."

She quieted.

"Alice, karma is going to have a field day with your ass when it's time to pay up for the shit you've done. You don't say shit like that to your child, and you especially don't say shit like that to my girl. As much as you didn't want her, I do, and I'm going to make sure she knows, every fucking day, how much I want her, how much I love her, and how grateful I am that she's a part of my life. That's the only thing I have to thank you for, bringing her into this world. I've got it from here."

Alice stared at his face, breaths growing increasingly audible. Then, looking away, she moved to her husband's side. "Bailey, take your friend and go. You're out of place here."

"She's not out of place to me," Noble said.

"Same here," Faith echoed.

"Bailey," Alice sighed, never looking up, "he's not your

father. Nigel Green isn't your father. So, you need to go. You don't belong here."

Faith gasped.

Noble's jaw ticked.

Bailey spoke up. "We may not share DNA, but Nigel Green is my father."

"Did you hear what I said?"

"Alice, come on. I knew. Didn't you hear what *I* said? I don't care. Blood doesn't make someone family. Love and devotion do, and since I was a little girl, Nigel Green has loved and been devoted to me. That's all that matters."

Nigel's monitor beeped, going instantly from constant to erratic. A team of medical practitioners flooded the room, shoving them all out in the process.

"Kel, let's just go," Bailey said. "I'll come back later. I'm not trying to have a fight outside my father's hospital room and stress him out any further."

He laced their fingers together. "I'll get Henry to bring you up when you do. That way, you can have some time alone with your father."

They walked off.

Bailey kept everything together all the way to the parking lot, while getting into the car, and when they pulled into the garage at home.

Later that day, however, she tried to hide her tears behind the bathroom door in the owner's suite. Knowing they were coming, he'd stayed close by, and she let him come in, sit with her at the edge of the tub, and hold her as she cried.

CHAPTER TWENTY-NINE

Eventually, he had to return to work, and he did his best to be present, but all his quiet moments were occupied by thoughts of Bailey. The news about her father didn't come as a shock as she'd already had an idea. What bothered her most was that Bailey adored and idolized Nigel, so suspicions or not, it hurt not to be part of him.

Kellen looked away from his computer screen—he wasn't paying attention to it anyhow—when a knock sounded on his office door. Alexis poked her head in and stepped inside, carrying a sleeping Abigail in a carrier.

He stood, rounded his desk, and went to give her a hug. "Hey, 'Lexis. What brings you all the way here on a random weekday?"

She stared up at him, chewing on the inside of her bottom lip. "I hate to bring this down on you, but…I'm leaving David."

His heart slammed in his chest. "What? Why?"

She handed him her phone.

A video on the screen had been paused on a still image of David sitting at the edge of the lake behind the house. Nausea coiled in his stomach as he pressed the play button, which showed David bringing a glass bottle to his lips. The shape of the bottle alone told him exactly what his brother was drinking; Jim Beam had been David's go-to prior to his stint in AA. Now, it appeared old demons had resurfaced.

"I know you think I'm leaving him because he's drinking again, but it's not. It's because he lied about it. He looked me *dead in my face* and lied."

He watched the rest of the video, massaging his forehead. By his estimation, in only a few minutes, his brother had downed at least ten ounces of liquor.

"He goes out, drinks, comes back in and swishes with Listerine like I'm an idiot," she said. "Like I can't smell it when he's sleeping next to me or taste it when he kisses me. I'm his wife, and he thinks I'm so stupid that Listerine, *Listerine*, is enough to make a fool out of me."

"You've already packed your stuff?" he asked.

"He's been at a conference in Arizona for the last three days. I hired packers and movers who got everything together in less than twelve hours. Then I sent him the video while I was sitting in the parking lot."

"Will you tell me where you're staying? I won't say anything to David. I want to check in with you and Abbie."

"Kel, you don't always have to be Mr. Fix-It. I'm *David's* wife. Abbie's *David's* daughter. You can't keep cleaning up your brother's messes."

"I know, but—"

"Kel, if David has to hit rock bottom to learn," a cry stumbled out, "then David's going to have to hit rock bottom."

"You came here, though," he pointed out. "You came to me for a reason."

"Because I'm no better than your folks, apparently." Sighing, she grabbed a pen from his desk and scribbled the address on a Post-it. "Here. I got an apartment closer to work. Your parents' house is along the way, so I can drop Abbie off. He can see her there if he's sober enough to remember he has a kid."

A teardrop fell on the Post-it.

"Lexis, I'll fix this."

"Kel, he lied to my face. He lied to us both. Two of the people who love him most in this world. This *thing*, this addiction, is stronger than I am. It's stronger than my love for him. I don't want to leave him, but I have no choice. His wife? His daughter? We're not enough, and I can't live with it anymore."

What she'd put up with already was more than she should have, but in many ways, he and Alexis were alike. For them, things bent and twisted but never broke. They could be staring at a jagged crack down the middle of an issue, but in their minds, fixing the Grand Canyon was possible with enough Elmer's glue.

"When does he get back?"

The phone vibrated, lighting up with David's name.

"Tomorrow night," she said, staring at the screen. "And I know he's going to keep calling. He might even try to come back early. When he does, tell him I love him. I just couldn't do it anymore."

"You shouldn't be alone right now, though. Why don't you stay with a friend? What about your sister? If it wasn't because he'd show up at either place, I'd have you stay with me or our folks."

"How are things with Bailey?" she redirected.

An intertwined image of Bailey and Connor sparked behind his eyelids.

Bailey wouldn't hurt herself the way Connor had. It was what he recited to himself daily, but they'd all believed Connor would have never done what he'd done.

"Complicated."

Alexis looked around the office. "You still here, at the hospital, and teaching?"

"Yeah."

The corners of her mouth turned down. "Work, it's like alcohol, isn't it? Numbs everything. Takes your mind off your troubles."

He didn't reply.

"You love Bailey, and right now, you probably feel like I did. Like love will get you through. But if you succumb to your work addiction instead of facing, head on, what ails you, it'll be you," the phone vibrated again, "coming home expecting Bailey and finding an empty house."

Everyone in his family pretended the hours he kept were part of his personality. They made jokes, made light of his fatigue and restlessness and purposeful absences at family functions. No one had ever called him out on his bullshit like that, and it sent shockwaves through his system.

He watched, motionless, as Alexis headed for the door.

"'Lexis, I'll fix this. I promise."

"Kellen, the *only* thing I'll ask of you is that, the next time David comes to you begging for help despite not showing any inkling of wanting to change to be worthy of it, do one thing for me."

"Which is?"

She swiped at her eye. "Say no. I love you. See you later."

"I love you t—"

The door shut.

He returned to his seat, shoved down into the chair by an invisible hand. While he understood David was suffering, Connor had been his twin.

His *twin*.

Connor's death had been the driving force behind his pediatric specialty as they'd been subjected to twin-to-twin transfusion syndrome. Connor was born developmentally delayed and had walked with a slight, shuffling gait. As much as he and David had tried to stand up for him when kids bore down on his disabilities, Connor had always been more emotionally aware, and therefore, more emotionally sensitive.

Ten years after his death, there'd been a shift in the cosmos. Instead of getting better, he and David worsened. Where he turned to tiring hours, David had turned to alcohol.

Bailey had gotten him to slow down, see movies, and go on a boating trip. Hell, Bailey had gotten him to take a vacation.

Earlier, he'd emailed the HR administrator to light a fire under her with the slow hiring process. He wanted to spend more time with Bailey. It was why it was a no-brainer; right now, she was hurting. She needed him, and he would be there.

How could he get that concept to transfer to his brother? What would be enough, if anything?

Alexis had left her phone behind, and it had gone from intermittent buzzes to vibrating wildly on his desk. Restraining the worst of his anger, he picked it up.

"David, what the hell is wrong with you?"

"Where's Alexis?" David asked, tone panicked. "Why do you have her phone?"

"Because she doesn't want to talk to you."

"I called the house, and she didn't pick up there either." He paused. "Kel, did she leave?"

"Did you see the video?"

"Kellen, if I go home, will I find my wife and daughter?"

"No. You won't."

David released a long exhale into the phone speaker.

"David, disappointed isn't the word for what I feel right now. Sobriety is hard, but if you were struggling with it, you could've come to me. You could've talked to your wife. You fucking lied to her, David. To her face. Destroying trust is a risky business. You're assuming there'll be pieces left to put back together."

"I don't need you lecturing me."

"Sure about that?"

David hacked a laugh. "Fine. Everybody wants to turn their back on David because he messed up? Fine."

"Don't play that victim shit. You didn't have to lie. You could have come to me. I've *always* been there for you."

"Where are they?" he snapped. "I know she told you where she went."

"She told me, not you."

"So what, Bailey isn't enough for you? You have to have my wife too?"

"What the fuck did you just say?"

"Isn't that why she told you where she was? So you could go over there at night when my daughter's asleep and—"

"You need to think better of yourself, for one. And two, don't insult your wife. More so, if my woman's name is going to come out of your mouth, you better be singing her praises."

"Then send her to my house on her knees, and we'll see if—"

He ended the call.

The slur in David's voice, the familiar temper and the lascivious comments—they were all there. Even without the video, he would have known. To no longer be able to hide it from the people he cared about most meant David might be past the point of help.

But he couldn't give up on his brother. Giving up could mean his parents being left with one son when they'd brought three into the world, and he couldn't do that to them.

Bailey's image flashed across his phone screen, and he took a moment to quell his temper before answering.

"Hey, Bailey."

"Hi, Kel." She sounded the same, empty and exhausted. "I won't keep you long. I'm just calling to tell you I love you."

He stopped in the middle of rising from his chair. "I love you too. I love you too, Bailey. So much."

"With everything that's been going on, I just wanted you to know that I'll come back to you, emotionally, soon. You are the greatest thing to ever happen to me, and I understand that more now than ever. I don't want you to worry that I won't. I'm just processing, and I know you have your own stuff going on—"

"I'm coming home." David, he'd deal with later. "Cat and Sariyah can cover for me. I'm coming home. I need to hold you."

She cleared her throat. "Come hold me, then."

In under a half hour, he entered the house from the garage door. Bailey met him in the kitchen, and he dropped everything, picked her up, and went upstairs.

He took his time, touching her slowly, each brush of his fingers telling her a different story only his heart was privy to. He marked her with his tongue, his teeth, claiming her as he made a path from her mouth down to the very core of her. She cried his name, tears pooling into the curls at her temples, and he didn't stop until she came, gasping and shivering, pulling at him until he hovered over her.

She guided him inside her, and as he lost himself in her eyes and each breath expelled between her lips, he let himself forget that there was a world outside where conditions weren't always perfect. Where pasts haunted and plagued relationships, where family could sometimes be a burden, and where, often, there were no answers. Right now, it was just him, Bailey, and nothing else.

"I'll always come back to you," she whispered, tears on her lids.

"And I'll always be right here," he groaned, her arms around his neck as he spilled pure ecstasy deep, deep inside her.

CHAPTER THIRTY

Their naked limbs tangled, Bailey burrowed as far into Kellen's body as she possibly could while he slept. At least, she thought he was asleep until she felt his lips on her shoulder. She tilted her head so those lips could land on hers and nearly wept when they withdrew.

This was the love she'd been waiting for.

He rubbed the tip of his nose along her jaw. "How are you feeling?"

"A lot better," she said. "There's still the outstanding question of who my father is, at least biologically, and if he's the reason Alice hates me so much."

"Is there a reason you call your mother Alice and not something more…motherly?"

"She forbid it. My father thought it was a weird quirk I picked up and didn't like it for a while, but since Alice didn't seem to mind, he let it drop."

He kissed her cheek. "I love you."

"And that means everything." She turned so that when he went to kiss her again, his lips landed on her mouth. "But there's one more thing."

He climbed over her and parted her legs with his knees. "Can it wait?"

"Yes." She nodded, his teeth taking her lip hostage as he slowly entered her, allowing her to feel every ridge. "It can wait."

EVENTUALLY, THEY LEFT THE BEDROOM.

Seated on the living room floor, they searched their phones and Kellen's laptop for any further information on Daniel Bailey. Daniel was the missing link in the chain—she could sense it. Another thought tapped her on the shoulder and yanked on her earlobe, but she ignored it.

For now.

As she thumbed through the rest of the documents from the safe deposit box, Kellen moved next to her so she could see the laptop screen.

"What I've found so far about this Daniel Bailey is pretty twisted," he said. "He even stayed on the Most Wanted List for a few years after his disappearance because of how heinous his crimes were."

Although this was a different picture, there was no mistake about it. This was the man she'd seen at the house. The man whose emotions it felt like she experienced whenever her body went warm.

Kellen continued. "And look here. It says that they believe he fled to Barbados because his parents had a great standing there in the community. The FBI questioned Ada and Walter, but the FBI could never prove they were aware of their son's whereabouts. In fact, at one point, Ada had accused them of killing him and trying to hide it."

She sifted through the documents, most of them newspaper clippings of Daniel's different crimes. "So, did the crimes in the U.S. stop once he got to Barbados?" she asked. "Or did he do the same thing there?"

"It doesn't say."

They continued to search in silence until she looked up and noticed the strain on Kellen's face.

"How was your day, by the way?" she asked, skimming an article about Daniel's accomplishments in academics and on his college swim team. In her opinion, the moment he'd taken his first victim, none of that mattered any longer.

Kellen groaned.

"That bad?"

"David's drinking again, so Alexis left him."

Although everything appeared to now be out in the open, she felt obligated not to tell him she'd caught David drinking that afternoon on his birthday. They both already had pretty well-stocked plates of crap to deal with.

"He might show up here at some point." He rolled his shoulders. "If I'm not here when he does, don't open the door."

"You think he's dangerous?"

"When he's sober, he's my brother. When he's not, I don't know who he is, and I can't trust that."

"Are you okay?"

"Just wasn't something I wanted to deal with right now, or ever again." Before she could ask him anything else, he changed the subject. "Look at this. They did a story on Daniel Bailey in the States too. Apparently, his only surviving victim lives here in Atlanta. They tried to interview her recently for some kind of TV show, but she declined."

"Think she'll talk to me?"

His irises dimmed. "What are you talking about?"

"I can give her some closure by telling her he's dead."

"But how will you prove that? And what if she asks why you haven't gone to the police?" He set aside the laptop. "Bailey, the point was to uncover whatever makes you go on these…*psychogenic fugue states,* not reopen old wounds for you or this woman."

"But what are my options, Kel? Now that I know he has a surviving victim, I can't just ignore that. She should know. Plus, there's so much going on, it's like the universe is testing our relationship. If that's the case, I don't plan to fail."

He yanked the papers from her hands and tossed them somewhere behind her. "When you say things like that," he moved forward until she was forced to lie on her back, "you make me want to do things to you."

"Good things?" she asked, reaching for his waistband.

"Bad things." He kissed her neck. "Bad, *disgusting* things."

CHAPTER THIRTY-ONE

Alice stirred, awakened by something poking her in the arm. She'd fallen asleep at Nigel's bedside, but his body remained steady, chest rising and falling, his eyes closed.

"It's me, Aunt Alice."

She yawned. "Erwin? Is everything okay?"

"Can I talk to you?"

"Of course."

He pulled up a chair and sat, his gaze falling briefly to the clasped hands in his lap.

"I found out today that I have a tumor on one of my lungs," he quietly shared. "They said it's something called squamous cell carcinoma. Lung cancer. I've never even smoked a cigarette. Over the years, it's been one thing after the other, and this feels like the final scene of the very deluded play of my life."

She placed a hand on his. "Did you get a second opinion?"

"Don't need one. And I'm not telling you this because I want anything. I'm telling you because of the other reason I made the decision to come to the States. Why I came to live with you instead of staying down there. Alice, despite what you want to believe, he's in the house."

A chill ran up the back of her arms. "Don't be ridiculous, Erwin."

"I've seen him more than a dozen times. And, to be completely honest, I think he's the one doing this. All these bad things that have been happening to me can't be a coincidence. Nigel, the love of your life, in that bed can't be a coincidence."

"For you, it could be karma."

Erwin's eyes sparked with a tiny bit of anger. "Karma? For me? Alice, he knows what *we* did. What you did to him, and what I did to Bailey."

"Stop."

"You killed him, Alice."

"He drowned."

"In dirt?"

"I had no other choice."

"What are you saying, then? That he deserved to die for making love to you? For making the mistake of falling in love with you? For confessing why he was in Barbados? Or, no, for confessing that he didn't do what the papers accused him of."

She stood. "I didn't know if I could believe him."

"He told you that *before* you had sex with him. *Before* you pulled me into your little murder plot using that same lie. So, if you didn't believe him, then you fucked a murderer."

"Which would make me a what?" She flicked her fingers in

his direction. "Look at what you did to Bailey. Maybe others too."

"I never did anything to anyone else."

"Just my little girl."

"Oh, so she's your 'little girl' now? How convenient."

"Leave."

The muscle in his jaw twitched. "Admit it. You would have done anything to trap Nigel Green, the son of an admiral. The boy you loved since you were children. But then, you made a mistake you couldn't hide, never knowing how decent of a man Nigel was that he would have married you even if you'd had another man's child. Daniel Bailey could have been alive. Bailey could have been raised by her father, and you still would have had your happily ever after with Nigel."

She pointed to the door. "Leave. And I want your things out of my house before the end of the week."

"Gladly."

He stormed out of the room, and she returned to her position next to Nigel's bed, dread gnawing a hole in the pit of her stomach.

CHAPTER THIRTY-TWO

Bailey glanced at the clock on her laptop.

Six-fourteen.

She brought her coffee cup to her lips, quickly scanned the Starbucks interior, and returned to her blank word-processing screen.

It hadn't been as difficult as she would have liked to find where the survivor, Tammy Campbell, now lived through the double-edged sword of the internet. On her days off, like a detective—or, perhaps, a stalker—she parked on the curb a few houses down from Tammy's to get a handle on the woman's routine:

- Around seven in the morning, Tammy left the house to go to work for a major healthcare corporation.

- A little after four, she returned home and pulled into her one-car driveway—she never parked in the garage.
- Two hours later, she biked to the gym, which was located less than two miles from the subdivision.
- After the gym, she returned home. Based on her changed attire, she showered at the gym.

Tammy Campbell didn't appear to be romantically involved with anyone, and there was no evidence of children. She'd been thirteen at the time of her attack, putting her somewhere in her early to mid-forties. Auburn hair, with more hints of red than brown, fell just below her shoulders. Hair she never wore in a ponytail.

"Is there a reason you've been watching me?"

Bailey looked over the laptop screen to find a pair of green eyes narrowed directly at her. "Excuse me?"

Tammy sat in the chair across from her. "I see you in the morning before I go to work and then when I come home. I know you're watching my house. What do you want? Are you another reporter?"

"No." She closed the laptop. "I'm not."

Tammy looked surprised for all of three seconds before her anger returned.

"Then what do you want?"

"I…I don't know how to explain it."

"Maybe you could explain it to the authorities."

"I probably couldn't then, either." Bailey squeezed her forehead. "Oh, God. When I tell you this, please don't call the crazy police."

"Can't. I've got warrants with them myself."

She laughed.

Tammy's expression cooled.

"My name's Bailey Green, and I recently found out that some way, somehow, my maternal grandparents were connected to Ada and Walter Bailey."

The look on Tammy's face said she recognized the names.

"But I'm not sure how, yet. The thing is, my paternal grandparents gave me a document that landed me in my birthplace of Barbados. Now that I think about it, I realize that the purpose of them giving me the information was for me to find out that Ada and Walter owned the house I grew up in. I also found out that they were the parents of a man named Daniel Bailey."

"Which led you to me," Tammy said.

"Yes."

"How did you find out where I lived?"

"Google."

Tammy snorted and looked off to the side.

"But I can assure you, I'm not here for anything crooked or malicious."

"So then, what do you want?"

"Well, first, I have reason to believe Daniel Bailey's dead."

Tammy stiffened. "What? How do you know? Is that why you're here? To tell me he's dead?"

"Partly. I, uh, don't know how to explain this next part, so I'll just tell you. Again, no crazy police, please." Bailey cleared her throat and straightened her spine. "I think I saw him, or at least his spirit, in the house I grew up in."

Tammy stared at her, blinked, and leaned back in her chair, folding her hands on top of her washboard stomach. "His...spirit?"

"I know it sounds crazy, but it's the truth. There's no other way to explain what I saw. And I have a boyfriend who's an MD who can testify to my sanity...somewhat. At least to the extent a boyfriend can. I'm sure he thinks I'm crazy in other ways."

Tammy smiled, huffed a laugh, but then sucked in a deep breath, voice falling to a near whisper.

"I was walking home from school when it happened," she said, gaze faraway. "When you're thirteen and grow up in a stable, loving household, it never dawns on you that taking a different path home could be dangerous. Especially when the path is an open field right behind your school."

Tammy closed her eyes, drew in another long inhale, and held it. As the air left her lips, she opened her eyes.

"I don't claim to know the inner workings of the universe. People say they see things. We capture odd things on camera, on video. Personally, I believe in horoscopes and numerology. Obviously, what you saw and what's been going on with your childhood home led you here, so there's that. Problem is, there's a flaw in your theory."

Bailey cocked her head to the side. "A flaw?"

"Daniel didn't do it."

"But they had a DNA match."

"Bailey, DNA in the eighties is nothing like it is today. Matter of fact, testing started becoming routine right around the same time the attacks started happening. However, after a tipster called the police hotline, they started looking into Daniel Bailey. It turned out that he fit the FBI's criminal profile and lived close to the 'comfort zone.' They argued it was enough probable cause and got a judge to sign off on a warrant to search his folks' place, where he lived at the time."

"And they found evidence in the house."

"Not exactly. Evidence would have been a murder weapon or a trophy from one of the victims. They found his hairbrush and used it to compare his DNA to what they…found on me and the other women. But I survived. I saw my attacker's face. And it wasn't Daniel."

"I'm assuming you told them," Bailey said.

"I did, right before they said I was too emotional to be sure."

Bailey, rolling her eyes, fell back in her chair.

Tammy shook her head and released a snort of disbelief. "Exactly. But, years later, I contacted one of the detectives who handled the case, the one who worked directly with my family, and he told me that by today's standards, that DNA wouldn't have cut it. It was only a partial match. Unfortunately, at the time, the case had grown so large that his hands had been tied. When he brought up the possibility of a mismatch, the district attorney told him to 'make it stick.'"

Bailey stared at her, blinking rapidly, her brain piecing all the new information together.

She hadn't prepared for this bit of news.

Truthfully, she hadn't been prepared to be cornered at Starbucks, but this was even more left field. Tammy spoke with certainty, but the man she'd seen at the house in Barbados was the one who'd been featured in those articles.

Tammy continued. "Daniel was in the 'comfort zone' because his family lived next to mine. I've been," she held up a forefinger and thumb, "*this* close to Daniel Bailey, and this person, the one who did those awful things, didn't have his scent. Or his shoulders. Or his fucking face."

She started to reach for Tammy's hand but changed her mind at the last minute. Regardless of the circumstances that had brought them together, they didn't know each other.

"So why flee?" she asked. "Why not stand trial?"

"There was too much evidence against him," Tammy argued. "And I was a kid at the time, so the police didn't want to hear whatever I had to say. They thought I was confused and in shock. One even scolded me for not being happy they'd identified my attacker. If you had that much stacked against you, and the means to run, wouldn't you? Not only guilty men run."

Bailey closed her eyes, allowing the words to penetrate. "Well, he disappeared in Barbados," she said. "No one's seen him in over thirty years, and there's no evidence of him leaving the island. He simply 'vanished,' but I know he died there."

"Are you thinking he was killed?"

She was. She also now believed she knew who'd killed him, and why.

"How are you doing, by the way?" she asked Tammy. "In general. I know it's been quite some time since the events. I also know, from personal experience, that those types of things can have a lifetime impact. I think you noticed me because you notice everything about your surroundings."

"Or you'd suck as a stalker."

Bailey laughed. "That too."

Tammy tilted her head to the side. "Let's just say, before it happened, I couldn't tell you what color the sky was. Now, I could tell you about a cloud formation from two weeks ago at half-past two on I-75."

"Or if there's a terrible stalker on your street."

Tammy snickered. "That too."

Of the many different ways she'd envisioned finally meeting Tammy Campbell to go, this never made the list. She'd imagined being ignored, Tammy putting up rightful wall after wall until, weary, she broke down and listened to what the crazy woman following her had to say.

"Today, my horoscope said that I would find guidance in someone unexpected but relevant to a major part of my life," Tammy said. "Me and you, Bailey, we were supposed to meet. I firmly believe that. Do you mind if we meet up again?"

Bailey shook her head. "Not at all."

"How about next week, same time, same place?"

"Are you going to show up with the paddy wagon and strait jackets?"

Tammy choked on a laugh, her entire face lighting up. "If I do, they'll end up putting you in the back next to me. But, no. Today's the twenty-second, a number that means accomplishing the impossible. In terms of signs from the universe, that's two for two."

They both stood.

"Can I ask you something, though?" Tammy asked. "It's about your name."

"It's about the 'Bailey' and 'Daniel Bailey' thing, isn't it?"

"Would you be offended if I said yes?"

"No, because my middle name is Danielle."

Tammy froze. "So then—"

"I think so, but I haven't confirmed it yet."

"So you might have part of his DNA." Tammy pushed in her chair. "Holy...hell. I'm serious, Bailey. Next week. Please come."

"I will."

Tammy, nodding, headed for the exit, hair swinging around her shoulders.

CHAPTER THIRTY-THREE

Kellen breathed a sigh of relief as he hung up the phone. Finally, the hospital had hired not one, but two staff neonatologists. In about a week's time, his roles and responsibilities would decrease, which would mean a ton of extra time.

It was only logical; he planned to marry Bailey, and they would probably have children someday. There was no way he could be the father and husband he hoped if he continued to work himself the way he did. He didn't want to come home one day and find his wife and little girl gone.

He left the office and said his goodbyes, eager to head home. Before, the house's eerie stillness and cold quietness used to drive him insane, which had led to barely manageable restlessness and insomnia.

Now, he had Bailey.

However, when he pulled up in front of his house, he found David sitting outside the front door. Even from a distance, he spotted the disheveled clothing, the slouch to his brother's shoulders, and the way David's hair cascaded to one side.

"She won't open the door," David mumbled as he approached.

"Who, Alexis? How'd you find her?"

"No. Bailey. She won't open the door."

"I told her not to."

David looked up, and he wondered how his brother could see him with the veins in his eyes so prominent.

"Why didn't you tell me she was living with you?"

"Let's go inside and get you cleaned up."

"Kel, did you get married? Please don't tell me my kid brother got married, and I didn't know."

Kellen pulled a light from his pocket and shined it into David's eyes.

"We used to be close, Kel."

"Come on." He put away the light and opened the front door. "You need to clean yourself up."

They stumbled inside.

He dropped his things in the entryway, and Bailey appeared when she heard the commotion, looking from him to his brother, sympathy written all over her face.

"You guys hungry?" she asked. "I made dinner."

"What'd you make?" David slurred. "Alexis isn't the greatest cook on her own, but she can follow a recipe. She made this turkey tenderloin once..." His eyes filled. "But I came home drunk and threw the plate against the wall. The husband of the year award goes to...this fuck up."

Kellen ground his teeth together.

Bailey looked at him, eyes pleading.

After a heavy sigh, he let her know he would be down for dinner and helped David up the stairs, all but tossing him into the guest bathroom. He dragged clothes from his dresser, chucked them onto the bed, and then joined Bailey in the dining room.

He walked up behind her and wrapped his arms around her waist. She turned around, returned the hug, and they remained that way until he'd had his fill of her—for now.

They finished setting the table.

David, looking a bit more refreshed than the catastrophe that had been on the doorstep, entered the dining room, took a seat, and reached for a dinner roll. Bailey had made barbecued chicken thighs, rice, and pigeon peas with a salad on the side. Something about the silence worked for them, at least at the moment, so Kellen thanked her by squeezing her thigh underneath the table.

"You have anything to drink?" David asked, shattering the quiet.

"I know you didn't just ask me to give you alcohol in my own damn house," Kellen growled. He'd been irritated since the moment he'd pulled up, but he also knew he was supposed to be gentle with David and try to understand where he was coming from. It was what they'd learned in family therapy all those years ago, before David's bitterness had turned into addiction.

"Damn, maybe some juice or water." David bit into his chicken thigh. "Some lemonade or something to wash down this dry ass chicken."

Bailey looked down at her plate.

"Mon chou," Kellen gave her thigh another squeeze, "you already know you can cook. Don't let this asshole get to you."

"Asshole?" David pushed his chair back from the table and dropped the chicken on the plate, sending rice scattering across the wooden tabletop. "So what, the minute I'm not the perfect brother, you give up on me?"

"Give up on you?" Kellen stood, his anger threadbare. "I've always been on the front lines fighting for your ignorant ass. When you're like this, do you think you're easy to deal with? Do you think I really don't want to take your fucking head off with the first thing I can get my hands on? If you weren't my brother, do you think I would be here yelling at you like this, or would I tell you to get the fuck out of my house?"

David, seething, stormed out of the dining room.

Kellen followed.

Instead of heading for the front door, David headed for the stairs, but Kellen grabbed him by the shoulder before he could begin his ascent. David turned and swung a fist toward his head, but he ducked the sluggish movement, grabbed his brother around the middle, and slammed him to the floor.

He stood, expecting the fight to be over, but David swept his feet, knocking him to the floor, climbed on top of him, and began pummeling him.

Bailey entered the room, yelling, but the blood boiling in his ears drowned out her words. He could only imagine how they looked, two adult men tousling on the floor like children.

Even in family therapy, he hadn't been allowed to hurt. Even in family therapy, he'd had to restrain himself.

"You're not like that, Kellen," they'd all said, parroting one

another. *"Kellen never gets angry. Kellen never gets upset. Kellen's fine."*

But Kellen wasn't fine.

He hadn't been fine since that day.

David, his mother, his father—they weren't the only ones who'd lost someone they'd loved. Despite the physical differences between them, he'd never seen himself as different from Connor. What had made things worse was that, as his twin, he was the one who'd made his brother that way. In the womb, *he'd* robbed Connor of what he'd needed, resulting in Connor's disabilities and challenges. And those disabilities and challenges had directly led to Connor's death.

He'd killed his brother.

"I said, stop it!" Bailey screamed. "Please don't make me call the police."

"Bitch, you stay out of this." David rose and stalked toward her. "This is between me and my brother. Our *family.* You're not even his fucking wife. You're just up in here acting like it."

Kellen rolled into a pushup, and slightly dazed, looked up just as David reached for her. She ducked, but bigger and longer, David lunged and grabbed her around the waist. He picked her up and sent her crashing into, then through, an end table made of glass and wood.

Kellen saw red.

He charged David, shoving him to the floor, and struck David in the side of his face with a tight fist. As though the fist brought with it some clarity, David held up both hands in a defensive posture.

"Kellen, I'm sorry. I didn't mean to—"

"I'm done."

"Kel—"

"Get out." He went to Bailey, who let him know she was fine, and lifted her into his arms. "Tell me what hurts."

"I'm fine."

Blood on her forearm caught his eye.

"Just a scratch," she said. "But your eye's beginning to swell. We need to get some ice on that."

"Don't lie to me," he warned. "Don't lie to me to save him. And don't listen to any of his shit, either. This is *our* home. Me and you."

David called out to him, voice gone weak. "Kellen? Kellen, I'm sorry. I'm so sorry. I'm so, so sorry. Bailey, I didn't mean to—"

"David, get the fuck out of my house." He didn't bother turning around. "Don't contact me. Ever again."

"You can't be serious."

Tears burned in his eyes, and his heart had only hurt like this once before in his life. He'd never given up, on anything, and he'd vowed to never give up on family, but too much was at stake.

Alexis was right; if he didn't get a handle on what was most important to him, right now, he would lose everything. His family, though they loved him, leaned on him far too much because he let them.

He'd never told them he had nothing left to give, so they'd drained and drained, needed and needed, assuming he had an endless supply of shouldering their darkest moments. Yet, in *his* darkest moments, he'd opened his eyes to find himself alone.

Until Bailey.

Whether it was following him to his brother's house, knowing she might walk into chaos, or remembering his favorite cake on a day that hadn't been his in a long time, with Bailey, it was always *them*.

Us.

Together.

"David, I'm done rescuing you," he said. "This is on you now. From here on out, it'll be up to you if you want to live without Alexis and Abbie. From here on out, it'll be up to you if you want to lose another brother."

"Kel—"

"David, I've got nothing left. Nothing." His voice cracked, but it was too late to rein it in, not that he could suppress this much pain. "Just…go."

"Where, Kellen? And what am I supposed to do without you? You're my brother, my best friend. I love you. What am I supposed to do without you?"

He started up the stairs.

At the top of the landing, he heard the front door open and close.

BAILEY SAT ON THE EDGE OF THE BED WHILE HE SEARCHED FOR any wayward shards of glass. He checked for any breaks or sprains, and besides a couple of scratches, she was okay. In fact, as he examined her, she kept asking if he was okay.

"I'm fine," he said, for the umpteenth time, sinking to his knees in front of her. "I'm okay."

She grabbed the sides of his face. "You're not."

"No. I'm not."

"What happened with Connor?"

He tilted his head back, filling his lungs with air, tears running down the sides of his face.

"Connor was my twin brother, as you already know. There's this thing called twin-to-twin transfusion syndrome, and basically, what that means is that there's unequal blood flow in the womb coming from the mother to the fetus. So, while I was getting nourished, Connor was being deprived. Because of it, he was born several pounds lighter than I was. He had heart and brain defects. He didn't learn to walk until he was three or talk until he was five. He walked with a slight shuffle that people made fun of. They called him retarded, slow, everything under the sun, and we tried to constantly make sure he understood his importance in our lives, but…"

He shook his head and looked up at the ceiling.

She joined their fingers.

"When we were seventeen, Connor hooked up with some guy on the internet who specialized in helping people end their lives. Like a modern-day Kevorkian, but instead of the terminally ill, he targeted kids with disabilities. The guy was eventually arrested, but not before he got to Connor. David and I, coming home from the basketball court one night, found him… and the pain, Bailey. That fucking pain. We went to tons of family counseling. We said his name openly, talked about him. We visited his grave. Things seemed to be better, but then, ten years after it happened, it's like something snapped. I couldn't cope anymore unless I was putting in eighteen, twenty-hour days, and David started drinking when he hadn't been even a social drinker to begin with."

"What happened in those ten years?" she asked, thumbs swiping along the corners of his eyes.

He shrugged. "We graduated. We went on with our lives. We stopped saying his name. I guess we weren't doing as well as we thought we were."

"Lie down with me?"

He joined her on the mattress.

She positioned herself so that her head was slightly above his and kissed his hairline, alternating between wiping his tears and smoothing his hair.

"Are you really done with David?" she asked.

"No, but I need…I need a break. It's too much."

"Whatever you decide to do, I'll support you, okay?"

He pulled her closer. "Let's talk about something else."

"Later," she whispered. "Right now, just feel. Let me be there for you, the way you're always there for me."

"I love you, Bailey."

She kissed the top of his head. "I love you too."

CHAPTER THIRTY-FOUR

When he opened his eyes again, it was to a semi-dark room. Bailey lay awake, stroking his hair, staring at the wall behind his head.

"Did I fall asleep?"

She looked down at him, gaze slightly off to the side of his face. "For a…little. Your eye actually doesn't look bad. I put some ice on it while you were asleep, but," she lightly touched the corner of the eye in question, "I'll keep an eye on it."

"Yes, Doctor."

"I actually like nurse better. I was thinking about getting a nurse's uniform."

He kissed the hollow of her throat. "I'm listening."

"Then, when you're in the upstairs office working, I'll walk in like, 'I put the orders in, Dr. Edwards.' But, the orders will be wrong."

"And I'll have to 'teach you a lesson.'"

"For that, and because I keep coming to work without panties when you explicitly have a sign up that says coming to work without them 'will get you fucked.'"

He laughed.

She chased her fingers through his hair. "How are you feeling?"

"I'm all right. I really am."

"I'm here whenever you need me. You know that, right?"

"I do." He touched another kiss to her throat. "But tell me now how your meeting with Tammy went."

"Did I say 'meeting' in my text?" She wrinkled her nose, squinting. "I meant more like, she caught me following her. But it went well. It was interesting. She's incredibly sweet. I like her. I told her I think Daniel's dead, and then she told me he wasn't the man who attacked her."

He leaned back. "What?"

"She said she knew the family well. And Kel, she saw the guy who attacked her. It wasn't Daniel. I even told her that I saw his ghost in Barbados and—"

"Bailey, no." He groaned, eyes closing. "You can't just…you can't go around telling people you saw what you thought was his ghost. It makes you sound crazy."

"I know what I saw, though." She pushed up into a seated position. "I thought you were with me on this. As a matter of fact, if you didn't search for missing cases in Barbados, none of this would have even happened."

He slid off the bed. "I know."

"Babe, you're dealing with a lot. You don't have to deal with this too."

"But we're in this together."

"No, we're in this," she motioned between them, "together. This relationship. I'm perfectly capable of handling my own stuff while you deal with what's going on with your family. No need to shoulder two burdens."

"But—"

"Do you think I'm crazy?" She left the bed and walked over to stand directly in front of him. "Do you think I have some sort of psychotic mental illness?"

He looked down into the beautiful dark eyes he loved so much, lucid and aware, and shook his head.

"No."

"So then, let me do this. I can handle it on my own, but I need you to trust me."

His hand spanned her lower back, tipping her closer. "I trust you."

"Good. Now, can I borrow some money to go back to Barbados?"

"Okay."

"There are more questions that need to be answered there," she went on, smiling up at him. "Problem is, only one of us is in a position to buy a ticket right now. I'll pay you bac...did you say 'okay'?"

"I did, and you don't have to pay me back."

"Not even with," she motioned to her body, "my Bailey Express card?"

He let out another laugh. "I don't buy you things in exchange for sex. I buy you things because I love you, and you're worth more than I could ever spend. Plus, your pussy already belongs to me."

"I can offer you my heart."

"Belongs to me."

"What about my love?"

He narrowed his eyes. "Just how much are you holding back?"

"You're right. You have it all." She wrinkled her nose and managed to pass off an expression of genuine disappointment. "Even when I find more to give, I immediately funnel it all into you. Must have something to do with how wonderful you are."

He stared at her and shook his head, biting down on his bottom lip. "B, you don't 'borrow' money from me. My wallet's in the nightstand. Do what you have to."

She searched his face, no doubt to see if he was serious.

And he was.

He was taking care of her now.

Out of everyone he'd ever sacrificed anything for, she was the one who'd given him the most in return. Whatever she wanted, he would give her. Although she might not have asked for it—at least, not right then—in a minute, he was going to give her some dick for that little "how wonderful you are" comment. And for listening to him, laying with him, and providing the comfort of her soft words and silken touch, he was going to bury his tongue in her pussy until she needed an oxygen tank to recover.

"I can come with you," he said.

"I can handle going back by myself," she insisted. "Trust me. Please."

"This makes me uncomfortable."

"I know."

"But I'm going to trust you."

She nodded. "I know."

"Oh?" He raised a brow. "You 'know'?"

"Kel, you could never say no to this face."

He scooped her up and headed for the shower. "Nope. Never."

CHAPTER THIRTY-FIVE

Tammy set her luggage down and looked around, her hands on her hips. "Where'd you say you met Kellen?"

Bailey did the same, the door to the villa shutting behind her. It wasn't the same one as before, and slightly smaller, but it was just as nice.

"Starbucks."

Over the last several weeks, she and Tammy had sent texts back and forth, exchanging information that eventually became friendly texts, checking up on one another. When she'd brought up that she'd be returning to Barbados, Tammy had hopped on the chance to tag along.

"Is he good to you? I mean," Tammy motioned around, "not just financially. Does he treat you well, as a person?"

"I've never felt more safe, appreciated, and loved."

"Starbucks, huh?" Tammy tucked a strand of hair behind her

ear as she made her way to the floor-to-ceiling windows over-looking the North Atlantic.

"I hope you don't mind my asking you this, but did what happened influence your approach to relationships? And not just the romantic ones."

Tammy flicked her wrist. "Oh, definitely. I mean, there were attempts over the years, at both. Some got closer than others. But when things started getting too close, too serious, that's when I chickened out. After that, I got content with being alone."

Bailey joined her at the window.

She knew that excuse well. It was among those she'd told herself, at least before she met Kellen. And she didn't deny that there were people who were content with being single, but she didn't believe any human found contentedness in loneliness.

Being alone was intentional.

However, yearning hid inside loneliness.

While explaining, a look had sparked in Tammy's eyes. One she'd seen before, staring back at her in the mirror. It was a look that said, "Stay away. People are dangerous," and in order to live a comfortable life, they had to be avoided at all costs.

Someone had broken what had once been Tammy's free, kind spirit, turning her into a hypersensitive shell of a person. The world, Tammy had learned too early, was less safe than she'd ever thought it could be.

"So what, I guess, is our game plan?" Tammy asked, her face transforming entirely, all her previous sorrow evaporating like vapors.

Bailey shrugged. "I really don't have a game plan, but I want to go back to the house. Even now, I feel like I have to be there. I know I have some sort of connection to the place."

"What about to the entity?"

"You already think he's my father, don't you?"

Tammy chewed on her bottom lip.

"Don't worry," Bailey reassured her. "I do too."

"So, when do you want to go?"

"Are you hungry?"

"No."

"Then, right now."

Tammy grinned. "Well, let's get to it. What's the worst that could happen?"

CHAPTER THIRTY-SIX

She was able to request Leo's services again for her stay. Apparently, despite all the drama she and Kellen had brought, he'd jumped at the chance to help, claiming that every other driver on the island would only take advantage of her. However, when they pulled up to the house, he remained at the end of the long driveway.

As usual.

Tammy followed her to the front door, barely a step behind.

Bailey reached for the handle, and the scent of roses wafted under her nose. Although the rest of the yard was well kept, the roses were in impeccable condition, standing out in bright bushels of pink, red, and white. Since her last visit, someone had built a trellis out of white wood, the perfect centerpiece for the floral backdrop. By its placement and the way the roses grew, over time, they would curl and hug the trellis, creating a beautiful seating area.

"Are you ready?" she asked, looking down at the fingers Tammy had curled around her upper arm. She'd shared what had happened during her last visit to the house, expecting it to change Tammy's mind, but Tammy had argued that, without Kellen with them, nothing similar should happen.

"Um," Tammy moistened her lips, "yeah. I think so."

Bailey opened the door.

The house invited them into its chill.

The tiny hairs on her arms stood on end, but she knew her old bedroom would be colder. This time, it was the first place she went.

Partway down the hallway, Tammy's grip tightened.

"Do you feel that?"

"That heavy feeling in your stomach?" Bailey said, inching forward. "That feeling like you're off your equilibrium and walking into pure, static electricity? No, I don't feel a thing."

Tammy nudged her and flashed her a smile.

They stopped in front of her old bedroom door. Today could result in absolutely nothing, and she knew that. She'd promised Kellen that, if nothing came of her adventure, she would drop the whole thing—as best as she could.

She placed her palm flat on the door and pushed. It didn't creak, which would have put her a bit at ease because she would have felt as though she was in the middle of a corny horror movie. Instead, it glided open, and once it reached a certain distance, it no longer needed the force of her hand; it simply swung back to the wall and remained there.

"It's so cold in here," Tammy said, her words a white mist.

Bailey scanned the room and lingered on the outline from

where she'd torn the mirror. However, the shards were nowhere to be found.

"Has somebody been here?" Tammy asked, on cue, grip still tight. "It's a lot cleaner than I expected it to be."

"I'm assuming someone cleans it."

A scent wafted beneath her nose, and she looked to her left. A few roses appeared, as though peeking, through the window. It was the first time she noticed how close the roses were to her old room.

"He's not here," she said, deflated. "He didn't show."

Tammy slackened her grip. "Think it's me?"

"Honestly, I don't even know what I was expecting. An apparition to appear, pointing to...what? Treasure? I sound like a Robert Louis Stevenson novel."

A few silent moments passed between them, and she looked up to Tammy staring at the bare spot on the wall, her head cocked to the side.

"What is it?"

"Someone did a patch job," Tammy said. "And from what I can see, it's a sorry patch job. Didn't you say your father was a contractor? So this couldn't have been his work." Tammy released her, walked over to the wall, and touched the surface. "Do you remember a hole being here?"

Bailey joined her, picking up on the slight indentation. "Not since I lived here, but my cousin lived here for a little while after we left."

She touched the wall, and a shock tore through the entire limb, from fingertips to shoulder.

"What just happened?" Tammy asked.

The wind shifted, and the roses' perfumed scent wafted into the room, circling them.

"Tammy, do you smell that? The roses."

Tammy tilted her nose in the air. "No, but the windows are closed. How can *you* smell them?"

"He's here. He's trying to tell me something." She looked around the empty room, and then her attention went back to the wall. "My father used to keep a shed out back. Maybe there's still some stuff left inside. I want to bust that part of the wall open."

"Isn't that concrete?"

"We have to try."

They turned toward the door, but a figure in the doorway stopped them dead in their tracks.

"Miss Inez? What are you doing here?"

"I heard voices," Inez said, her voice calm but her eyes intense. "I was outside tending to the rose garden."

"So you're the one who's been keeping them?" Bailey asked.

"Yes. Did you find what you were looking for?"

"I think so. By the way, this is my friend Tammy."

Inez tilted her head in greeting. "Hello, Tammy. And where's the handsome boyfriend?"

"Back home. Hey, you wouldn't happen to have a shovel or something, would you? Maybe a hammer? Something to knock this wall out."

Inez tapped her chin, disappeared, and came back with a pruning saw. "This might work," she said. "Looks weak there. Don't think that part's solid concrete."

Bailey went to work, piercing and sawing with a lot more

ease than expected. Tammy crouched next to her, sneezing and swatting away dust. As the wall crumbled, it revealed an opening that held a box fitted between two studs.

Tammy reached in and retrieved the box, brown and wooden and heavily scarred on the lid. It looked like something that, one hundred years ago, would have played music when opened.

Tammy dusted off the lid. "This is some cool shit."

Bailey set the saw on the ground and crouched next to her. "I can't believe this was behind the wall. Behind the mirror I tore from the wall."

"You *tore* the mirror from the wall? You didn't tell me that part."

"I promise I will later. Open it."

Tammy opened the lid, which, ironically, released a loud creak. A few stacks of folded papers were inside, some with the ink bleeding through.

"I swear, if these are love letters," Bailey said, carefully retrieving one. Her pulse beat so hard in her ears, it left behind a slight ache. Everything faded to a low buzz. Their surroundings grew faint, fuzzy, and as she read, she heard the voice of the man who'd written the words on that sheet of unlined paper.

 *Alice.*

For a moment, her eyes couldn't deviate from the name. She'd known she would see it, penned in unfamiliar yet intimate handwriting.

Thank you for believing me.

Thank you for seeing the truth that I couldn't have done those things I'm being accused of. I love you, and I can't wait to meet our baby girl.

Remember our bet?

I still say it's going to be a girl.

Yours truly,

- Daniel

"Who's Alice?" Tammy asked.

"Her mother."

They looked up.

A tall man stood in the doorway behind Inez, and their features were so alike, Bailey blinked, several times, to distinguish the ethereal from reality. She'd never known Daniel Bailey. Until several weeks ago, she'd had no idea he existed. Yet, somehow, she'd fallen for a man who favored him as though, through Kellen, he'd found a way to keep his promise to protect her.

"Did you really think I wouldn't come?" Kellen asked.

"Are you the boyfriend?" Tammy waved. "Hi, Kellen. It's nice to finally meet you. I'm Tammy."

He raised both brows. "Tammy? What are you doing here? Bailey didn't mention…"

Bailey drowned them out and reached for another letter.

Daniel,

I love Nigel.

- Alice

She reached for a third.

Alice,

You've stopped answering my calls. And where are you? Please write back. What do you mean you love Nigel? Since when? You told me you loved me. I know you do.

Is it the baby?

Is she okay?

If it's truly a girl, can we name her Danielle? Or is that too close to my name?

- Daniel

Alice,

Please write me back. Call me. Come to see me. I told both your mother and mine about our baby, and your mother found you at that woman's house. What were you trying to do?

No matter what anyone says, I want our baby.

- Daniel

Alice,

Where are you? Tell me where you are so I can come to you. We can leave Barbados. Why Nigel? Is it money? My family has money. Lots of money. We can go to Mexico and raise Danielle there.

I love you. Please write me back or call or come see me.
    -Daniel

Kellen crouched next to her. "Bailey?"

 *Alice,*

If you're done with me, tell me to my face. With everything we've shared, everything you've said to me, I deserve at least that. You told me you'd be mine forever.

Was that a lie?

Erwin told me you're getting my letters. He's handing them to you. He watches you read them. I won't have him continue to run back and forth for nothing.

Answer me.

Please, God, I can't sleep. If you don't want Danielle, I want her. I want my daughter. Please don't get rid of my baby girl. I love her already.
    -Daniel

She wiped her tears before they fell and possibly ruined the paper.

 Daniel,

You're right. You deserve a face-to-face explanation.
    I love you.
    - Alice

"Kel, he seemed kind of sweet."
He kissed her temple. "A lot like you, baby."

"And innocent. I know they were barely eighteen at the time, but these letters make him seem like Ada and Walter sheltered him. Maybe too much." She swiped at her nose. "Erwin must have kept them. There's no way Alice knows they still exist. She would have gotten rid of them. If Erwin was their messenger, he kept the letters."

"Want to know the story now?" Inez asked. "I can tell you now, my dear. Now that everything has been revealed."

The three of them nodded.

"Alice said she met up with Daniel Bailey to tell him she loved Nigel," Inez explained. "She said he showed up in a rage she had never seen, and she believed it was the same rage he was in when he killed all those people. She then said he took her out on a boat ride. While they were out there, he left her, swam to a second boat, and disappeared."

Bailey folded the letters and placed them back inside the box. "That's a shitty alibi, but he was already a suspected criminal. Any story would have sufficed. It also didn't help that he was a champion swimmer. Did anyone ever report seeing another boat?"

"No, but it was nighttime," Inez said. "When Alice didn't come home, Nigel and his father went looking. They found her floating aimlessly in the middle of the boat, haggard and emotional."

"She was pregnant by then," Kellen pointed out. "What happened when she started to show?"

"She said Daniel forced himself on her in the same rage. The island wept for her because her mother, and Ada, encouraged her to have the child. To bear a child of great sin. People used to whisper when you were out, but you were too young to notice. If it looked like Alice loved you, they would say she willingly gave herself to Daniel. If it looked like Alice loathed you, then they would say her story was true. She came from a good family big in the church. It would have been a huge scandal if it was proven that she'd let a man like that into her body."

"Did you believe her?" Bailey asked.

"I tried not to form opinions. I wasn't a stranger to the herb woman's house. And, out of shame, I've said untrue things."

"Were abortions still illegal?"

"Not at that time, but good women did not lie with men who weren't their husbands. And, God forbid somebody saw you at a clinic. Lord, the shame. We're not the smallest island, but everybody still knows everybody's business."

Bailey looked around the room. If, all this time, she'd been channeling her father, why'd he bring her here? What had she missed that he wanted her to see?

The roses perfumed the air.

She sprung to her feet and raced outside, Kellen, Tammy, and Inez on her heels. First, she searched the earth beneath the rose vines. Then she dropped to all fours and picked up hand-fuls of the ebony dirt.

"Kel? Tammy? Help me dig."

Both, without hesitation, kneeled next to her and plunged their hands into the soil.

"He's here," she said. "My father never left Barbados."

CHAPTER THIRTY-SEVEN

"If you love him, why did you let me...why did we...I wouldn't have given that to just anyone, Alice. You're the first woman I've ever made love to, and I want you to be the last."

Daniel ran his fingers through his hair, tugging slightly at the roots. He'd assumed Alice had put together this boat ride, this midnight picnic, to tell him what he'd been waiting to hear —that she would run away with him, and they would raise their child together.

The branches behind her rustled.

Erwin appeared from the brush and made his way to where they stood, his shoes further flattening a bushel of dying roses.

"So you don't love me," Daniel prefaced. "At least let me raise my daughter."

"It won't be a girl," Alice said.

"Still, let me have her. I'll handle it. At the end of this, no one will have a bad word to say about you."

"You can't make that promise."

"Yes, I can. I can make it with my entire heart."

She wiped away tears. "Tonight, I can give you this boat ride. I can give you this one last time because of what we've meant to each other. Then, once the baby's here, I'll let you have it. I've already talked to your mother."

Erwin's head snapped around. "But that's not what you s—"

"Will you agree to that?"

Daniel stared at her, unable to see what he'd done wrong. Where he'd gone wrong. He didn't want to leave without her, but she'd agreed to the most important stipulation, which was better than nothing. His mother wanted to take the baby, but he could raise Danielle. He could do a lot more than they gave him credit for. What he couldn't do, and hadn't done, was force himself on those girls, and he certainly hadn't killed them, either.

"As long as my little girl comes with me," he said.

"Okay." Alice sighed. "Could you get the boat ready?"

Nodding, he turned around.

The next thing he knew, he was on the ground. The world spun, and a headache larger than the land mass they lived on pounded in his skull.

"Alice, what did you do?" he heard Erwin whisper.

"Help me dig."

"I...I can't."

"We've always been close, more like brother and sister than nephew and aunt."

"Alice, I—"

"Please help me, Erwin."

"What about the baby?"

"I didn't want this baby."

"Alice, no. To you too? He did the same things they're saying he did in the States?"

"Yes."

"But he said he didn't do them. In his letters, he said—"

"Before you came, he confessed that he did, and that he was sorry. But there's no apology to erase something like that."

"Will you have it?"

"My mother knows. Now, she's watching me. I don't have a choice, but I can't let him do this to anyone else."

Daniel, groaning, raised his head and tried to look around. "Alice?" he called, but his voice carried no farther than a few inches in front of him. "Alice, what's going on?"

"For what it's worth," she knelt next to him and stroked his hair, "I really like you, Daniel, and I wish I didn't have to do this. But I love Nigel. I've loved him since I was seven."

A tear tickled the bridge of his nose. "Alice…"

"And I know you said you didn't do those things, but what if you did? What if you did and everybody finds out? I should have never given you something I was supposed to give to Nigel on my wedding night. I lost my head. Nobody ever taught me how to control passion once it's gripped you, just how to avoid it. You shouldn't have to pay for that, but look how big your scandal had to be to ruin you. All I had to do was lie down."

"Alice...please..."

"I'm sorry." She sniffed, tear drops falling onto his cheek. "I'm so sorry."

"Please have the baby, Alice. And please make sure she knows how much I wanted her."

CHAPTER THIRTY-EIGHT

Bailey continued to thrash in her sleep when the sedative he'd given her should have knocked her out for longer than the three hours she'd slept so far, but it had been a unique past few weeks.

He, Bailey, and Tammy had unearthed a well-preserved skull.

A human skull.

In forty-eight hours, the FBI had both decided that the case warranted their attention and arrived on scene in Barbados; Bailey had helped to convince them by giving them background on who she was, whose skull it could be, and sharing that she had evidence linking her to Ada and Walter.

The FBI and Forensic Sciences Centre in Barbados worked together to dig up the rest of the skeletal remains. The FBI had then placed a rush on the DNA, and the results had confirmed not only was it Daniel Bailey, but also that Bailey was indeed his daughter. In addition, they'd confirmed the initial DNA, which had implicated Daniel, hadn't belonged to him.

The case officially reopened.

With the partial DNA match and Tammy's statement placed into consideration, they were now looking at one of Daniel's relatives, who'd been in the area at the time of the homicides. During the initial investigation, the relative was brought up as a suspect, but by then, the DA's office had been convinced they'd found their man.

All that had happened in a matter of *weeks*.

Neither he nor Bailey had slept more than a few hours per night since, but he was used to trudging through sleepless nights like a ship sailing through molasses. However, he hadn't been able to stomach watching her do the same.

The doorbell chimed.

Kellen kissed the top of Bailey's head, regretfully left the warmth of her body, and headed downstairs. Alice Green stood on his front stoop, wearing a fashionable, knee-length dress covered by a cardigan, her purse slung over her forearm.

"Is Bailey home?" Alice asked. "This is where Noble and Faith told me she's been staying."

He crossed his arms over his chest. "She's asleep. And she's not 'staying' here. She lives here. This is her home. Our home."

"Oh."

"I'm not waking her up."

"I wasn't expecting you to."

"Then why haven't you left?"

"Your name is Kellen, right? Kellen, could I please talk to her for a minute?"

"Nope."

"It's okay, babe," Bailey said from behind him. "Let her in. I'll talk to her."

He didn't step aside right away.

Alice stared at the doorway, waiting.

"Try anything, and I'll make sure you live to regret it," he warned. "As much as Bailey's father wanted her, to raise and love her so she wouldn't have had to deal with your shit, I want her *one hundred times more,* to love and to cherish. Are we clear?"

Alice took a half step backward. "Yes."

"It's okay, Kel." Bailey's hand warmed the center of his back. "Let her in."

Slowly, he stepped aside.

Alice entered.

Bailey directed her mother to the living room, where they both took a seat. He sat next to Bailey and leaned back into the cushions, one long arm stretched behind her head. She cupped his knee and squeezed.

Alice looked around. "This is a lovely home you two have."

"Thanks," Bailey said. "Now, why are you here?"

"To…well, to explain. I heard the Daniel Bailey case has been reopened, and they are looking at a relative of his as a suspect."

Bailey nodded. "That's correct."

"Some things might come out with all of that resurfacing. Things I want to tell you myself so you won't have to hear it from the news or wherever. But first, I want to say this. I know I was never good to you."

Bailey remained quiet.

Just because, he planted a kiss on her cheek. In response, she gave his knee another squeeze.

"Daniel Bailey is your real father," Alice said.

Bailey tipped her head in another nod. "I know that already, Alice. They reopened the case because of me. I found his remains."

Alice's frame went stock-still. "How did you know he was buried at the house?"

"I never said anything about the house." Bailey leaned forward, clasped her hands, and sighed. "But I know about that too. Those letters you two exchanged? Erwin kept them. He hid them in a wall in my old room. Everything else, I pieced together."

Alice swallowed, eyes filling and her voice considerably quieter. "I didn't hate your father."

"I know he loved you."

"And I cared for him, I really did, but there was no future for me with him. Once I learned why he was in Barbados, even though he told me it wasn't true, I was conflicted. What if he'd done the things they were saying?"

"Then everyone would have known you'd lain with a devil."

"And you know how things are down there, Bailey. Even to this day. It would have ruined my family and my chances with Nigel. I would have never been able to provide what I've provided for you, Noble, and Faith if I'd made a different choice."

"You didn't even want me."

Alice's bottom lip trembled. "Sometimes I did. God, some-times I did."

Bailey swiped at her eyes, gnawing away at her top lip.

Kellen leaned forward. "You okay?"

"I'm okay."

"I'm here."

She stared into his eyes. "I love you."

"I love you too."

Alice retrieved a cloth tissue from her purse and dabbed at her eyes. "Bailey, sometimes it took God's strength not to crush you to me when you cried. I'm not proud of how I treated you, but you were my baby. It was hard to forget that."

"Why wouldn't you want to hold me?"

"Because I didn't choose you."

"And that's why you hate me? Because I was a mistake?"

"I don't hate you."

"Alice, you taught yourself not to care about me. Your instinct was to hold me, to comfort me, and you forced yourself not to."

"That doesn't mean I hate you. My feelings for you are simply different from my feelings for Noble and Faith. The love I have for them isn't what I feel for you, but I don't hate you. And seeing you hurt...oh God, it kills me to see you hurt."

"Did you think people would question your story if they saw you being affectionate with me?"

"Oh, I know they would have, and that was part of it. I had a truth to hide. But I didn't want you. I just didn't. It never made sense to me how I could want to care for something so badly that I never wanted to bring into this world."

Teardrops dripped from the bottom of Bailey's chin. Kellen swiped them away with an index finger, kissed her temple, and whispered his support to temporarily bolster her. She was getting the answers she'd longed for, but they'd both known those answers would cause pain.

"You don't like seeing me hurt," Bailey said. "But you did some of the hurting."

Alice swatted the air. "Those are words, Bailey. Words are nothing like watching you swell up from a bee sting. Or watching you get hurt at a construction site."

"What about watching a book fly into my head? Did that hurt you too?"

Tear droplets darkened the skirt of Alice's dress.

"Alice, I didn't let you in for you to spend the afternoon lying to me."

"Bailey, I've forgotten nothing of what I've done. I remember that day, clearly, and I couldn't eat. I couldn't sleep. Then when Nigel asked me what happened...I can't remember the story I gave him, but he knew it wasn't true. Some days, I wanted to die knowing how I treated you. Knowing the things I did, and," she swallowed, "the things I let happen to you. Father, forgive me. But just because I never wanted you doesn't mean I hate you. Hate is a strong word I've never felt for you. I did my best with you. I fed you and gave you a good home."

Bailey stood, walked to the stairs, and leaned against the metal railing. "Parents are supposed to feed and shelter their kids. What do you want, a medal? For doing the bare minimum? You could have done even a little more by stopping Erwin."

"I couldn't. I thought he'd turn on me. Tell everyone what I did. So, yes," a hard cry sputtered between Alice's lips, "I let that happen to you to hide my secret, and I'm sorry. It's not enough, and it'll never be enough. But, for what it's worth, I'm sorry you were born to a mother like me."

"I forgive you for what you went through," Bailey said. "And I understand how young you were when everything happened. But you made my life much more difficult than it needed to be. The level of healing I've had to undergo has all been because of you. That, I can't forgive you for. So you don't hate me. That's fine. That makes it easy to no longer see myself as your daughter."

Alice wiped her face, but it only smeared her tears.

Sensing Bailey had nothing left in the tank, Kellen stood. "I think we're done here," he said. "If Bailey wants to talk to you again, fine, but today, we're done. I'm not going to have you stressing my girl out in our house."

Alice rose, situating her purse across her arm. "Wait. There's one more thing. If you want to give them the letters, I won't run. I've lived with this burden for thirty years. I don't want to live with it any longer."

"I won't give them the letters," Bailey said. "Honestly, the only thing they prove is that you lied about your consent."

"Please don't say anything to Nigel, however. The only thing I'm truly afraid of is losing my family. Even if they have to visit me in prison, I don't want to lose their trust."

"You mean Nigel, Faith, and Noble, right?"

"Bailey…"

Kellen ticked his head at the door. "Come on. I can walk you out or put you out. Your choice."

Alice studied his face.

"I'm not related to Daniel Bailey too, if that's what you're wondering."

"I wasn't," she said. "But it's almost like God chose you to do what Daniel couldn't."

"And what you wouldn't."

He walked her to the door.

After taking one last long look at Bailey, she left.

He shut the door, and he'd barely turned around before Bailey wrapped her arms around him. Knowing he'd forever love the way she felt holding him, he closed her into his embrace and wiped away any remaining tears that lingered behind.

"Bailey, I have to admit. I come from a petty background. I wouldn't have forgiven her, and I would already be on the phone with Nigel, Faith, and Noble."

"Well, I'm not as forgiving as I appear," she said. "I called Nigel when I heard her voice downstairs. I explained the situation, and he said he could handle it. My phone was on the whole time, and he heard everything."

He dropped a hard kiss on her lovely mouth. "How are you feeling?"

"Much, much better. Amazing. Lighter. Happy. Kel, you make me so happy."

"That's because my lady's gorgeous *and* incredible."

"And what does your lady get for being both gorgeous and incredible?"

"First, a bath," he brushed her lips with another kiss, "and then an oil massage. After the oil massage, by the time I'm done with you, my tongue is going to be as strong as my biceps. After that, we'll take a shower where I'll…okay, so pretty much, I'm planning to fuck you for the rest of the night."

"Can we use whipped cream?"

"On your nipples? Please say on your nipples."

"On my nipples."

"You get the can," he graced her with one more kiss, "and I'll start your bath."

She released him, and he hurried up the stairs. Before his foot hit the landing, he heard the front door open, and a thud followed by a scream.

CHAPTER THIRTY-NINE

David's mind replayed the events of what had happened with Kellen and had been doing so in the weeks since it occurred, each time revealing even more of the terrible aspects of his addiction. Swallowing tears, he tossed back what he'd decided would be his final shot of vodka, paid his tab, and made sure not to stumble as he made his way to the parking lot.

When he reached the car, he fought his way behind the steering wheel. Tears poured from his eyes as he gripped the circle of leather with one hand and pressed the Bluetooth button to call Alexis with the other. She'd been ignoring his calls, but she needed to pick up this time.

She *had* to.

Her voice filled the cabin interior. "David?"

"Hi, sweetie."

"You're slurring."

"It's because I'm drunk."

"I'm hanging up no—"

"Wait, that's not why I called." He inhaled and gripped the steering wheel with both hands. "I called to tell you that I love you, Alexis."

Her voice mellowed. "I love you too, David."

"You still do?"

"Of course. Do you know how much we've been through? How much we mean to each other?"

He let his head fall back against the seat. "I've been hurting you. I've been hurting you and Abbie, and you've been so strong through it all. I don't know what's wrong with me. Why I can't let this go. Do you think it's hopeless? That I might be hopeless?"

"No. I don't think you're hopeless. It's hard. This is hard. I understand that. I didn't leave because I don't think this is hard for you."

"I still see him."

"I know, and I wish you hadn't found him that way."

"And Alexis, babe, I know you had to leave. I'm not mad at you about it. I never was. You're an amazing mother, thinking about our daughter when I was too selfish to."

"David—"

"Anyway, I called to tell you I love you, one last time. To hear that voice, one last time. God, you're so sweet. I remember the day we got married, the way you wore your hair, your dress. My jaw dropped. Do you remember that? Kellen nearly passed out from laughing so hard because he'd never, literally, seen someone's jaw drop."

"David, what do you mean by one last time?"

"Then came Abbie." He went from tears to sobbing, his words slowly becoming incomprehensible. "How did a lump of a man like me not only snag a drop-dead gorgeous wife, but then have a daughter like Abigail?"

"Babe, where are you? Tell me where you are. I'll come meet you."

"I love you, Alexis. Kiss Abbie for me."

"David, tell me where you are. I'll come. I swear I'll co—"

He ended the call and dialed Kellen next, pressing ignore each time Alexis' call tried to come through.

Kellen didn't pick up.

"Kel, it's me," he said, starting the ignition. "I wish I didn't have to leave this in a voicemail, but it might be easier this way. You've always been the rock of our family, keeping everything together in a burning house. I used to think that was brave. Commendable. But I never realized what it might be doing to you. Until that day at your place, I'd never seen you cry. Even after Connor, you stood tall while the rest of us crumbled around you. Now, I realize you should have been able to crumble too."

He backed out of the parking space.

"Kellen, I'm sorry for not being your older brother and stepping in when the family continued to place load after load on your shoulders. I'm sorry for the things I said to Bailey, what I did to her. Please apologize to her for me, okay? I didn't mean any of it, and I'm grateful you have her in your life. I love you, little brother. I love you...so damn much."

Ending the call, he pulled out onto the main road. On the other side of the street, he spotted a large, thick tree.

CHAPTER FORTY

Kellen tempered his breathing.

Tried to remember his training.

But it was Bailey lying at the bottom of the stairs, blood pooling at the back of her head. It was Bailey lying motionless as the pool grew larger underneath her.

Alice kneeled next to her, crying, smoothing Bailey's hair and touching her forehead to Bailey's, repeatedly.

"Move, Alice."

"My little girl—"

"Alice."

She moved aside.

"What happened?"

She mumbled, through tears, "I was so upset. Nigel called me, and I was so upset. I wanted to know why she didn't tell me he heard our conversation. Why she told me she wouldn't say anything. But she was on the stairs, and when she heard the door—

"Did you push her?"

"No. I swear I didn't. I tried to run to catch her. She slipped, but she was holding something, so she couldn't grab the railing."

The can of whipped cream.

He should have grabbed it from the fridge. He should have waited for her before going upstairs. He should have remembered to lock the fucking door.

"Did you already call 911?" he asked. "Call 911."

Alice scrambled for her purse, pulled out her phone, dialed, and held it up to her ear.

"B, open your eyes for me, beautiful," he said. "Look at me. Let me see those pretty eyes."

"Kel?"

It was a rare occurrence where he found himself praying it was "only" a concussion.

"Hey, gorgeous. Open your eyes for me."

She opened them a fraction of a centimeter. Behind him, Alice relayed the incident to the dispatcher. He quickly rattled off his address and coached her through how to explain the situation, as well as the symptoms of Bailey's he'd observed so far.

"A Grande, medium roast, nothing fancy," Bailey quietly groaned, her eyes unfocused. "For the doc."

He forced a shaky smile. "First words you ever said to me. I'm inscribing them on our wedding rings. Script font okay with you?"

"Kel, I have to close my eyes."

"Is it the light? Does it hurt?"

"My head hurts."

"I know it does, and I'm sorry."

"I fell."

"I know, baby. I should have been here to catch you."

Alice reappeared next to him. "Is she awake? Bailey, don't close your eyes. I know I wasn't a good mother, but you cannot die, sweetheart. I'm sorry. I'm so sorry. I should have held you. I should have held you and rocked you and kissed your little nose—"

"Alice, save it. Now's not the time. See that bag near the entryway? My stethoscope's inside. Go bring it."

She hurried off.

"Does anything else hurt, baby?" he asked.

Bailey coughed, and her breathing grew noticeably more shallow. Her lips looked like they were changing color, and he used every ounce of strength he could muster to keep it together.

"B, does your chest hurt? Did you hit more than your head? Alice, did you see if she hit her back or chest wall?"

Alice returned with the stethoscope. "I don't know."

"I'm going to show you how to hold her so I can listen to her lungs."

She did as instructed, and he didn't like what he heard.

"*Fuck.*"

"What?" Alice asked. "What's wrong? What did you hear?"

"Diminished lung sounds."

"What does that mean?"

"I hear sirens, Alice. Go direct the ambulance."

"What does that mean?"

"Alice, go direct that fucking ambulance because, I swear to God, if my girl dies, you're joining her."

Alice ran off.

"Bailey, I'm going to need you to fight, okay?" he whispered. "You can hold on. I know you can. Do it for yourself, for Tammy, your sisters, Nigel, and Daniel. Do it for me and the truckload of kids I'm going to put inside you."

Her eyelids rose, more slightly than before. "A," she gasped for air, "truckload?"

"So you don't answer when I call your name, but the minute I start talking about us having a shit ton of kids, you open your eyes."

She managed a faint smile.

"That's my girl." He kissed her forehead. "Help's here."

CHAPTER FORTY-ONE

Kellen paced the hospital waiting room. Although he didn't know the neurologist who'd be tending to Bailey, Sariyah was familiar with him. Sariyah had vetted him.

She'd also promised that, once they were done at the office, they would join him. He'd started to tell them it wasn't necessary; however, today, he needed the extra support.

Today, he would need as much support as possible because when he walked through the emergency room entrance, he'd nearly collided with his sister-in-law. Once Alexis had explained why she was there, his heart had nearly burst from his chest.

Pride wouldn't get in the way of him asking for help.

Not today.

Not anymore.

"They're keeping him for seventy-two hours," Alexis said, her puffy eyes following his movements, dark circles underneath. Despite her obvious fatigue, she looked immaculate, as usual, in an oversized sweater, leggings, and flat boots. Straightened hair cascaded past her shoulders.

"Kellen, let's sit."

His immediate instinct was to argue, to say he was fine.

But he wasn't.

So, he sat.

Alexis took the seat next to him and, sighing, stretched her legs out in front of her.

"David called me," she began. "He'd been drinking. At first, I was upset. Then he said something about telling me he loved one 'one last time,' and I knew why he'd called."

Kellen tapped the back of his head on the wall behind them.

"I traced his location from his phone, and he was out near Lenox Park. He didn't know where I'd moved, but he ended up three minutes away from my new place. What are the freakin' odds?"

Outstanding.

Now, he needed those same odds to work in Bailey's favor.

"When I got there, he was still in the car, looking at his phone. Then I tapped on the window, and when he looked up and saw me, he bawled. He cried so hard, I started crying. I'm grateful Abbie was with your parents. I needed to be one hundred percent present for him."

The hospital doors swung open.

Kellen looked up, but it wasn't the neurologist.

"Did he call you?" she asked.

"Yeah," he scrubbed a hand down his face, "but he called when I was...when all the stuff with Bailey happened, so we didn't talk. He left a voicemail, but I'm not sure I want to listen to it now that I've talked to you."

"Don't blame yourself."

"Trying not to."

She squeezed his forearm. "I know what happened at your house. I know what he did to Bailey. He called me right after it happened and left a long, incoherent voicemail about how he'd lost you."

At the mention of Bailey's name, his stomach tightened.

"He called your parents too," Alexis went on. "Your mother called me and asked me what he meant by his goodbye message. I told her what I thought, and she told me she tried reaching you, but you didn't pick up. Kel, she asked me to call you before she asked me to call 911. She called you, couldn't reach you, and still didn't call 911."

"That's how it was. I trained them to rely on me."

"You did what you thought you needed to do. Even I leaned on you too much sometimes. Not anymore. I was talking to David about it, and I realized that you never let him fall. He's never truly been afraid of losing everything until you stopped saving him. And," she cleared her throat, "he finally opened up to me about Connor in a way he never has. Something tells me you've been fighting the same demons."

Technically, he was, but the fight was no longer one-sided. Now that he'd chosen to no longer kill himself being strong for everyone, he had the energy to do things for himself. When his energy got low, he had someone to lean on. Someone who made up his whole world.

"I am, but I'm working on them," he said. "As far as David, what's going to happen after the psych hold?"

It took her close to a minute to respond.

"There's a place in Midtown. They're not only alcohol-rehab-based. They do therapy, nutrition, fitness. A whole-person approach, I think they call it. It's a sober living program. He'll live there while undergoing treatment."

"That's good."

"I think so too."

"How's Abbie?"

"She misses him. I miss him too."

The doors opened again, and a face he recognized walked through. This particular physician worked in neurosurgery, and the last person he wanted to see was a neurosurgeon.

A family rushed forward to talk to the neurosurgeon, and he sighed so hard, it emptied his lungs. Leaning forward, he thrust his hands in his hair and pressed his elbows into his thighs.

Alexis stroked the middle of his back. "Kel, David's stable. Lean on me for support right now. You've done all the heavy lifting. Now, it's time for us to be there for you."

"Honestly, 'Lexis, all I want is for Bailey to be okay. I should have never left her alone downstairs, and I should have remembered to lock the fucking door."

"Would she blame you?"

He shook his head. "No."

"Of course not."

"'Lexis," he raised his head, "you know that point in a relationship where you realize you want the person in your life to be there for a long time?

"I do."

"For me, it happened pretty early on. Probably that night Bailey came with me to help you with David. The next day, I woke up, and I just *knew.* So, in my mind, that's not my girlfriend back there. In my mind, she's the rest of my life."

FOUR HOURS LATER, WHEN THE DOORS OPENED, THE NEUROLOGIST finally walked through. And when he spotted the smile on her face, Kellen's knees nearly buckled as he rose to his feet. Alexis had left to pick up Abbie.

"Kellen?"

They shook hands.

"Nice to meet you," he said.

"Same to you. Any friend of Sariyah's is a friend of mine. And it's all good news. The MRI's clean. However, Bailey does have a concussion. Did the ER doctor talk to you about the pulmonary contusion?"

"Yeah, and it's just the bruised lung. No fractures."

"On my end, I'd like to observe her for twenty-four hours, but she's going to be just fine. I did suggest that she be careful on those stairs, though."

He'd ordered stair grips while waiting and sent emails to three contractors about changing the railing. He'd have no time to do it himself. He had a priceless patient to tend to.

"Is she awake?" he asked.

"Oh, yeah, and the first thing she said when she opened her eyes was, 'Where's my Kel?'"

CHAPTER FORTY-TWO

Bailey, for what felt like the millionth time, told Kellen she was fine to get the door, but since the accident, he'd had a field day taking care of her.

"You rest, B," he said. "It's your father."

He opened the door.

Nigel and Kellen exchanged a handshake before Kellen ushered him inside.

Nigel looked much better since the last time she'd seen him, which was when he'd come to visit her at the hospital. Henry had been taking good care of him, and without Alice around, he'd managed to step up and start taking better care of himself.

"Hi, Sweet pea." He walked over to her, gave her a gentle hug, and kissed her forehead. "How are you feeling today?"

"I'm all right, Daddy."

He grinned.

"What?"

"You still call me 'Daddy,' and that makes me so happy. No matter what, you're my baby girl. Now, let's sit. Come, let me help you."

She'd learned to stop arguing when he, her sisters, Kellen, his friends, and Tammy tried to help. They all merely acted like she made the request in a different language.

He helped her onto a cushion and took a seat next to her. Kellen asked them if they wanted anything to drink, and after they declined, he disappeared into the kitchen. He'd made her promise to let him take care of her, and once she agreed, he asked her to quit her job.

So far, she hadn't given him an answer.

"So, the forensics determined Daniel died of a head injury," Nigel said. "Blunt force trauma. Also, Erwin told the authorities he was the one who killed Daniel. He figured it would be better for him to take the charge, considering his health status." He took both of her hands in his. "Bailey, I love Alice, I do, but you're my daughter. If she pushed you, I'm not giving her another dime of my help. I barely want to now, knowing how she hurt you. She says I knew. The standoffishness, yes, but I never knew she physically hurt you."

"She didn't push me. She only turned herself in, saying she did, out of guilt."

"The attorney says it'll be next to impossible to prove intent."

"Because she didn't push me. Now, don't get me wrong, I think she should face charges for what she did to Daniel, but if Erwin's copping to that, so be it. Honestly, I'm tired. Daniel's spirit can finally rest in peace knowing his name was cleared, and his daughter had a chance at life."

It wasn't until weeks after digging up Daniel's body that she realized she no longer went into what Kellen referred to as *fugue* states. She no longer felt like one of her limbs threatened to burn right off her body. With Daniel now settled, she felt like herself again. Better than herself.

"Are you staying for dinner, by the way?" she asked.

He helped her to her feet and held her hand on the way to the kitchen. "Well, that's actually the real reason I'm here."

"Oh, *wow*. But your Sweet pea is," she faked a cough, "sick."

"I know, but that man of yours can throw down. Noble and Faith are on their way too."

"They don't live in Atlanta."

"I told them Kellen invited me to dinner, and that he's cooking. But," he playfully patted her forearm, "I'm sure they're coming to see you too."

Bailey laughed, shaking her head.

CHAPTER FORTY-THREE

"Bailey, I'm home!"

Bailey set aside her laptop, scrambled from the upstairs office, and raced down the stairs. Kellen, smiling, held his arms wide open, but she stopped in front of him.

"What's that?" she asked.

"What's," he looked at the envelope in his left hand, "this? Your letter from Emory."

She tapped her phone screen. "I was going to check the status online."

"Oh. So, do you want to do that instead?"

"Give me that letter."

"I want a kiss for my hard work getting it from the mailbox."

She rose onto her toes.

He bent.

"On second thought..." She snatched the letter from his

hand and tried to run off, but he grabbed her around the waist and dropped a kiss on her neck.

Then another.

His tongue followed, and the envelope slipped from her fingers.

"A quickie might help settle my nerves," she suggested.

He released her, picked the letter up off the floor, and handed it over. "Know what else might help settle your nerves? Opening the letter."

"You're the one who got me all warmed up, kissing and licking on my spot and everything."

"You should've just kissed me."

She tore at the flap, then paused. "What if this is a rejection letter?"

"It's not the only school in the area you applied to. Open it. Now, I'm getting nervous."

"My heart's pounding so hard. Wait." She turned, facing away from him. "I want to read it first. That way, if it's bad news, I can rein in the ugly cry."

Taking a deep breath, she retrieved the letter, first noticing the official university logo at the top.

 *Dear Bailey,*

> *Before you open your actual letter to Emory, I wanted to give this to you. I couldn't wait another moment to tell you how much I love you, and how much these last several months with you have changed my life.*

With you, I never feel alone.

With you, I never feel incapable.

I can depend on you, trust you. You're beautiful, amazing, and the strongest person I know. Having you in my life has allowed me to see the world the way I've always hoped to see it, the way Connor saw it, a lens through which all good things exist.

From the first moment I saw you, I knew. I can't explain it, but I knew I wanted you as part of my life for a very long time. Bailey, I'm convinced we were created to love one another, and I promise I will do everything in my power to make you happy.

However, this isn't just a letter to let you know how much you mean to me, and how much I love you. After that wall opened up in Barbados, after I saw those letters, I knew. I knew I wanted to give you the day I ask you to be my wife in the palm of your hand to hold on to forever, as my promise to you, that you are the woman I've been waiting for.

You are the woman I want, the woman I love, and the woman I plan to love for an eternity.
  - Kel

"So, what's it say, B?" he asked.

She stared at the paper, hands trembling. Then, slowly, she faced him, and he was there, on one knee, his beautiful eyes full of light and hope.

"Bailey Danielle Green," he said, choking up, "will you marry me?"

She opened her mouth, but not even a squeak made it out. So, she frantically nodded her head.

"Yes?" he asked. "It's a yes?"

For the first time, she noticed the ring. Of course, there was a ring. There was usually a ring present for these occasions, but all she'd seen was him.

He slid the sparkling, elegant pink diamond onto her finger.

"Yes." She threw herself into his arms. "Yes, yes, yes."

"The letter wasn't cheesy?"

"It was perfect, baby. So perfect. I love you, love you, love you."

He picked her up, and she wrapped her legs around him. Their lips came together, and she slid her tongue into his mouth as deep as it could go.

"I want you," she sucked on his bottom lip, "right now."

"Check your application first."

"But I need you."

"And I'll give you more than you can handle...after you check your application."

She groaned.

He gave her a quick kiss and set her down.

"Just so you know," she unlocked her phone, "nothing can top that. I'm still shaking."

She tapped her email app, took a steadying breath, and opened the email.

"Ho-ly crap." She looked up at him. "I got in. *I got in!*"

"And I didn't pull any strings," he said. "This is all you."

"I wouldn't have cared. You're amazing. The best. I wouldn't have cared." She took his hand and headed for the stairs. "Now, come. Let me show you a *mouthful* of my gratitude."

CHAPTER FORTY-FOUR

Six months later

Bailey apologized to the makeup artist for the third time, but she couldn't stop crying. She was so happy, she couldn't stop the tears from falling.

"I don't think we'll make it through the first five minutes," Tammy said, dabbing at her eyes.

The makeup artist laughed and shook her head. "I'm gonna bring my stuff to the ceremony. Something tells me I'll be doing full faces before the reception."

Bailey nodded. "Please do."

She'd opted for an ivory, strapless custom-made ballgown. Alexis, who was freakishly talented at doing hair, checked her curls and coils one last time. With ease, Alexis had tamed and elongated the usually untameable strands, setting the style off with a gorgeous floral hairpiece.

Abigail sat on Noble's lap on the other side of the room in a champagne-colored flower girl's dress, matching the rest of the bridal party. Faith, next to them, gushed over how adorable Abigail looked in that little flower girl dress.

As Bailey stared out at her bridal party, she took in the ways her life had changed. In less than a year, she'd made two close friends in Alexis and Tammy, and she'd gotten the answers to the questions that had danced in her mind for years.

Alice's attorney had eventually gotten Alice's charges dismissed. Erwin, on the other hand, was currently in limbo with how he was to be tried considering he was a naturalized citizen, who'd committed a crime, as a minor, against a U.S. citizen, in Barbados.

The state of Nigel and Alice's marriage currently hung in the balance, and she'd asked to accompany him to the wedding, but he'd declined.

None of that mattered today.

It didn't matter anymore.

She had Kellen.

Wonderful, amazing, Kellen.

Her future husband.

Nigel knocked on the door and pushed it open a smidge. "Sweet pea. It's time."

Bailey opened her arms for a group hug, got a final approval on her dress and hair from the room, and then went out to meet her man at the altar.

CHAPTER FORTY-FIVE

Kellen burst out laughing as one of his closest friends, Tayler Diaz, straightened his tie. A flawless engagement ring glittered on her finger, and a small mound poked at her forest green, one-shoulder strap dress. Their third friend, Ethan Stewart, and his wife, Alexandra, had a baby girl a few months ago.

"I'm so serious," she mumbled.

Ethan entered the hotel room. "Looks like it's about that time. Nervous?"

Kellen faced the mirror to check out Tayler's handiwork. "Nope. Not nervous at all."

Tayler snorted. "Yeah, right. Let me see the inside corner of your cheek."

He smiled.

"Bailey's so freakin' lovely," she half said, half squealed. "E, I was just telling Kellen that my friendship with you two is what spawned this love and appreciation for Black women."

Kellen stifled a laugh.

Ethan rolled his eyes.

"What?" she asked.

"You say that as if Black women haven't always been beautiful and worthy of said love and appreciation," Ethan argued. "You remember Tia Morris from medical school? If Alexandra wasn't in the picture—"

"Tia's happily married with four children," Kellen cut in. "But I'll tell Alexandra you said that."

"Please, don't. Actually, I wanted to ask you guys if you wanted to collaborate on a paper on the inhuman strength of nursing mothers."

"Sure." Tayler glanced at him. "I'll even be a case study once I have this kid. All you need to do is say something stupid."

"So Gage can separate my spine from my body?"

Kellen laughed, more nervous than he'd ever been in his life, but he wasn't sure why. He was marrying the love of his life.

Maybe he wasn't nervous.

Maybe he was eager for it all to be over so they could finally start their journey as husband and wife.

Maybe it was because of the redemption he'd seen in his family with David's extreme commitment to his treatment program, instilling hope that David and Alexis might make their way back to each other someday.

Maybe it was the fact that Abbie was getting bigger, and he could see traces of Connor whenever she made certain faces, all of them ridiculously adorable.

Or maybe it was seeing his best friends starting families, and it made him think about the family he couldn't wait to start with Bailey.

"*Como se dio*s, are you crying?" Tayler asked.

He quickly swiped at his eyes. "No…and como se what? What exactly are you trying to say, and where did you learn to speak Spanish, in Ireland? You're half-Cuban, Tay."

"And half Ghanaian, but I don't know any Akan, either." She stood on a chair to dab at his eyes with a tissue. "I do know this. I know, *te amo*, my best friend. I'm so happy you've found someone to love you as much as you love them, and as much as we," she motioned to herself and Ethan, "love you."

He gave her a tight hug before embracing Ethan.

"Let's go make this thing official," he said, his knees slightly wobbly as he followed them out of the room to prepare for the longest wait of his life.

But it was more than worth it.

Everyone stood.

His future wife raised her head, their eyes met, and his mind took him back to the first time he'd seen her. The first time he'd seen those eyes, heard her laugh.

She didn't break their gaze as she walked toward him. Tears spilled from his eyes, and tears dripped onto her cheeks.

He took her hand, and she came to him.

He reached beneath her chin, tilting her face up to his, her eyes dark and gleaming and full of more love than he ever knew someone was capable of feeling for him. From the very first time he'd laid eyes on her, he'd known—she was the woman he wanted, and he would gladly spend his life proving just how grateful he was to have her.

EPILOGUE

Kellen, heart so full he was afraid it might burst, watched as Bailey leaned over their son, Christian Connor Edwards, and blew air against his stomach while Christian giggled and grabbed for her face. A perfect autumn had descended on Atlanta, prompting their little family outing in Piedmont Park.

Families had gathered.

Vendors were out in abundance.

Dogs chased butterflies and caught Frisbees.

Yet, all he could focus on was the beautiful woman in front of him and their even more beautiful four-month-old son.

Bailey gave up on the ponytail most days, wearing her hair in its naturally curly state, complete with his favorite layer of frizz. She was also holding down the fort as a wife, mother, and Ph.D. student in the Emory English program with plans of doing a two-year fellowship in creative writing.

She kissed the tip of their son's nose. "Pooh, I love you so freakin' much. I can't believe I have such a beautiful son and," she glanced over, "the sexiest husband in all of Atlanta."

Kellen, grinning, scratched at his jaw. "I do what I can."

"And, baby, you do it well."

Tammy waved as she headed over, hand in hand with her first attempt at a real relationship.

"Look, Pooh, it's Auntie Tammy!" Bailey lifted Christian into the air and waved one of his tiny hands.

"Sorry we're late." Tammy reached for Christian, who eagerly leaned in her direction. "We had a," she extended her ring finger, "stop to make."

Bailey's hands flew to her mouth. With his wife temporarily baby free, Kellen pulled her onto his lap and inhaled her scent.

"Give us the deets, Tam," she said. "How'd it happen?"

While Tammy explained, Kellen reveled in the feeling of his wife leaning back against his chest, his son's smile, and the beauty of the day outside. He'd never known this could be for him, and for that, he was more than grateful.

Everything was almost perfect.

"Uncle Kel! Titi Bailey! I'm here!"

Abigail raced toward them.

David and Alexis trailed her, smiling and laughing, their hands clasped. Strapped to David's chest was his and Alexis' ten-month-old son, Kian.

Kellen kissed Bailey's temple. She tipped her chin up, and he dropped one on her mouth.

Now, things were perfect.

Thank you for reading.

xoxo,

Alex

ABOUT THE AUTHOR

I'm a creative creature from the Caribbean who likes animals, Star Wars, quirky humor, and any kind of media that deals with people finding love in an otherwise impossible time.

Connect With Me:

Mailing List:
Text BOOKADDICT to 66866!

Blog - http://www.kalexwalker.com
Website - http://www.kalexwrites.com
Amazon - amazon.com/k-alex-walker
Instagram - instagram.com/kalexwrites
Facebook - facebook.com/mskalexwalker
Bookbub - bookbub.com/authors/k-alex-walker

Looking for exclusive stories, updates, giveaways, one on ones, and more? How about writing a book *with* me?
Join me on Patreon!

ALSO BY K. ALEX WALKER

International Mafia

Prince of The Brotherhood

Moonlight Retribution

Myths, Legends, and Monsters

The Gatekeeper

Elias The Wicked

The Girl in the Mountains

Jonah's Ghost

The Game of Love

The Game of Love

The Game of Love - Sequel

Angels and Assassins

The Wolf

The Protector

The Anarchist

The Dark Knight

The Shadow

The Darkest Knight

Hidden In The Shadows

www.ingramcontent.com/pod-product-compliance
Lightning Source LLC
Chambersburg PA
CBHW020931260626
47169CB00006B/1666